Spirit Song Prequel

OSS'STERA

An Epic Fantasy

ROSS HIGHTOWER &
DEB HEIM

Black Rose Writing | Texas

ISBN: 978-1-68513-646-8
LIBRARY OF CONGRESS CONTROL NUMBER: 2025933754
PUBLISHED BY BLACK ROSE WRITING
www.blackrosewriting.com

Printed in the United States of America
Suggested Retail Price (SRP) $21.95

Oss'Stera is printed in Andalus

*As a planet-friendly publisher, Black Rose Writing does its best to eliminate unnecessary waste to reduce paper usage and energy costs, while never compromising the reading experience. As a result, the final word count vs. page count may not meet common expectations.

Praise for
Oss'Stera

"An epic fantasy delight that reads like a standalone. The authors deliver a plot like Sanderson's *Mistborn* and romantic matchmaking mischief like Marillier's *The Harp of Kings.*"
—Cam Torrens, author of the *Tyler Zahn series*

We would be remiss if we didn't acknowledge the support of our biggest (and in her own words, our oldest) fan, Betsy MacDougal. She has been tireless in her support, reading every manuscript, and buying every book. She has told us in no uncertain terms that we need to complete the Spirit Song Saga "while she's still alive". We mean to do just that.

Maps

You can find maps and more at rosshightower.com/argren

Books in the Spirit Song Saga

Prequels

Argren Blue

Desulti

Oss'stera

Spirit Song Trilogy

Spirit Sight Volumes One and Two

Spirit Light Volume One

For a complete list of the books in the Spirit Song Saga and updates on availability, check rosshightower.com/spiritsongsaga

Characters

Alle'oss

Alar	Leader of *Oss'stera*, in a relationship with Scilla
Fin	An orphan who looks after Sigurd and Olafson
Inga	Bergamot's chief cook
Keth	Member of *Oss'stera*
Lief	Member of *Oss'stera*
Old Jep	An elder in the Ishien River Valley
Olson	Manager of Bergamot's estate
Scilla	Artist, Member of *Oss'stera*, in a relationship with Alar, Ukrit's sister
Tove	Member of *Oss'stera*
Trell	Servant on Bergamot's estate
Ukrit	Artist, Member of *Oss'stera*, Scilla's brother
Zaina	Member of *Oss'stera*

Volloch

About-That	Pretentious artist
Adelbart	Imperial Governor of Argren
Anton Bergamot	Volloch lord
Belden Brucher	Brennerman's tormentor, son of Lord Brucher
Brennerman	Captain of Imperial Cavalry in Agren
Brie	Murtair
Eirin	Murtair
Gerold	Adelbart's beleaguered assistant
Heinz	About-That's apprentice
Helmut	Guard on Bergamot's estate
Holden Mueller	The groom
Krueger	Command of the Inquisition in Richeleau
Ragan	Former Imperial witch
Sofria	Chief Financial Officer of the Desulti

| Vint | Inquisition spy on Bergamot's estate |
| Violette Bergamot | The bride |

Others

| Chekka | Lord Bergamot's blacksmith |

Oss'Stera

Prologue

The murtair crept along the stone passageway, hugging the wall to stay out of her quarry's sight. The wind's low whistle masked the feather light scuffs of her boots. Most people believed the members of her order were simply assassins, but murder was only one of their tools. She wasn't often called on to take a life, but she wasn't squeamish when the situation called for it. Most of her victims deserved their fate.

The old monk assured her the one she was looking for would be here. Rounding a corner, she saw him. The corridor ended abruptly. Instead of a stone wall, an opening looked out over a valley high in the Northern Mountains. No barrier existed to prevent someone from falling. The hallway simply ended. The boy sat on the edge, his back to her, his feet dangling over a sheer drop. He wore the loose tunic and trousers the monks wore, and his amber hair was shorn close to this scalp.

She crouched, and took a step toward him.

"You're getting better." He looked at her over his shoulder, gracing her with a rare, toothy smile.

Tove returned his smile, prowled to the edge, leaned out, and looked down. A hundred paces below the boy's bare feet, the granite bones of the mountain gleamed in the summer sun. She sank to sit cross-legged and gazed out over the valley. The only signs of life were tiny figures in the Tituun village on the valley floor and a pair of the great vultures riding thermals thrust up by the mountains across the valley.

"It's been a long time since you visited," the boy said, letting a faint note of reproach in his voice.

"A year," Tove said. She studied his profile. He had only seven summers, but already he had the deep serenity of the brothers who inhabited this monastery. "You haven't changed."

He frowned at her. "I see no reason for insults." He let the smallest of grins take the sting from the rebuke. "How long are you staying?"

"Two days." Tove looked out at the valley again. "Brother Xander told me this is your favorite spot in the monastery."

His head tipped to the side, then he looked up at a blue sky dotted by high wispy clouds. "When the wind is just right, the air is still here and this time of day, the sun warms the stones." He pressed his hand flat on the ancient red granite.

"Better than the dining hall with one of Brother Lucian's sweet rolls?"

"Well…" He glanced at her, the corners of his lips quivering. "I can think here." He returned his gaze to the valley and let his eyes close. "Tell me about when Alar, Scilla, and Ukrit went to Lachton."

"Again? You must have heard that story a thousand times."

He nodded slowly. "Again."

Tove looked up at the sky. The boy was right; it was a pleasant spot. "Where to start?"

The boy didn't answer.

"It was seven years ago. Alar was the leader of the rebels who called themselves *Oss'stera.*"

"Our struggle."

"That's right. *Oss'stera* means our struggle in the *Alle'oss* language." Tove let her thoughts sift through her time with the rebels. "We were a pretty pitiful lot. Until Alar took charge."

"And Alar discovered he was a realm walker."

"Yes." Realm walkers could enter *annen'heim*, the realm of the dead, and return. While in that bleak realm, time seemed to stop in the physical realm, so it appeared as if the realm walker could move instantly from one place to another. "Because he was a realm walker, we began to have some success against our Imperial oppressors."

"The supply caravan to Ka'tan."

"Yes. The Imperial Rangers who guarded that caravan would have defeated us without Alar. But we won and obtained the supplies that got us through that first winter."

"And the *Alle'oss* art."

The art was intended as a payment by the Imperial Governor of Argen for the debt he owed the Desulti. The Desulti, or the Order as it was known to the women who were members, was founded by women who fled the Imperial patriarchy. They knew they could never defend themselves from the Empire's armies, so they sought economic power and weren't afraid to wield it.

The *Alle'oss* intercepting the art set off a complicated series of events that found the rebels fighting alongside Imperial Cavalry against mercenaries from the Union. "Yes, we recovered the art. Our cultural heritage." The boy knew this, of course. She didn't know why he always asked to hear stories he knew by heart, but she was happy to oblige. His quiet serenity was a balm that soothed the psychic wounds her violent life inflicted. Besides, she liked him and cherished their rare moments together.

"Why did Alar go to Lachton?"

Rousing herself from her thoughts, Tove squinted across the valley. "Despite our successes, Alar knew it would never be enough to rid Argren of Imperial domination." She fell silent, remembering the comrades they lost. And the lives she took. "It's easy to take a life. Impossible to give it back."

The boy nodded.

"So, when the Imperial witch —"

"Ragan," the boy said with a wide smile.

"Yes, Ragan," Tove said, unable to prevent the slight twist to her lips.

The boy's expression suggested he noticed her disapproval. "She speaks highly of you."

"When did you see her last?"

The boy's lips pursed, and he squinted up at the sky. "She came to see me and my mother a month ago."

"Does she ever ask anything of you?" Ragan never came to Tove unless she needed something and was always full of dire warnings about what would happen if she refused.

"No. She comes to tell the monks what she wants them to teach me. She doesn't want me to know that, but after she leaves, they always have new lessons for me."

"What new lessons did she leave for you this time?"

"Tsadan philosophy."

Tove stared at him. "How *old* are you?"

The boy chuckled. "Brother Xander says I'm older than I have any right to be." He glanced at her. "Alar and Lachton?"

"Yes, anyway," Tove said, "Ragan told Alar he should follow the Desulti's example and seek power through wealth."

The boy nodded solemnly. "Are you happy Alar made the deal for you to become Desulti?"

"Yes," Tove said. "More than I can ever say." She paused, letting herself enjoy the sun's warmth and the absence of wind. Even at the height of summer, the monastery perched on top of a mountain could be chilly.

"How *is* Danu?" the boy asked, a brow hitching.

"She is impatient for me to return," Tove said, feeling her face warm.

The boy returned her smile. "So, Alar listened to Ragan's advice."

"Yes," Tove said. "Alar rescued the Imperial governor's daughter from Union mercenaries. The governor was willing to do anything to express his gratitude. Alar asked him to allow *Oss'sfera* to export *Alle'oss* products from Argen free of Imperial taxes and regulations."

"A black market," the boy said with a mischievous grin.

"Where did you hear that term?"

"Brother Xander."

"Well, Brother Xander is right. It was a black market that should have given *Oss'stera* a commercial advantage."

"Should have?"

"Yes. Alar and his fellow rebels, Scilla and Ukrit, went to the Imperial city of Lachton to make their fortune. But they knew nothing about commerce."

Lika turned his head to look directly at her. "But Alar is not like other men."

Tove let a soft grin soften her features. "No, Alar is a man who sees possibilities where no one else does."

The child let a satisfied smile bloom on his serene face and looked out over the valley.

They sat quietly for a time, then Tove asked, "When was the last time you heard this story?"

"Ragan told it to me when she came. But I like to hear you tell it." He paused and said, "Tell me the rest."

The full story is told in Argren Blue: A Spirit Song Story by Ross Hightower and Deb Heim.

1

Rebellion

Governor Adelbart sat stiffly, hands in his lap, eyes on a rectangle of sunlight on the spotless surface of his office desk. He put this meeting off as long as he could. He hoped the cooperation between the cavalry and the *Alle'oss* rebels during the battle at the fort would tame Captain Brennerman's virulent bigotry. But it only seemed to have the opposite effect. When the captain's troopers began harassing peaceful *Alle'oss*, searching for the rebels who were so recently his allies, Gerold, Adelbart's assistant, insisted the governor act. After all, Adelbart promised the rebel leader, Alar, he would rein in the captain of his cavalry.

It was all part of a complicated arrangement he and Gerold made with Alar after he rescued the governor's daughter from Union mercenaries. In exchange for allowing the rebels to bypass Imperial taxes and regulations, they would pay a fee directly to Adelbart. The rebels agreed to cease attacking Imperial forces, and Adelbart agreed to restrict Brennerman's bullying of the *Alle'oss.*

The trouble was, Brennerman terrified him. Though the captain had hidden his contempt for the governor behind a thin veil in the past, after the recent troubles, the veil had been lifted. It was Adelbart's mother after the disastrous ball for his eighteenth birthday all over again.

"You are the Imperial Governor of the Military District of Argren, for Daga's sake," Adelbart mumbled to himself with a sharp nod. "And he is a mere captain relegated to an Imperial backwater."

Adelbart let out a yelp at a sharp knock on his office door. Hand to his chest, he chastised himself. It was the knock Gerold used when he was alone.

"Come," Adelbart said, embarrassed when his voice cracked.

Gerold entered and moved briskly to stand before the desk. His eyes roved the governor's sweat-slicked face, then he extracted a handkerchief and handed it over. "Are you ready?"

Adelbart nodded, mopping his brow.

"You remember what to say?" Gerold asked. When the governor nodded, he said, "You are the governor. The *captain* serves *you*. Stick to what we discussed. Don't let him draw you into an argument." Gerold's brows drew together as he studied Adelbart. "If he balks, tell him you have the authority to relieve him of his command."

"Yes, I remember all that," Adelbart said testily, handing the damp handkerchief to his assistant.

"You need this deal with the rebels."

"Me?"

"We. We need this deal," Gerold amended. "Your debts —"

"Yes, yes. I am well aware of my financial difficulties."

Before Gerold could respond, someone behind Gerold spoke. "Ahem."

Gerold whirled. Adelbart leaned out to see around his assistant. Captain Brennerman stood in the doorway. The captain was taller and thinner than most men, allowing him to peer imperiously down his long nose from a greater height. His graying hair was cropped close to his scalp. He wore the blue uniform of the Imperial Cavalry, but he adorned it with far more gold than normal. Adelbart was sure it wasn't regulation.

"Captain," Gerold said. He stepped hurriedly to the side and gestured to the spot he vacated. "Thank you for coming early."

"Yes," said the captain. He stepped up to Adelbart's desk and clasped his hands behind his back. His eyes roved the office, lingering on the painting by the *Alle'oss* master, Omar, on the wall behind the governor. Only then did he meet the governor's eyes and give a shallow nod. "Governor. You asked to see me."

The insulting demeanor was almost enough for Adelbart's anger to shoulder his fear aside. Almost.

"Captain Brennerman." Adelbart was so surprised at how steady his voice was, he paused, his eyes opening a little wider. Noticing Brennerman watching him uncertainly, he started again. "Captain Brennerman," he squeaked. *Zut.* He gave his head a shake. "We," he said, gesturing to Gerold, "have had reports of your men harassing the *Alle'oss*—"

"Yes," Brennerman said and sniffed. "All part of an overarching effort to root out the rebels who call themselves *Oss'stera.*" His brows rose. "Self-admitted rebels."

"The same *Alle'oss* who assisted your cavalry in preventing the Union mercenaries from making off with Imperial treasures," Adelbart said, startled by the edge that found its way unbidden into his voice.

The captain's eyes narrowed slightly. "Yes. I've been meaning to ask about that. Those supposedly priceless paintings seem to have gone missing. Where are they?"

"That is not your concern. They are hidden in an undisclosed location where no one can find them for safekeeping." Sweat beaded on Adelbart's brow while he replayed the confusing sentence in his mind. It was almost true. The *Alle'oss* hadn't disclosed to *him* where they hid the paintings he allowed them to keep. He assumed they were safe.

Brennerman eyed him. "Yes. Well, I'm quite confident my men would have made short work of the Union filth without the negligible assistance of the rebels."

"You mean your men who were hiding in the barracks at the time?" Gerold blurted. His face drained of color and his eyes opened wide.

Adelbart and Brennerman stared at him.

"Governor, I'm sorr —"

Adelbart waved away his apology. In the tense atmosphere, surprise at his normally stolid assistant's embarrassed expression forced a giggle from the governor. Before the captain could launch into a tirade at the governor's laughter, Adelbart interrupted him.

"Captain," he said sharply. "Let me see if I understand you. You believe the group of *Alle'oss* who assisted your cavalry at the battle at the fort are rebels against the Empire."

"That is correct."

"Yes." Adelbart adopted a curious frown. "Pray tell me, what acts of rebellion have these *Alle'oss* committed?" The clops of a horse's hooves on cobbles outside the governor's mansion were audible in the silent office as he and Gerold watched the captain expectantly.

Finally, his face darkening, Brennerman said, "*Someone* must have attacked the company of rangers you sent to guard the supply caravan to Ka'tan." He waved a hand. "It can be the only explanation for why it didn't arrive. The rangers couldn't have simply vanished into thin air."

Adelbart chuckled and gave Gerold a look to encourage him to join in. "Captain, surely, you aren't implying a ragtag band of *Alle'oss* wiped out an entire company of Imperial Rangers. You, yourself, said they were of *negligible* assistance during the battle at the fort."

Brennerman became still, then his mouth opened slowly. But before he could command it what to say, Adelbart spoke again.

"No, I think it's safe to assume it was the Union mercenaries who attacked the supply caravan. After all, the mercenaries *were* in possession of those Imperial treasures you spoke of. Treasures they could only have obtained from the caravan."

Adelbart and Gerold watched Brennerman struggling to overcome this logic. Of course, the captain couldn't know the rebels who called themselves *Oss'stera did* wipe out the ranger company and hijack the caravan, which included the priceless art, among more mundane supplies. The art was intended to pay Adelbart's substantial debt to the Desulti. It wasn't until later the mercenaries stole the art from the *Alle'oss*. The idea it was the mercenaries who attacked the caravan was a lie Gerold and Alar concocted to cover the rebels' involvement.

Finding the lie insurmountable, Brennerman adjusted course. "Nevertheless, there *are* rumors of rebel activity. We must not turn a blind eye —"

"Captain Brennerman," Adelbart said. "Until you can produce evidence that consists of more than rumors and your own speculations, I must insist that you and your men cease harassing the local inhabitants. If you can't abide by this directive, I will be forced to remove you from your command."

Brennerman's mouth slammed shut. His eyes cut to Gerold, then returned to the governor. Something more primal rippled through his usual sour expression before he gained control of his face. He gave a crisp nod and said, "Of course, sir. Is there anything else? Sir?"

"No," the governor said. "You may return to your duties."

Gerold and Adelbart listened to the captain's footsteps receding down the hallway. Two heartbeats after they faded from hearing, Gerold rushed to shut the door. Adelbart gasped and started to hyperventilate.

"Governor!" Gerold exclaimed, turning away from the door. "I — your mother would be so proud of you right now." Apparently noticing the governor's distress, he hurried around his desk and rested a hand on the governor's back. "Breathe, sir. Slow breaths. There, there."

Finally gaining control of his breath, Adelbart slumped back in his chair and took the handkerchief Gerold offered him. Mopping his face, he glanced up at his assistant. "You think so? About my mother?"

"It was a masterful performance," Gerold said with a wide smile. "Worthy of an Imperial Governor."

"Thank you, Gerold." He gestured with the hand holding the handkerchief. "Shame I can't actually tell her, what with the rebels and all." He gave Gerold a weak grin and handed over the soaked handkerchief. Standing, he swayed and took a moment to gain his balance. "Now, if there is nothing else… I'm off in search of a quiet place and a stiff drink."

"Of course, Your Excellency."

***

Brennerman stopped at the bottom of the steps in front of the governor's mansion. He was so angry he barely acknowledged the soldiers standing guard watching him uncertainly. When he did notice them slouching, he pivoted and glared until they lifted their hands in salute. They were infantry, and he was cavalry, but he still deserved more respect than their limp salutes implied. After demonstrating a proper salute, he turned away, dismissing them, and gazed across the paved plaza in front of the mansion.

He would never allow such impertinent behavior in his command. If he had to guess, the commander of the infantry unit guarding the governor's mansion allowed his men to fraternize with the locals. Brennerman set strict limits on his troopers and made sure they understood who were the rulers and who were the ruled.

Setting off across the plaza, he replayed his meeting with the governor. Like it or not, the stooge was right; he could remove Brennerman from his command. He briefly considered forcibly removing the governor for incompetence. The problem was, Adelbart's mother was the emperor's sister. Despite the fact many in the Empire would sympathize with his actions, Brennerman wouldn't survive the resulting storm.

He stopped in the middle of the plaza and gazed into space. A chill spring breeze raised goosebumps on his exposed neck. Could he follow the governor's directive and ignore the rebel threat? No. The rebel leader, Alar, may be arrogant and disrespectful, but he was a dangerous man. It was clear from the adoration his fellow rebels heaped on him, he had the charisma the most dangerous fanatics possessed. If left free to operate unmolested, he would attract more troublemakers and eventually *Oss'stera* would be more than a minor irritant.

What he needed was to find another way to root out the rebels. Some way that didn't implicate him or his men. Pivoting on his heel, he strode back the way he came. The answer was so obvious, he didn't know why he didn't think of it before. The Inquisition. In Brennerman's mind, the inquisitors spent far too much energy hunting down little girls they claimed were witches and not enough rooting out rebellion. The normally peaceful *Alle'oss* had lured them into complacency. Allowing these *Oss'stera* rebels to go unmolested was proof. The Inquisition sent a novice to investigate the rebels the previous winter but chose to do nothing. It was time Brennerman rang the alarm bells and shook them out of their false sense of security.

*****

"Rebels?" the commander of the local Inquisition house asked incredulously. "*Alle'oss* rebels?"

It took Brennerman hours to fight his way through the Inquisition bureaucracy to reach Commander Krueger, encountering the same skepticism at every level. He peered down at the man, seeing his hopes for a vigorous investigation dissolving.

The Imperial capital in Argren had only recently been transferred from Kartok to Richeleau. But, while it was relatively easy for the governor to move, it was a much more complex affair to transfer the extensive Inquisition apparatus headquartered in Kartok. Krueger was a functionary. An administrator with little investigatory experience. He was a placeholder, assigned to Richeleau to establish the administrative structures the Inquisition would require when they moved.

"Yes. Rebels," Brennerman said, forging ahead despite his flagging hopes. There must be someone in this office who would take his concerns seriously. "The Inquisition headquarters in Brennan apparently took the idea seriously enough to send a novice to investigate. He must have produced a report."

Krueger stared at him, then nodded. "Ah, yes. I remember. The half-breed. Harold Wolfe." He sat back and laced his fingers over his belly. "Ask yourself, Captain Brennerman. How seriously did my superiors take this threat if they sent a half-breed novice to investigate? Without the supervision of an inquisitor, no less?"

Brennerman blinked. He threw out his hand. "He was there. Wolfe. With the rebels when I planned the attack on the mercenaries. Surely you heard about the battle at the fort."

The commander's smile widened. "When *you* planned the attack? *With Alle'oss* rebels?" He cocked his head. "Are you admitting to conspiring with rebels?" He waited while Brennerman struggled to respond. When it was clear he couldn't, the commander said, "In fact, our intelligence branch has concluded your men wouldn't have won the battle without the help of a group of *Alle'oss* hunters."

"There are rebels operating in and around Richeleau," Brennerman said mulishly. "Rooting out rebellion is within your purview. If you don't act while they are small and disorganized, it will be on your head."

The commander stiffened. Then his expression shifted, and he sat up. "You met these rebels? Know what they look like?"

"Yes, of course."

"Work with our artist to produce likenesses. We'll create dossiers, investigate, and keep you updated on any developments." He sat forward, retrieved his quill, and bent over the document on his desk. "Now, if that is all."

2

People Like Us

Alar watched the back of the barge captain receding as he made his way to the exit. A shaft of light speared the interior of the tavern when he opened the door. He exited without a backward glance, pulling the door closed and restoring the gloom.

"That was the last one," Alar said, peering glumly into his empty tankard.

"There will be others," Scilla said, trying a weak smile. "I'm sure there are barges working the river that aren't in Lachton."

"I'm sure there are," Alar said, setting the tankard on the table. "But that man was one of the few who even agreed to talk to us, and Ukrit will be here with the first shipment soon."

"Pelts, honey, wool cloth," Scilla said. "Nothing perishable."

Alar tipped his chair and rested his back against the wall. "No, but since no one will give us warehouse space, we have nowhere to put it."

"Can't really blame them," Scilla said. "I'm not sure my father would have leased space to people like us."

Alar lifted a brow. "People like us?"

"Destitute, broke and with few prospects."

"Ah," Alar said with a nod. "I thought you meant *Alle'oss.*"

"I suspect that's part of it as well," Scilla said, letting her gaze drift across the nearly empty room. "Lachton may have been an *Alle'oss* city at some point, but it's clear who rules the roost now. All the captains we've talked to are Volloch. Not all of them have called us *l'oss,* but you could tell they were thinking it."

They sat with their own thoughts for a time, listening to the sounds of the nearby harbor through an open window. They came to Lachton with the goal of becoming wealthy. Not for themselves, but for *Oss'stera,* the rebel group they led. For most of their history, the rebels of *Oss'stera* lived hand to mouth, often going days with nothing to eat. After rising to lead the group, several violent encounters with Imperial forces convinced Alar if they were to stand toe to toe with the Empire, they would need to think beyond their next meal. It was Ragan, the former Imperial witch, who encouraged Alar to follow the Desulti's example and seek power through wealth.

Alar attacked the problem with the same vigor with which he attacked every obstacle. He made the deal with a grateful governor that would give them an advantage over competitors. Imperial export taxes were exorbitant, and the complex export regulations were a means of cutting the *Alle'oss* out of the business of exporting goods from their own land. Under their deal with the governor, his assistant, Gerold, would provide the documentation they needed and since it came from an official Imperial source, it would pass muster with any Imperial inspector.

With the agreement in hand, Alar and his fellow rebels, Scilla and Ukrit set off for the prosperous Ishien River Valley to find goods to sell. They were sure the *Alle'oss* living in the Valley would jump at the opportunity. After all, Scilla and Ukrit grew up there and their parents had been well respected merchants in the Valley. Unfortunately, their countrymen made the same assessment of their prospects as the Volloch in Lachton. It took all of Alar's charm and Ukrit's and Scilla's reputations to convince a few people to agree to a single shipment. It was a trial. If they didn't turn a handsome profit, they were out of business.

While Ukrit remained behind to gather the merchandise, Alar and Scilla headed to Lachton to find customers. At one point, Lachton was a small *Alle'oss* outpost which grew wealthy on fish from the nearby Lake Vitaeshu. When the Empire came, Lachton grew into a major commercial center. The surrounding hills were rich in minerals, pelts, and lumber. Imperials shipped it all from Lachton's port on the Odun River south to Hast and the seaport in Lubern.

Alar and Scilla arrived in Lachton, brimming with optimism. It wasn't long before reality set in. The first problem was neither of them had the slightest idea how commerce worked in the Empire. It took them a week to grasp something as simple as leasing warehouse space. Alar hoped Scilla learned such things from her parents, who ran a successful business before Imperial soldiers killed them. Unfortunately, commerce in the Empire was on a completely different scale than in a small town in Argren. Every transaction involved contracts and legalities that were beyond them. It didn't help that, being artists, neither Scilla nor her brother Ukrit absorbed much of their father's business acumen.

But the biggest problem was that most people in Lachton, like most Imperials, harbored deep-seated prejudices against the *Alle'oss*. A few successful *Alle'oss* merchants remained in Lachton, but it was only because they were familiar to other merchants, and they did what was necessary to blend in with the Volloch.

"Perhaps a little planning would have been advisable this time," Alar said.

"What, and break with tradition?" Scilla asked with a small grin.

"What we need is leverage."

Scilla nodded slowly. "Like we had with Governor Adelbart."

"Exactly. Either that or enough coin to overcome prejudices."

"Chicken and egg," Scilla said. After another pause, she pursed her lips and said, "We could always borrow the coin."

"The banks in Lachton are all Imperial," Alar said. "And besides, like you said, who would lend to destitute *Alle'oss?*"

"Well, actually, I was thinking of —"

"Don't say it," Alar said.

"Say what?"

"You were going to say the Desulti."

"They do have the coin. Obviously," Scilla said. "And they might be interested in being part of the deal we made with the governor."

"I'm sure they would jump at the chance to be a part of our deal. But if recent events have taught me anything, it's to be very wary of going into business with the Desulti. I suspect they would find they don't have much use for us. And who could blame them? What exactly do we bring to the table?"

"Good looks and charm?" Scilla asked with a smile, then waved a hand. "Just an idea. Not sure we have many options left at this point." They sat quietly for a time, then Scilla said, "Do you miss her?"

Alar nodded. The mention of the Desulti brought their fellow rebel, Tove, to both of their minds. When Alar rescued the governor's daughter, he also rescued the Desulti, Brie. Hoping to make contacts within that secretive organization, Alar made a deal with Brie to sponsor Tove's induction into the Desulti. "I knew I would miss her, but I was unprepared for how much. I forgot how much I relied on her cynical snark to keep me level-headed."

"Maybe Tove will decide being Desulti isn't for her," Scilla said with a shrug. "I imagine they won't make it easy for her."

"Oh, I know they won't make it easy," Alar said. The Desulti were Imperial women. They fled the Imperial patriarchy to become Desulti, but many of them retained Imperial prejudices. "Brie said as much." He rested his elbows on the table. "But no matter what they do to Tove, it'll just make her mad. She'll never give up, no matter how bad it is."

"I worry about her," Scilla said.

"Me too."

Alar noticed the proprietor eyeing them. They put out word they could be found at the Tipsy Rooster in case any barge captain wanted to talk. They spent long hours in the tavern, but the most they could afford was a single ale between the two of them each day. "I think we've worn out our welcome."

Scilla glanced back at the man. "I don't think I can face that shack," she said. "You want to walk along the harbor? Maybe another barge arrived."

Unable to afford a room in an inn, they had been sleeping in an abandoned shack in a derelict part of the warehouse district. If they huddled together under their blankets for warmth and it didn't rain, it wasn't awful. They'd slept in much worse places.

"That sounds lovely." Alar stood, gave the proprietor a cheery wave and followed Scilla.

***

Brennerman gazed down at the map table in his office, only vaguely aware of the sounds of his men drilling in the inner ward of the fort drifting through his open window. Though he would never admit it to anyone, he was honest enough with himself to admit his men would have lost the battle at the fort without the *Alle'oss* rebels. When he first encountered that ragtag gang, he dismissed them. But they surprised him. They were few, for now, but they were far more formidable than anyone else acknowledged.

Returning from his thoughts, he focused on the map of the eastern Empire, his eyes moving to the bottom left corner where he had sketched what he knew of the Empire's front lines facing the Kaileuk. That's where he should be rather than in a backwater like Argren. It was where he was until the Imperial advance bogged down in the swamps. Cavalry was of little use in the heavily forested bogs. Though the Empire retained a few cavalry units to patrol the vast plains behind the lines, his company wasn't one of the lucky few.

He let his gaze drift across the rugged terrain around Richeleau. Cavalry wasn't any more suited to the mountains than the swamps. Horses were usually confined to the roads, a situation that filled him with disquiet. Drawn out into long lines, cavalry were vulnerable and weren't able to take advantage of their strengths. A competent force, well positioned in the dense forest, would devastate their columns and there would be little they could do to respond. Other than flee. Despite what the governor said, he was sure the rebels were responsible for the disappearance of the supply caravan to Ka'tan. They needed the supplies to survive the winter. That they destroyed an entire company of Imperial Rangers proved how dangerous they were. That was precisely why he was so worried. And why he intended to sidestep the governor's instructions.

He spent hours with the Inquisition artist perfecting the depictions of as many of the rebels as he could remember. For all the good it would do. That buffoon, Commander Krueger, was as blind as Adelbart.

So, it was left to him to root out the threat. He shuffled through the maps until he found one of Richeleau and the surrounding territory. An index finger tapping his chin, he studied the map. Nestled in the foothills of the Eastern Mountains, Richeleau was surrounded by forested, hilly terrain on the north, south and west. The land to the east was much more rugged, rising quickly to low mountains.

From their garb and their facility with bows, he didn't believe the rebels were city dwellers. They would have to feed themselves, and it would be much easier in the forest. If he were a rebel, he would make his base to the east. There were far more places to hide in defensible terrain. But to be sure, he would increase his patrols in the hills to the north, west and south. He couldn't use horses in the mountainous terrain east of the city, but he could increase his patrols on the road that headed east toward Ka'tan.

A company of Imperial Rangers, replacements for the previous company, were due in Richeleau within the week. Operating in mountainous terrain was why the rangers existed. Surely, the commander of that company would want revenge. Brennerman would prepare a briefing, outlining a joint operation to find and destroy *Oss'stera*.

He pivoted on his heel and called to his adjutant, then rounded his desk and dropped into his chair. They would find the rebels, and when they did, he would find evidence of the supplies they stole from the Empire in the caravan. Not even an idiot like Adelbart could deny that.

3

Lies

Since Ukrit couldn't know where Alar and Scilla were staying, they agreed to meet at the ferry station on the Odun River at the sixteenth bell. The Odun River wound its way around the eastern side of Lachton. Canals connected the harbor in the city to the river. Every day, Alar and Scilla made their way across the city to the ferry station, and every day, they were disappointed. Finally, on the day that marked the end of their first month in Lachton, they caught sight of Ukrit's red tresses among the passengers on the ferry.

Scilla's brother drove his wagon off the ferry and guided it past the line waiting to board for the return trip. When he spotted Scilla waving, he gave them a wide, toothy smile, and pulled off the road, out of the way of traffic.

Alar frowned up at Ukrit, who peered down at them from the wagon's bench. "One wagon?" he asked.

Ukrit grimaced, set the brake on the big wagon, and climbed stiffly to the ground. "We were lucky to get this. After you left the Valley, people started having second thoughts."

"Did they forget they could avoid Imperial taxes?" Scilla asked.

"No," Ukrit said, looking affronted. "I reminded them. Repeatedly. The problem is Adelbart. They don't trust him, and after what he did to Lirantok, who can blame them?"

"So, what's this for?" Alar asked, waving a hand at the wagon.

"Old Jep convinced them to give us a try. All we have to do is make a profit on this load. Earn some credibility. The next shipment will be bigger."

Alar exchanged a look with Scilla.

"You got it all lined up, right?" Ukrit asked, noticing their disquiet.

"We're in negotiations," Alar said.

"Negotiations?" Ukrit asked, looking from Alar to Scilla.

"Yeah, we were, just now, negotiating what to tell you when you got here," Scilla said.

"Tell me?"

"Still undecided," Alar said, then set to untying the ropes holding down one corner of the canvas covering the wagon's bed.

"You don't have a buyer," Ukrit said.

"We don't," Scilla said. "We thought about shipping it all down to Hast or Lubern and finding a buyer there, but we can't find a captain willing to take us on. No one in Lachton wants to do business with ragged looking *Alle'oss.*"

"Huh." Ukrit looked Scilla up and down. "Can see their point, now you mention it." He looked up at Alar, who was standing on the spokes of the wagon's wheel, peering under the canvas. "What do you suggest we do?"

Alar dropped to the ground and brushed his palms together. "First, we get this unloaded."

"You have any ideas where we put it?" Scilla asked.

"That shack where we're sleeping," Alar said.

Scilla stared at him, then snapped her mouth shut and examined the wagon. "All of this? In that leaky, decrepit shack?"

"The bright side of it being only one wagon load is that it'll fit," Alar said. "Probably. We'll throw the canvas over it to keep it dry. Sleep on top of it."

"What about the wagon?" Ukrit said. "And the horses? I only have enough feed for another week."

"There's a yard behind the shack that's out of sight of the road," Alar said.

"And how do we feed them?"

"They can graze in the yard for now. The second thing we have to do is sell the honey," Alar said. "When we were walking along the canal, I saw a sign in front of a cafe advertising Argren honey." When Scilla and Ukrit stared at him, he said, "If they're advertising it, it must be in demand."

"But will they buy it from us?" Scilla asked.

"We may look scruffy, but honey's honey, right?" Alar asked.

"They'll pay us half what it's worth," Ukrit said.

"Probably," Alar said. "But we need some coin to clean ourselves up. New clothes, baths, for a start. We can't help being *Alle'oss*, but we can, at least, look respectable."

They were silent for a bit, then Ukrit glanced over his shoulder at traffic on the road. "You know, you could..." He walked his fingers in the air. "Go into *annen'heim*, slip inside some of these rich Imp houses —"

"No," Alar said.

Ukrit scowled. "What good is a magical ability if you aren't going to use it? Besides, they're Imps. The same ones that won't do business with us only because we're *Alle'oss*." Alar shook his head, but before he could speak, Ukrit held up a hand to stop him. "Let me see if I understand your calculation. You don't mind using this ability to *kill* Imps, but you won't steal from them."

"Yeah," Scilla said, picking up a foot and displaying the boot Alar stole for her. "It's an inopportune moment to grow scruples."

"Oh, no, no, no," Alar said, waving his hands in a dismissive gesture. "You misunderstand. I have no problem stealing from Imperials." Taking in their skeptical frowns, he said, "I've given this some thought, so bear with me."

Scilla lifted a brow, shifted her weight onto one foot and crossed her arms. Ukrit settled back against the wagon and gazed expectantly at him. "We're listening."

"The Inquisition, the military, the vast bureaucracy that makes our lives a nightmare. All the things that make the Empire run. I don't know exactly how it works, but I do know it all requires coin. A lot of coin. Not even the emperor could be that wealthy. The coin comes from somewhere, and I'm guessing a lot of it comes from the people with the most. The only people with an interest in keeping the whole thing afloat. Wealthy Volloch lords. So, without a relatively few obscenely wealthy lords, the Empire would crumble. Wealth, I might add, accumulated on the backs of the unwilling poor. Like us. From that point of view, for a band of rebels — like us — stealing from wealthy Imperials is a moral imperative."

Frowning, Scilla and Ukrit exchanged a look. "So, what's the problem?" Ukrit asked.

"We can't — ever — forget our goal," Alar said. "We're seeking riches not for ourselves but for *Oss'stera* and Argren."

"Right. So?" Scilla asked.

"Common thieves don't become rich, and they eventually get caught." Their frowns smoothed. Alar gave them a big smile. "Our goal is to become *extraordinary* thieves. The kind who can buy their way out of trouble. Like the Desulti." Understanding entered their expressions. "You steal a loaf of bread, the Imps throw you into prison for years. You're as wealthy as the Desulti, the Imps ignore an occasional assassination." He paused, looking from Ukrit to Scilla. "It's a question of scale."

"Huh," Ukrit said. "It's a good point. Still, it would be nice to have some coin. Would make this easier."

"It would," Scilla said. "I wouldn't mind a bath and a bed to sleep in."

"We'd all be happy about that," Ukrit said. "The bath, that is. Hard to sell honey when you smell like a goat."

"It's a well-reasoned argument," Alar said, grinning at Scilla's scowl. "Okay, as a means of acquiring some startup funds, let's explore our options." He glanced up at the wagon. "But first, let's get this unloaded."

***

The merchandise tucked away in their shack, Alar, Scilla, and Ukrit decided an ale and a meal would spark their creativity while they explored their options. Ensconced in a booth in the Tipsy Rooster, it didn't take them long to exhaust the limited possibilities, prompting an impatient Ukrit to return to the top of the short list.

"I still say we should just pick one of those big Imp mansions." He gestured in the general direction of the wealthy neighborhoods. "You go into *annen'heim* and see what you can find."

Alar peered into his tankard, lamenting its nearly empty state. "While you and Scilla wait safely outside."

"Keeping watch," Ukrit said, "in case… Well, in case the residents come home."

"And if they do?"

Ukrit sat back, waved a hand, and glanced at Scilla. "You know. We'll warn you. That screech owl thing Tove does."

Alar chuckled. "Even if that *would* work, the problem remains the same. It won't do us much good to steal anything other than hard coin. I don't have any idea how to liquidate stolen goods. Do you?"

"There's places," Ukrit said.

"Where?"

"Places," Ukrit said. "You don't know."

Alar grinned. "And you do?"

"So, we have to find the right people first."

"What do you think, Scilla?" Alar asked.

"I think, in the long run, it would make sense to know those kinds of people."

Ukrit gestured to his sister triumphantly.

"In the long run," Scilla said. "But I agree with Alar. I'm not sure how it works, but I imagine those people would take one look at us and know they can cheat us. It's a lot of risk for uncertain gain. Our goals are much bigger than making a bit of coin."

"It's just this one time," Ukrit grumbled.

"As long as it *is* just the one time," Alar said. He started to sip his ale, then decided to save the last swallow. "*One* job. It's got to be a guaranteed payoff."

Ukrit started to speak, then closed his mouth and gazed around the small tavern. The Tipsy Rooster was one of the few *Alle'oss* owned establishments in the neighborhood around the harbor. It was a favorite hangout of *Alle'oss* who served rich Imperials. The tables were filling up with the dinner crowd, and the indescribably delicious aromas of an *Alle'oss* stew permeated the room.

Alar fished a hard penny from his pocket and set it in the center of the table. They gazed at it forlornly. It was their last coin, enough for them to split one bowl of stew.

Light from the opening door fell across the coin, prompting Alar to look up at a man and woman entering the tavern. They dressed like most *Alle'oss* in Lachton, looking more like Imperials than the *Alle'oss* who lived in Richeleau. But something about them was different. He watched them making their way to his side of the tavern, trying to decide what caught his attention. Only when they neared did he realize it was because they displayed the subtle markers of wealth so important in Imperial society. The superior cut of their clothes, the gold cufflinks at the man's wrists, the silver pin that held the woman's bun in check, to name a few. And most important, the air of casual superiority every *Alle'oss* recognized. It was such a convincing impression, Alar checked the color of their hair when they drew close enough in the low light. The man's close-cropped hair was blond and the woman's was auburn. They were *Alle'oss.*

As they passed, the man looked back at the woman and asked, "Did you see them bringing the dowry?" Before she could answer, they slid into the next booth.

Alar, Ukrit and Scilla looked at one another. Alar swallowed the last of his ale, put the tankard against the thin wood partition between the booths, and pressed his ear to it.

"— didn't," the woman said. "But I heard about it. They say the chest was so heavy, it took four men to carry it."

"That's right," the man said. "Lord Bergamot has to pay that much to marry off his daughter. She's getting up there, you know. Twenty-eight summers." There was a pause while they gave their orders to a server, then the man said, "Don't worry about Bergamot. He can afford it."

"Why?" the woman asked. "I mean, why the big dowry? I saw his daughter when she came to the Spring Ball last year. She's attractive enough."

"Oh, that's not the problem. You know how these Volloch marriages work. It's all about making connections. Politics, business, influence. They sell their daughters for advantage. Looks only play a small part."

"So, what's the problem?"

The man's answer was so quiet, Alar had to press his ear tighter against the tankard to hear.

"The parents are very careful to keep it a secret, but you can't help hearing the arguments the three of them have. When Lady Violette was younger, she always found a problem with the matches her father found for her. They were too ugly, or too arrogant, too stupid, too shy… always something. Not that her feelings mattered. Those matches didn't work because the grooms rejected her."

"My master said she's too difficult."

"That's exactly what the suitors said," the man said, speaking in a normal tone. "Last month her father told her time was running out, that she was too old, and he would have to take whatever he could find."

"What did she say?"

"She said, 'Good, then we can stop this charade and let me get on with my life.'"

There was a slight pause, then both of them broke into laughter.

When their mirth subsided, the woman asked, "So, how did her father find this match?"

"No one's really sure. Lady Violette and the groom have traveled in the same social circles for years. They're friendly enough, but there's certainly no spark. But for some reason, she hasn't chased him away like the others. If you ask me, I think her parents wore her down. She and her mother are at each other like cats and dogs." There was a slight pause when the server returned. "It's my guess she's just trying to escape her mother."

"Sounds like a marriage made in heaven."

"Imperials."

"Right." They were quiet for a moment, then the woman asked, "Why doesn't she just run away and join the Desulti?"

They snickered.

"Anyway, the wedding will be quite the fest. It's put a lot on my plate. The celebration lasts a full week. Everyone, who is anyone, will be there. The most prominent are staying at the estate. There are feasts every day, balls every night, entertainment, an art show. I don't know how I'll get it all done."

"Art?"

"Oh, yes. You know what a patron of the arts Lord Bergamot is. He's inviting twenty of the best artists in the Empire to create paintings for the event. He'll buy every work. The only thing is, they have just one week to finish."

Alar slammed his tankard down, stood on the narrow bench, and leapt over a startled Scilla. The man and woman jumped when Alar landed beside their table.

"*Lehasa,*" he said to blank looks. Apparently, they didn't speak *Alle'oss.* "Good evening," he said.

They mumbled greetings, frowns chasing the surprise from their expressions as they took in his clothes.

Noticing the woman's nose wrinkling, Alar took a half step back. "I apologize, but I couldn't help overhearing the last bit of your conversation, only because you mentioned art." He rushed on before they could respond. "I, myself, am not an artist." He held his hand where Ukrit and Scilla could see it and beckoned urgently. "But I represent two masters of the *Alle'oss* new school artistic movement. *Akana si.*" The furrows in the man's brow smoothed at the mention of the new school.

Scilla and Ukrit appeared at his side and Alar moved over to make room. He gestured to them and said, "May I introduce Scilla and Ukrit Woodsmith, students of the renowned new school master, Sune. Scilla is a painter and Ukrit is a sculptor."

"I'm sor —" the man started before Alar interrupted him.

"I can see from your expression you've heard of the new school, so I'm sure you understand how pleased your lord would be to have two masters at the wedding." He waved to Ukrit and Scilla's clothes. "As you know, some new school artists have been…" He glanced around, leaned forward and spoke confidentially, "persecuted by the Inquisition." He straightened and said in a normal voice, "Unjustly so in our case. That explains our present impoverished condition, but I can assure you the rags on the outside merely mask the genius within." He gave them his widest smile and waited while they gaped at him.

Finally, the man gestured to Scilla and Ukrit and said, "Even if they are who you say they are, why would Lord Bergamot invite the wrath of the Inquisition to host new school artists?"

"Yes, well, as you know," Alar said. "The new school invited Inquisition attention by choosing forbidden subjects for their paintings. Quite rightly, as many would agree. But as Scilla and Ukrit will use the wedding celebration for inspiration, this will not be a problem. So, your lord will own works with all the flair and revolutionary technique of the new school, but the subjects will be such that no inquisitor could complain." Alar paused to emphasize his next words. "Imagine what your prestigious guests will think. It will be a sensation." He could see the man was intrigued.

"Do you have samples of their work?"

"Alas, no," Alar said, letting his expression and stance convey the tragedy of their situation. "In our haste to leave Argren, we were forced to leave much behind." When a skeptical frown appeared on the man's face, Alar rushed on, "But they will be happy to produce a small sample for your evaluation."

"We will?" Scilla muttered.

Alar ignored her. "All we need are the supplies — paints, canvas, sculpting materials, and such — because, as you have no doubt noticed, we find ourselves short of resources since arriving in your fair city." Alar could see in the glance the man and woman exchanged, he almost had them. "What do you risk? A little coin. You provide the supplies, a place for us to stay for a few days, modest sustenance. If you discover I'm lying, we leave, and your lord is no wiser. But I'm confident a patron of the arts like Lord Bergamot will be more than grateful if you were to bring masters of *akana si* to depict his daughter's long-awaited nuptials."

Alar waited while the man stared at him. Finally, the man said, "Come to Sylvan Lane tomorrow morning at the eighth bell. The house in the neo-imperial style. Around back at the servant's gate. Don't be late."

Alar bowed. "Of course. Your master will be forever grateful." He herded Scilla and Ukrit toward the tavern door.

"What about the stew?" Ukrit asked.

Alar scooped up their last coin and whispered, "We'll get a sausage on the street."

"I didn't finish my ale," Ukrit grumbled as Alar shoved him out the door.

When they were standing on the street in the gathering darkness, Ukrit and Scilla glowered at Alar's grin. "New school masters?" Scilla asked.

"You remember what Sune said," Alar said as he started walking. He adopted Sune's affected gestures and speech. "Already, there is great promissse." Sune, Scilla's and Ukrit's mentor, owned a gallery in Richeleau.

"Promise, he said. Promise." Scilla said, falling in beside him.

"What will these rubes know?" Alar asked, grinning at the irony of using a term the Volloch often used for the *Alle'oss*. It was an apt appellation for Volloch when it came to art. "You've seen what Imperials call art. You'll be fine."

"You didn't even ask him how long we have to produce this sample," Ukrit said. "Painting's one thing, but I don't think I could produce a decent sculpture in a week."

"Tell us," Scilla said, "why you got us into this?"

Alar stopped, held up a hand and ticked the reasons off on his fingers. "We get a decent place to sleep. For a bit anyway. We get decent meals. For free, mind you. The lord will buy your works. Assuming they're good enough." When Scilla frowned at him, he rushed to add, "Which, of course, they will be. *And* we will have access to the estate on which a very large, very heavy chest of coin is hidden. The dowry." He held up his index finger. "One job." He extended his arms to his sides and grinned.

"Clever," Ukrit said.

"But how do we get the coin out and how do we get away?" Scilla asked. "There has to be all kinds of security and you've seen those estates. There are walls, gates, guards everywhere."

Alar waved his hands. "Details." He resumed walking. "All we have to do is get in, see what's what, then we come up with a plan."

"A plan?" Ukrit asked. "I don't like the sound of that."

"Have we ever failed?" Alar asked.

"Repeatedly," Scilla said.

"We've just been lucky," Ukrit said. "Mostly."

"Spirit's luck," Alar said. "I expect we'll need it, but it hasn't failed us yet."

"No," Scilla said. "Not yet."

4

Truth

"That sausage last night wasn't nearly enough." It was the old Ukrit who rose from his bedroll in the morning. The one Alar met on the road to Lirantok as Alar was fleeing an Imp slaver. The one full of grumbles.

Alar stopped and peered up at the street sign. "I'm aware. Was thinking of it all night, as my stomach wouldn't shut up long enough to let me sleep." They passed around a crock of honey before they left the shack, dipping into it with their fingers, but it barely touched their hunger.

Scilla pointed down a street and started walking. "We heard you the first five times you mentioned it," she said to Ukrit, the ragged state of her patience obvious in her tone.

"Just hungry, is all," Ukrit said under his breath as he followed.

Scilla whirled on him. "Oh! Is that the problem? You're hungry. Well, why didn't you say so before? Let me see if I can rustle you up some breakfast." She extended her arms to her sides. "Oh, wait! There *is* nothing I or Alar can do about you being hungry!"

Ukrit pulled up and glared at her. But instead of responding in kind, like the old grumbly Ukrit would, he glanced around at the expensive neighborhood. "Just nervous, is all. Hungry. And nervous."

"Nervous?"

"I've never sculpted for anyone but Sune and family." He rotated his shoulders. "And the truth is, I'm slow." When he looked up and found Alar and Scilla grinning at him, he said, "Slow at sculpting, smart asses."

Alar slapped him on the shoulder. "Don't worry. You heard what the man said. Lord Bergamot only buys the pieces he likes. If yours is rubbish, it's not a problem."

As Alar and Scilla turned away, Ukrit said, "I didn't say it would be rubbish. I said it wouldn't be *finished.*" Setting off after them, he muttered, "Smart asses."

They left most of the buildings behind and walked for what seemed a long time along a winding wooded road before they found the correct street. "This is it," Alar said.

They left the small shack before dawn to make it to the neighborhood on the northern outskirts of Lachton by the eighth bell. Even so, they were cutting it close. They heard the seventh bell nearly half an hour earlier. Still, they paused and gazed down the street, unsure how to proceed. They passed other residential neighborhoods with increasingly expensive looking houses as they walked. But the only thing they saw on this street was a tall stone wall that extended into the distance. An ornate iron gate a hundred paces down the street was the only entrance. Two men in gray and green livery guarded it.

"Is this it?" Ukrit asked.

"He said it was the one in the neo-Imperial style," Scilla said.

"Oh, that one," Ukrit said. "How does that help?"

Alar took hold of Scilla's arm and walked briskly down the street toward the gate. The guards watched them warily as they approached. When they were even with the gate, Alar stopped and studied the house at the end of a long drive. He settled a hand on his hip, then threw the other toward the house. "Now this," he said loudly, "is a lovely home. A perfect exemplar of the austere lines of the neo-imperial style." He gave Scilla an expectant look and flicked his eyes to the guards.

"Oh!" Adopting a thoughtful frown, she rested a finger on her chin and said, "I don't believe you're right about that. This home is clearly *not* neo-imperial."

Alar humphed, tilted his head, and peered at the house. "What do you think, Ukrit?"

Ukrit started. "I… uh… agree with Scilla. This house is more likely from the late Davorian period."

"Late Davorian?" Scilla said and laughed. "You must have had too much ale last night, Ukrit. Your eyes are bleary." She looked at the frowning guards as if seeing them for the first time. "Let's ask these gentlemen."

"Sir," Alar said, waving a hand at one of the guards as if trying to get his attention. "Tell my friends that this house is in the neo-Imperial style, will you?"

The guards glanced at one another, then one of them said, "I'm not sure what your game is, but by the looks of you three, you're in the wrong neighborhood. I suggest you move along before we move you."

"Nice try," Scilla muttered. She approached the guard who spoke. "We were told to appear at the servant's entrance of an estate on Sylvan Lane by the eighth bell. The only directions he gave us was the house was in the neo-Imperial style."

"Who told you this?" the other guard asked.

"He, uh, didn't give us a name. He was tall, thin, short hair, well dressed. *Alle'oss.*" The guards smirked, but before they could speak, Scilla rushed on. "We're artists trying out for an art show for a wedding. If we're late, we lose an opportunity to lift us from our obviously desperate state."

Noticing the shift in their expressions when Scilla mentioned the wedding, Alar asked, "So, the wedding is here?"

"Maybe."

"All we want to know is how to find the servant's entrance," Alar said. "If we're lying, no one will let us in, and whoever is guarding that gate can move us along."

After a pause, the guard pointed back in the direction they came from. "Go up to the intersection, turn left twice. You'll find the gate in the back wall."

A bell somewhere on the estate began tolling the eighth hour as they turned onto the alley at the back of the estate. They broke into a sprint and arrived, sweaty and panting, at the servant's gate as the last note was dying in the morning air. The man they met in the tavern the previous night was just disappearing.

"Good morning," Alar said between ragged breaths. "Right on time."

The man peered at them, his eyes roving over their worn clothes. "You look even worse in the light of day."

Alar couldn't think of anything to say to that, so he let his smile widen and kept quiet.

After studying them for a few more moments, the man sighed. "Well, as I've already assembled the supplies." He grew stern. "But you will follow me to the stables, and you will remain there until I've evaluated your claims. Afterwards, regardless of the outcome, guards will escort you off the estate, whereupon you will leave peacefully."

Even after they all nodded, he gazed at them, his expression full of doubt. Finally, he sighed again, turned and walked down a path that ran along the inside of the wall. Alar, Scilla and Ukrit fell in behind him, followed by three guards.

"Excuse me," Alar said. "I'm afraid we didn't get your name last night."

"That's because I didn't give it to you," he said over his shoulder.

Alar looked back at Scilla with wide eyes and arched his eyebrows. Catching his eye, one of the guards snorted.

Majestic elms, clothed in pale green spring leaves, bordered the well-manicured path, their limbs arching over their heads and extending beyond the wall. When they emerged from the shadows of the trees, they crossed a grassy sward, toward a building that was larger than any house Alar had seen in Richeleau. Horses in an attached corral watched them approach, tossing their heads and whinnying.

Just before they arrived at the wide-open door to the stables, a man and woman riding a pair of white horses emerged. The woman wore black knee-high boots that glinted in the morning light, cream colored riding pants, a blue blouse and a red riding helmet. Both the man and woman had the characteristic black hair of Volloch. The woman glanced to her right as they rode past, her eyes locking with Alar's. Just before she looked away, her top lip curled slightly.

"Who was that?" Alar asked.

The man, leading them into the interior, said over his shoulder, "The Lady Violette, the bride, and her father, Lord Anton Bergamot."

They passed down a wide aisle flanked by stalls, many of them occupied, then climbed a wooden staircase at the back of the building. The top floor was mostly one immense room. Their arrival swirled dust, which was caught in sun beams emitted by rows of windows on two walls. Crates, the disassembled parts of carriages, various bits of tack were all organized neatly. They followed a trail recently plowed through a thick layer of dust to one end of the room.

Stopping outside a door at the end of the trail, the man gave Alar an impatient look, then addressed Scilla and Ukrit. "You have four hours. You can use only the supplies in this room. When I return, I will judge how valid your claims are. My word is final." He paused, staring sternly at them, until they nodded. "You are not to leave this room. The guards will see that you don't."

"What would you like us to do?" Ukrit asked.

"Do?"

"The subjects of our works."

"Oh, yes." His lips pursed for a moment. "You walked across the back of the estate. Do something you saw."

"Can we go back and look one more time?" Scilla asked.

"No."

He was turning to leave when Alar asked, "Sir, might I ask? We had to hurry to arrive on time and were not able to procure breakfast."

"I will have something brought up," he said and turned away.

A guard opened the door and gestured inside. There were no windows on the bare walls. The only light came from pairs of lamps in sconces mounted on three of the walls. An easel with a canvas sat in one corner. Paints, rags, a palette, brushes and other items Alar didn't recognize rested on a table beside the easel. In the opposite corner, a pedestal sat beside a table on which various tools rested beside brick shaped lumps of clay stacked in a pyramid.

Scilla stood in front of the canvas, staring down at the table. She picked up a brush and ran the bristles across her fingers. Holding the brush close to her eyes, she plucked a loose bristle free with delicate fingers and stared at it. Throwing the brush down, she whirled on Alar. "This is impossible! I can barely see the colors in this light, and these brushes are pathetic."

"Clay," Ukrit said, pushing his index finger into one of the bricks. "I've never worked with clay." He picked up one of the instruments. "I don't even know what any of these are for."

They glared accusations at Alar.

"Worse than any of that," he said. "I'm going to need to pee pretty soon."

***

Captain Brennerman looked up as his adjutant, Jan, entered his office. Before Jan spoke, Brennerman caught sight of two of the recently arrived rangers in their green uniforms passing outside his window that looked out onto the inner ward of the fortress.

"Captain," his adjutant said. "Three of the additional patrols have returned."

"Three?"

"The patrol of the road to Ka'tan is late."

Brennerman looked away from the window and focused on his adjutant.

"They are only two hours late," Jan said.

Brennerman glanced at the window, but the rangers had disappeared. The ranger company arrived a week before, and their commander hadn't reported to him. When he noticed Jan speaking, he focused on him and asked, "Excuse me?"

"I said the Ka'tan road patrol got a late start, so it's not surprising they aren't back."

"Right, of course. Anything to report from the other patrols?"

"No, sir. Nothing unusual."

"Thank you." When he was alone again, Brennerman gazed out the window. As the commandant of the fort, the ranger company fell under his command. The captain of the ranger company, Hoch, should have reported to him as soon as he arrived. It was galling. But none of his patrols found any sign of the rebels. That left one blank spot on the map; the rugged terrain east of Richeleau. He needed Hoch's cooperation, so it was up to him to be the bigger man.

Standing, he retrieved his jacket and headed out the door. With a brief word to his adjutant, he stepped into the fort's inner ward. The sun was nearing the top of the western wall, leaving a third of the ward in twilight. His men, who had just returned from patrol, were nearing the dining hall. A group of rangers were on an intercepting course. The rangers were hard men, veterans of the tough battles in the mountains of Styria. Brennerman's troopers were good men, but they hadn't had the same opportunities to prove themselves. From the reports he was getting from his lieutenants, the rangers showed little respect for the cavalrymen. Brennerman admonished them against responding in kind. They were to show no deference to the rangers but should treat them with respect.

Brennerman watched the two groups converge on the entrance to the dining hall. There was a tense moment, then one of his lieutenants stepped forward and extended a hand. The rangers turned and entered the dining hall, leaving the trooper standing with his hand extended. The other troopers laughed and clapped the offended man on the back, then followed the rangers. Brennerman allowed himself a moment of pride. At least *his* men showed some military professionalism.

Hoch's adjutant looked up as Brennerman entered his office. "Sir," he said, but he didn't rise.

Swallowing his pique at the man's disrespect, Brennerman said, "I wish to see Captain Hoch."

"Yes, sir. I'm afraid I don't have an appointment for you."

"An appointment? I am the commandant of this fort. I don't need an appointment." Suddenly, the anger that simmered since the rangers arrived surged. "You stand at attention when a superior officer enters the room, Lieutenant!"

The man got slowly to his feet.

Brennerman stared at him until he offered a sloppy salute. "The next time you fail to come to attention and offer a proper salute, you'll spend a month in the guardhouse."

"What is going on here?"

Brennerman looked away from the lieutenant to find Captain Hoch standing in the door to his office. He was half a head shorter than Brennerman, thick armed and barrel chested. Scars on his forehead and chin testified to his long career in the rangers. He wore the same simple green uniform as his men. Only the twin bars on his collar indicated his rank.

"Captain Hoch," Brennerman said. "Your men apparently take after your example."

"Excuse me?"

"Lack of respect for the chain of command."

Hoch glanced at his adjutant, then came further into the room. "Chain of command?"

"I am the commandant of this fort and have been for the past year. You arrived a week ago and couldn't bother reporting to me."

Hoch gazed at him for a long moment, then his eyes flicked down to Brennerman's uniform. "I apologize. If I had known the amount of gold on a uniform indicated seniority, I would have paid more attention to those embellishments."

Brennerman felt his face blanch. Out of the corner of his eye, he noticed the lieutenant suppressing a smile. Technically, though they were the same rank, Captain Hoch had seniority, having been a captain longer. But Brennerman was the commandant of the fort, so he outranked Hoch. By rights, Brennerman could relieve him of his command for such blatant disrespect. But it would be better if he had his willing cooperation, so with an effort, he ignored the insult. "I wish to discuss a task for which your unit is well suited."

Hoch's brows quivered. "A… task?"

"Yes. If you could come to my office so we can examine a map of the area."

"That won't be necessary. I have my orders, and I doubt very much if they overlap with your *task*."

"Orders? I should have been informed of any orders. Who gave them?"

"I'm to discover what happened to the previous ranger unit under *your* command."

Ignoring for the moment that Hoch didn't answer his question, Brennerman said, "They were ambushed on the road to Ka'tan."

"Ambushed? By whom?"

"I suspect it was an *Alle'oss* rebel group who call themselves *Oss'stera*."

"*Alle'oss* rebels?" Hoch asked and exchanged a grin with his lieutenant. "You believe Alle'oss rebels eliminated an entire company of Imperial Rangers. Leaving no trace?"

Brennerman opened his mouth to respond, but Hoch put up a hand to stop him. "And what have you done to respond to this threat? Are these rebels still at large?"

"That is the task I wish to discuss with you. We are conducting a search —"

"Waste of time," Hoch said dismissively. "I read the Inquisition report on what occurred here over the winter. That business with the mercenaries and the *rebels.*"

Brennerman gaped at him. "Inquisition… What report?"

"The report Inquisitor Harold Wolfe filed on his return from Richeleau."

"Inquisitor? Wolfe is only a novice."

Hoch shrugged. "He's an Inquisitor now."

Brennerman met Wolfe when he coerced Brennerman to join forces with the rebels. He assumed it was only an expedient, that the novice would deal with the rebels after using them in the battle. But Wolfe showed what Brennerman considered undue respect for the *Alle'oss* before the battle and disappeared afterward without taking any action. Brennerman heard nothing about a report. "What… Why…" he spluttered.

"I suggest you read it," Hoch said with a knowing grin. "I'm sure a copy has been filed with the local Inquisition house." His expression hardened. "Now, as far as the chain of command goes, I've read your file, Brennerman. We both know why you *command* a fort in a backwater like Argren. From now on we keep to our own business. I have my orders, and you have your wild goose chase." He started to turn away, then caught the eye of his adjutant and turned back to Brennerman. "And the next time you raise your voice to one of my men, I'll pull the rank that matters." He turned his back on Brennerman and entered his office.

Brennerman gaped at his open door.

"Do you wish to make an appointment?"

Brennerman's head swiveled to the lieutenant in time to see his grin before he suppressed it. Gathering himself, he gave his jacket a tug, turned on his heel, and strode through the exit. He was halfway to his office before he became aware of his surroundings. Ignoring his men's salutes, he entered his adjutant's office. "No interruptions for the next half hour," he mumbled, then hurried into his office, shut the door and froze.

His gaze drifted until it came to rest on the framed certificate he received when he graduated from the Imperial Military Academy. Top of his class. The most highly decorated cavalry graduate ever. Victor Storm, the general who stood atop the Empire's cavalry forces, a man Brennerman admired more than any other, presented it to Brennerman himself. The general told him he expected great things from him. It was no more than Brennerman expected of himself.

But here he was, years later, relegated to a backwater, dismissed and ridiculed, still needing to prove himself.

Sensing weakness, the grief he kept at bay most days clawed its way free. He managed to arrest an undignified sob by pressing a fist against his mouth and biting down on a knuckle until it bled. Moments passed, then, with an enormous effort, he donned the armor he so carefully constructed. Competence and professionalism. It was the only thing that kept him upright some days.

Back in control, he took a breath and let it sigh out. With or without Hoch's cooperation, he still had a job to do. Straightening, he gave his jacket a tug and stepped into his adjutant's office. "Schedule a meeting with my lieutenants for tomorrow morning."

5

Invitation

Alar peered over Scilla's shoulder. "Shouldn't it be… bigger?" Scilla and Ukrit had been at it for over three hours. The odor of paints, turpentine and sweat was overpowering in the small, stuffy room. The canvas on which Scilla was creating her work was four feet tall and three feet wide, but the image that was emerging under her brushes occupied only a small portion in the center.

Scilla whirled around, forcing Alar to leap away from the brush she brandished. "I told you before," she said through clenched teeth. "Stay over there!" She pointed with her paintbrush to the other side of the room beside the table on which a guard laid out their breakfast.

"Right," Alar said, backing away, hands in a defensive gesture. "Getting edgy is all. A lot riding on this. No pressure, though."

Scilla glared at him, until he neared the opposite wall, then turned back to the easel.

Alar watched her for a few moments, then turned his attention on Ukrit, who was sweating profusely over his emerging sculpture. Ukrit claimed he never worked with clay before and, based on the volume of his swearing the first two hours, Alar believed him. He started over twice. But even though he had only finished the head, neck, forelegs, back and part of the tail, Alar had to admit the horse emerging from the clay was remarkable. Neck bent, ears pinned back, nostrils flaring. It was as if the animal struggled to burst forth from the mound of clay. Alar didn't know what standards the man who left them here would apply, but he had to be impressed.

He edged sideways, so he could peer at Scilla's painting, one eyebrow rising and lips twisting. The image emerging of the couple they saw riding out of the stables, though admittedly quite good, was dwarfed by the canvas. He would feel awful if the man disparaged Scilla's efforts, but he was pretty sure that was what would happen.

The door swung open. Alar jumped and turned in time to see a guard step out of the way, revealing their judge holding a lantern in one hand. He entered, breezed past Alar without a word and went to stand next to the pedestal on which Ukrit's sculpture rested. Ukrit stepped back, clay-streaked forearms at his side, one of the sculpting tools dangling from a limp hand. Sighing heavily, he caught Alar's eye and shrugged.

The man held the lantern up, bent over, and put his face close to the horse. He edged around the pedestal, his head tilting one way, then another. Straightening, he lifted his gaze from the sculpture, a slight arch of surprise in his brows. When he saw Alar watching him, his expression cleared, and he said, "This is acceptable."

Ukrit dropped the tool.

"Never had a doubt," Alar said, grinning at Ukrit's stunned expression.

"Yes, well… let us see what we have here," the man said and crossed the room to Scilla's canvas.

Scilla stood aside, a frazzled expression on her face, the pallet and brush still in her hands. Paint and sweat blotched her face, arms, dress, and hair. Alar held his breath, keeping his face blank, but readying a sympathetic frown.

The man stared at the painting. He lifted his lantern and leaned forward until his nose was inches from the canvas. After what seemed a long time, he straightened, murmured something unintelligible, then thrust the lantern at Scilla. She threw the pallet at the table and took the lantern. The man grasped the sides of the canvas, lifted it from the easel, then hurried to the door, brushing Alar aside as he passed.

Scilla gave Alar a panicked frown on her way out the door. The three of them and the guards streamed after the man and the painting across the enormous room, down the staircase, past the stable stalls and into the sunlight. The canvas in his hands, the man cast about until he found Ukrit.

"Here," he said, thrusting the canvas at him.

Ukrit grasped the canvas and held it up.

The man rotated the canvas around until the sun fell fully on the painting, then said, "Stay still." He bent forward again and studied the small painting.

Scilla caught Alar's eye and frowned. Remembering she still held the brush along with the lantern, she looked around for a place to put them, then absently held the brush out to Alar.

Alar took it and watched the man examining the painting.

After long, tense minutes, the man straightened and spun around. Finding Scilla, he approached her, seemed to gather himself, and asked, "Where did you study?"

"Excuse me?" she asked.

He waved a hand at the canvas. "Your technique. Where did you learn to paint like that?"

She looked past him toward Ukrit, who rotated around enough so he could see what was happening. "I don't know. I guess I learned most of it from Sune."

"Sune?" The man's brows knitted.

"He has a gallery in Richeleau."

He clasped his hands behind his back and gazed over Scilla's head. "And you've studied with no one else?" He lowered an intense gaze to her face.

"No. It's just been me and my brother, mostly."

He returned to the painting, nudging Ukrit around again so it faced the sun. Beckoning Scilla over to stand next to him, he swept his hand across the canvas. "The depth you've achieved in such a small work is really quite astounding." The amiable shift in his tone and stance was startling. "The colors… well, you could only work with what was provided. But even so, what you've achieved is remarkable. You will have to tell me sometime how you achieved this purple."

When he paused and smiled at Scilla, she stared back at him and mumbled, "Thank you." She extended her arm with the lantern and Alar hurried forward to take it.

The man looked furtively around, then leaned forward and spoke in a confidential tone. "I've had the great pleasure and honor of perusing a Valdemar." When Scilla looked up at his face, inches from her own, he nodded and winked. He straightened and held his hand above Scilla's painting, fingers splayed. "This lacks, shall we say, a certain maturity compared to the Valdemar, but its aspirations are in the same neighborhood." He cocked his head and peered at Scilla. "You are still quite young to have developed such startling technique." His fingers went to his lips and rested there as he gazed at the painting. "I will have to pay a visit to this Sune," he murmured, then he dropped his hand, gave her a wide smile and said, "You must let me purchase this painting."

"What?!" Scilla asked.

"Have you sold any other works?"

"No. I just…" She paused, mouth open, then she said, "Paint for myself."

"Oh, how delicious," he said, rubbing his hands together. "The first work of a budding master." He turned to gaze at the painting speculatively. After a moment, his eyes flicked toward Scilla, then he took in Alar's ragged clothing. "I wish you — and your brother, of course — to produce works for the wedding. But we must make you all presentable. If you will sell me this painting…" He fished in a pocket, a knowing smile on his face. When he withdrew his hand, something glinted between his fingers before he held up a gleaming golden coin and said, "I will pay you one gold Imperial Eagle."

Alar dropped the lantern. "Oh, *sheoda*!" he blurted. The man frowned as Alar scrambled to retrieve it.

Ukrit spun the canvas around until he could see Scilla, his head bobbing.

Scilla looked at Alar, stunned. "Up to you, Scilla," he said.

A matching grin grew slowly on her face. "Of course. That would be wonderful."

"Excellent!" He held out the coin and placed it in Scilla's trembling palm, then he waved a guard over and gave him instructions on where to take the canvas. He watched the guard retreating for a moment, then turned back to Scilla with a flourish.

"Thank you… again!" Scilla said, still looking stunned.

"No. It is entirely my honor." He took the paint-stained hand, not gripping the coin, and kissed it. When he straightened, he turned to Alar and said in a business-like tone, "You identified yourself as their manager… Alar?"

Alar nodded, "Yes, and Alar is correct."

The man stepped forward and offered his hand.

Alar hesitated. The *Alle'oss* grasped each other's forearms, but he had seen Imperial men grasping each other's hands. He took the man's hand and was relieved when he smiled.

"My name is Olson." He let go of Alar's hand. "Now, the wedding festivities begin four weeks from today and continue for one week. The artists are required to stay on the grounds for the duration and must produce their work the week *before* guests arrive. Therefore, you must have them at the servant's gate no later than the eighth bell, three weeks from today. Is that clear?" When Alar nodded, he added, "And please make sure you are all presentable to polite company." He took the lantern from Alar, kissed Scilla's hand once more, nodded to Ukrit, and said, "The guards will show you to the gate." With that, he strode across the lawn toward the manor house.

Alar, Scilla and Ukrit stared at one another.

"Mine was acceptable," Ukrit said with a wide smile.

***

The guards who led them to the front gate, rather than the servant's gate, were considerably more amiable than they were that morning. One of them, in particular, took an interest in Scilla, walking beside her and pointing out parts of the immense estate. Alar followed, more than a little annoyed by his attention.

Scilla stopped abruptly, reached out and took the guard's arm and pointed between two of the oaks lining the path. "What is that?" she asked.

He followed her gaze, then smiled down at her and said, "That's the Lady Violette's gardens." He stepped closer to Scilla than was strictly necessary. "Of course, it's early spring now, but in another week or two, the garden will be quite the spectacle. Blues, and reds, and yellows. The Lady does love the colorfullest flowers."

"Colorfullest?" Alar mumbled. He edged closer to Scilla until their arms touched and looked out at the garden. The oak trees and the pine straw mat beneath them were separated from the garden by a narrow lawn. Alar decided he would have to trust the guard on his assessment of the color, because most of the plants were just emerging from their winter slumber.

Scilla started to turn away, but hesitated as a couple appeared, ambling along a path through the garden. It was the bride and another man. Lady Violette still wore her riding outfit, providing some of the colors — blue, cream and red — the garden couldn't. They watched as the couple climbed a small wooden bridge which arched over a stream beside a small pond. They paused at the top, standing slightly apart, and gazed at the garden. It was not a picture of a happy couple. Remembering Olson's bleak assessment of the marriage from the previous night, Alar guessed the man was the groom.

"Best be getting on," the guard said. "Olson likes his directions followed precisely."

As they resumed walking, Alar asked the guard, "What's with this Olson?"

"What do you mean?"

Alar was amused that his voice didn't carry the gentle tone he used with Scilla. "He's *Alle'oss*, but he seems sort of…"

"Volloch," Urkit said, then he said to the guard, "No offense."

The guard looked as if he wasn't sure whether he should be offended, but then Scilla touched his arm and said, "Ukrit means he seems more refined than most *Alle'oss*."

"Oh, right," the guard said, pulling his shoulders back the smallest amount. "Well, Olson is a rare duck. He's *Alle'oss*, but he's in charge of the household."

"What does that mean?" Scilla asked the question Alar was mouthing to her behind the guard's back.

"He's in charge of everything that has to do with running the estate. The other servants, cooks, the household finances. Has a lot on his plate, he does, which, as you pointed out, is unusual for a *l'o*—" His eyes flicked to Scilla, and he cleared his throat before continuing. "An *Alle'oss*. But he's much more refined than usual. Knows wine, art, and such things." He chuckled and gave Scilla a lopsided grin. "Yeah, he's an odd duck, alright."

When they arrived at the gate, the guard opened it, then inserted himself between Alar and Scilla. "I assume you —"

Alar stepped around him, gave him a big grin, and slapped him on the shoulder. "Thank you for your hospitality." He cocked his head and asked, "What was your name again?"

"Uh, Helmut."

"Thank you, Helmut," Alar said. He nudged Scilla into motion and said to Helmut, "We can find our own way back to the city. See you in three weeks."

"Is he still there?" Scilla asked as they neared the intersection.

Alar turned around, walked backward for a few steps, waving to the guard. When he turned back around, he said, "Yep."

"I think he was going to ask to see you," Ukrit said, sounding slightly offended.

"Broad minded, our Helmut," Alar said, grinning at Scilla's frown. "I mean, considering he's a bit of a bigot." When they turned right off Sylvan Lane and the gate was no longer visible, he slipped an arm around her waist and pulled her close. "I'm… We're really proud of you." He fished the gold coin from his pocket and held it up to catch the light from the midday sun.

"We're going to eat, right?" Ukrit asked. "You don't have some harebrained plan for that coin, do you?"

Alar let Scilla go and returned the coin to his pocket. "I expect you would have learned by now the harebrained plan is not to be dismissed out of hand. But you need not be concerned, Ukrit. Tonight we celebrate. Food, ale and good company. What say you, Scilla?"

Scilla stopped, forcing Alar and Ukrit to stop as well. "I need some Argren Blue."

6

Ragan

Alar stared at Scilla, mentally calculating how long it would take him to reach the Ishien River Valley and return. He sympathized with her desire to have the precious blue pigment, Argren Blue. *Alle'oss* pigments were one of the reasons new school art was held in such high regard. But even on a fast horse, a horse that could run all day, there was no way he could make it back in time. When she started to speak, he held up his hand. "The only things on my mind at the moment are a warm bath, an ale and a bowl of stew." He paused and said, "Let's talk about this later."

She gave him an impatient frown, but then she nodded, turned and continued walking. Ukrit shrugged and followed.

Finding a tavern that offered baths, laundry services and could break the golden eagle proved difficult, but by flashing the coin, they finally found one on the edge of the posh district in the northern end of the city. The proprietor regarded them suspiciously and forced them to use the back door, but gold was gold, so he kept his questions to himself. Alar was so happy to feel clean, he didn't even mind when the man hustled them out the back door in damp clothes.

The warm sunny day matched their mood as they made their slow way back to their neighborhood. Alar watched Ukrit carefully at first, looking for any signs of envy. But he shouldn't have worried. He appeared even more proud of his sister's accomplishment than she did. Scilla did her best to deflect their flattery, but her pink cheeks revealed she wasn't entirely immune to it.

They arrived at the Tipsy Rooster tavern in the harbor district in time to beat the dinner crowd. Ensconced in their favorite booth, they shared good cheer, ales, crusty bread and bowls of *Alle'oss* stew. For Alar and Scilla, it was the first decent meal they had in a month.

After waddling back to their shack and caring for the horses, they lay on their backs atop the crates, gazing up at stars through the leaky roof and quietly marveling at their turn of fortune. There was only one fly in the ointment. Having pondered how to break the bad news to Scilla about the pigments all night, Alar knew what Ukrit meant when he broke the silence.

"Three weeks to get there and three weeks to get back. If you ride like your hair is on fire."

Three weeks would be a stretch, even if he could switch horses along the way. "We're supposed to show up at the estate in three weeks," Alar said. "The painting has to be done a week after that." Having delivered the verdict, he braced himself for Scilla's disappointment.

"You don't have to go all the way to the Valley," Scilla said. "There are some pigments in *Honutok*."

Alar rotated his head and found her gazing calmly at the ceiling. *Honutok* was the village *Oss'stera* founded east of Richeleau. When he and Scilla returned from the Ishien River Valley, Scilla brought back some of the pigments and left them in *Honutok* for safekeeping.

"That's right," Ukrit said. "I forgot about that. A week there and a week back if you walk. Plenty of time."

Alar couldn't hold his laughter back.

"What?" Scilla asked.

"You might have reminded me of that earlier."

"You didn't want to listen," Scilla said. "All you could think about was a bath and food."

"You're right," Alar said and chuckled. "I apologize." They fell silent. Pleasantly mellow, Alar's fingers sought out Scilla's. With warm thoughts of visiting *Honutok* in mind, the fingers of his other hand caressed the rough surface of the canvas covering the crate beneath him. "How much coin do we have left?" When Scilla told him, he asked Ukrit, "How much did Old Jep say we need to make on all this stuff?" He rapped on the crate with his knuckles.

The figure Ukrit told him was less than he feared.

"Are you thinking what I think you're thinking?" Scilla asked.

"I think so," Alar said with a grin.

"That would leave us with —"

"Just enough to get by," Alar said. "New clothes, so we're presentable. Might have to scrimp a bit, but it should be just enough."

Ukrit groaned. "And here I was looking forward to regular meals."

"We have plenty of honey," Alar said. "Now that we don't smell like goats, you could try selling that while I'm gone."

"You sure this is a good idea?" Scilla asked.

"No," Alar said. "But we'll pay them a little more than the minimum and they'll be impressed that we got it done so fast. I'll have Lief deliver the payment to Old Jep and get him organizing the next shipment. When we sell this…" He knocked on the crate again. "We'll make our coin back and maybe a little more."

They fell silent for a time. "It's not the stupidest thing we've done," Scilla said.

"Not sure that's a criterion we should get used to applying," Ukrit grumbled.

"I quite agree," Alar said. "But it's what we have to work with at the moment." He sat up and looked down at them. "Trust me, it will all work out. I'll leave first thing in the morning."

***

Rather than walking, Alar hopped a ride on a merchant's caravan to Richeleau. Then he left the city, heading east, and walked the rest of the way to *Honutok*. Nestled behind a row of hills, the village was surrounded by towering granite outcrops and could only be reached through two narrow ravines.

Lief, standing at the entrance to one of the ravines when Alar topped the hill, waved, not looking surprised at Alar's appearance. Alar descended the slope, trying to dismiss a sense of foreboding.

"How are things?" Alar asked when he drew close.

"Good," Lief said. "New people showing up pretty regular. Word's out. Got the summer gardens started."

Alar waited, but apparently that was all the news Lief had for him. "You, uh, you don't look surprised to see me."

"Heard you were coming."

Alar gazed at him, but Lief's expression was as inscrutable as always. "Uh-oh," he said finally.

Lief nodded. "She got here yesterday. She wants to talk to you."

Ragan. Only an Imperial witch with the gift of prophecy could know he was going to show up in *Honutok* at this moment. "She say what she wants?"

Lief shook his head. "I didn't ask."

"Probably the best policy," Alar murmured. "She here?"

"No, she's in Richeleau. She wants you to meet her at the Black Husky tonight." He gestured over his shoulder. "Brought a kid with her."

"Her daughter?" Ragan's daughter, Alyn, was born in *Honutok* the previous winter.

Lief shook his head and squinted up at the sky. "Boy named Aron," he said and returned his gaze to Alar. "Maybe ten summers. He, Zaina, and Keth are getting acquainted."

Deciding he didn't want to know why Ragan was traveling with a boy of ten summers, Alar murmured, "I don't have time for this." He looked up at the top of the granite outcrop and returned the sentry's wave.

"What *are* you doing here? Didn't expect you for a couple of months."

"I need the pigments Scilla left here." When Lief frowned, Alar added, "It's a long story. I'll tell you later. In the meantime, I have a favor to ask of you."

Lief's brows twitched up.

Alar reached into his pack, extracted the pouch containing the coin, lifted it, and shook it.

A small smile appeared on Lief's face at the soft clink of the coin within. "You sold everything?"

"Not exactly. Not everything. Yet." He handed the pouch to Lief. "Take this to Old Jep. Tell him we sold everything and ask him to start organizing another shipment for the summer."

Lief took the pouch and hefted it in his palm. "Where did you get the coin?"

"All part of the long story. I'll explain once it's all over."

"It's a lot of coin," Lief said.

"Yeah. I wouldn't expect any trouble in the mountains, but you might want to bring some others with you."

Lief nodded. "Wouldn't mind paying the family a visit."

Alar glanced up at the sun visible through the wind tossed canopy. "I got an hour before I have to head off to Richeleau. Why don't you show me around?"

***

It was all Alar could do to drag himself away from the warm welcome he received in *Honutok*. He worried constantly while he was away about the village, but he shouldn't have. He left good people in charge, including Lief. The residents wanted to hold a feast in his honor. It was more than a little amusing that when he told them he had an appointment in Richeleau, they decided to hold the feast anyway.

As he set off, festive music following him, he reflected on what awaited him in Richeleau. He was deeply ambivalent about getting involved with Ragan. If he was forced to, he would admit her sudden appearances benefited *Oss'stera* in the past. The first time she helped them rescue Scilla from the Inquisition. The second time led ultimately to the deal with the governor, helped them recover the priceless art by *Alle'oss* masters and gave him the leverage to make the deal that got Tove into the Desulti.

But both of those instances involved the kind of complicated violent encounters he hoped to leave behind. Still, it was Ragan who urged him to set his sights higher, to make *Oss'stera* more than a ragged band of rebels. That was the reason he, Scilla, and Ukrit were in Lachton. She was probably serving her own agenda, as usual, but maybe he owed her enough to listen to whatever crazy plan she had in mind.

Despite the fact *Oss'stera* was in business with the Imperial governor, Alar remained cautious as he made his way through Richeleau to the Black Husky tavern. He was still a wanted man. He never came to the attention of the Inquisition or civil intelligence services in Richeleau, but the captain of the Imperial Cavalry in Richeleau, Brennerman, knew who he was, and he hated the *Alle'oss*.

Fortunately, he made it to the tavern without encountering Imps. After checking to make sure he wasn't followed, he slipped into the tavern and surveyed the room. Ragan wasn't there yet. The proprietor, Jora, waved him over. By the time Alar got to his customary place at the shadowed end of the bar, Jora had an ale ready. Alar slapped a coin on the bar before Jora could say the ale was on the house.

"What's this?" Jora asked warily.

"Back payment for many ales. Consider it a partial payment for the repairs you had to make after the Inquisition tore up the place."

"You, uh, you aren't getting into trouble, are you?"

"Not at the moment," Alar said with a grin and took a sip. "Mmmmm. Still the best ale in Argren."

Jora swept the coin off the bar. "Not going to turn it down, but I'll keep it a bit. In case you need it back."

"Any news?" Alar asked, leaning his elbow on the bar so he could keep the door in view.

"Apparently, there was a battle up at the fort a few months back," Jora said, watching Alar carefully.

"Really?"

"Yeah, people are saying the cavalry finally got tired of the Union mercenaries lording it over them," Jora said slowly. When Alar only nodded, he said, "Course there's rumors about some *Alle'oss* being involved."

"Rumors?"

"Probably nothing." The rise in Jora's tone made it a question.

"Can't believe everything you hear," Alar said with a wink, and lifted the tankard in a toast.

"Right," Jora said and moved off to serve other customers.

Alar didn't have to wait long. Ragan entered the tavern and looked straight at him. She wore a cowl with a deep hood despite the warm day, probably to hide the tattoo near her left temple, a mark of her former status as a Seidi novice. She pointed to a table by the wall and made her way over to it. Alar joined her and took a seat with his back to the wall so he could watch the room.

"How's Alyn?" he asked. He hadn't expected her to show up with her infant daughter, but he was curious why she wasn't home with her.

She flinched, hesitated, then said, "With her father."

Alar waited, but she didn't elaborate. "Want an ale?"

Ragan waved Jenna, Jora's server, over. "I'll buy, if you want another."

They ordered ales and bowls of whatever soup was available. When they were alone again, Alar said, "I'm afraid to ask why you wanted to see me."

"I know I asked a lot from you last time. But you have to admit, it worked out well for *Oss'stera*."

"I will admit that," Alar said. "However, it was you who told me to set my sights higher. I was hoping I was past that sort of thing."

"You'll want to hear what I have to say."

Jenna set the ales and bowls in front of them. He drank the first ale on an empty stomach, and he was feeling it. Not a good time to talk to Ragan.

"Let's hear it," Alar said, dipping his spoon into a hearty barley soup.

"A representative of the Desulti is visiting Governor Adelbart."

Alar's spoon hovered above his bowl. "Why?"

"I suspect they want in on the deal you made with the governor."

"You mean, you don't know?"

"As I told you before," she said, irritation edging her voice, "the future is forever shifting, and I don't see everything." She paused to let her irritation dissipate. "But… if I had to guess, I would say yes, that is why she is here."

Alar noticed the spoon in his hand, set it down in the bowl, sat back and gazed around the room. "*Vo kustok*," he murmured. After a moment, he looked at Ragan. "Is this because I got Tove into the Desulti?"

"You did nothing of the sort. It's up to the Desulti council to allow her to join. You only gave her the opportunity to try. That she is now in the Order… well, frankly, I'm shocked."

Alar stared at her. "She's Desulti? Is she okay?"

Ragan nodded. "She is, and she's fine. But Tove being in the Order has nothing to do with them wanting in on this deal. I suspect the murtair you made the deal with, Brie, told them about it and this is what the Desulti do; they exploit opportunities."

"They'll push us out."

"Yes," Ragan said. "They don't like competition. The only advantage you have is they will underestimate you because you're *Alle'oss*."

"I should have known this would happen."

"It's my fault," Ragan said. "You're new to this kind of thing."

Alar gazed at Jora leaning against the bar and chatting with some of his regular customers. "Okay, I don't believe for a minute you're here out of the goodness of your heart." He was surprised at the hurt that appeared on her face. "You have your own reasons." Her face cleared. "What is it?"

"It's what you said to me. Set your sights higher."

Alar hesitated, reading her expression. "You're going after the Empire."

"And *Oss'stera* will have a part to play."

"You've seen this? In the future?"

"I can't tell you more," she said.

"Because you don't know, or you just don't want to tell me?"

"If I tell you, you'll try to fulfill my goals rather than your own. That will change what will happen."

He gazed at her sipping soup from her spoon, then watched a couple enter the tavern and take a table near the door. This was why dealing with Ragan was so frustrating. How helpful would it be to see into the future, to know which courses of action had the best chance of success? She always downplayed how useful it was, but he couldn't imagine knowing more about the possibilities wouldn't be helpful. Still, he knew from his previous dealings with the witch how difficult it was getting her to spill her secrets. Maybe it was enough that she felt *Oss'stera's* fortunes were tied to her own. "Fair enough," he said finally. "So, what's the plan?"

She sat forward, pushed the bowl of soup aside, and rested her elbows on the table. "First, we have to find out what the Desulti offer the governor."

"How are we going to do that?"

"Well, I would think that would be obvious," she said with a smirk.

"Right," he said, lifting a spoonful of soup to his mouth. Jora must have a new cook, because the soup was much better than usual. "You want me to, what, search her room?"

"That would work. Better yet, you can listen in on their meeting."

"That's going to be tough. I'm assuming they'll be behind closed doors. I'll have to get into the room and hide ahead of time."

"The governor is hosting a ball tonight," Ragan said. She reached down for a satchel, pulled out a bundle of cloth, and handed it to him.

"What's this?" he asked, taking the bundle.

"Servant's uniform."

He dropped a pair of pants into his lap and held up the shirt. "You don't think they'll notice an unfamiliar servant?"

"The governor hires *Alle'oss* vendors for his balls. There will be a lot of people they don't know mingling with guests."

"And one of them has agreed to hire me?"

"Already arranged," she said. "Once you're in, you slip away, find the Desulti's room and search it. Then find a way to listen in on the meeting and hide until they meet."

"When is the meeting?"

"Tomorrow morning. I would suggest you hit the privy before you hide."

"Good advice," Alar said. "You have any idea where her room is?"

"The guest rooms are on the second floor. The largest suite is on the northwest corner. I'm sure that would be where the governor put her."

"Or Gerold did," Alar said, referring to the governor's very efficient assistant.

"Right. The meeting will likely be in governor's office."

"The governor's office," Alar said flatly. When she didn't respond, he said, "The rooms will be locked."

She dipped into her satchel again and withdrew a heavy brass key. "All the doors in official Imperial buildings must be accessible to authorities. This is a skeleton key which should open every lock in the building."

Alar eyed the key. "Should?"

"I'm cert — Reasonably certain it will work."

"Sounding more and more like one of our plans." He took the key and slipped it into his pocket. "What was the other thing?"

Ragan lifted a brow.

"You said, 'first…'"

"Oh, right. The second thing is you need to remind the governor who he made the deal with."

"And how do I do that?"

"I suggest you show up in his bedroom in the middle of the night and scare the *sheoda* out of him. Nothing like someone appearing out of nowhere to put a scare into someone."

Alar stared at her, imagining the governor's reaction. "Murtair on one side, realm walker on the other." He grinned. "Poor guy."

They ate in silence for a bit, then Alar asked, "What do we do if the Desulti are trying to push us out? They don't seem like they take no for an answer very often, and I doubt we can rely on the governor to stand up to the Desulti for long."

"Let's find out what they're proposing," Ragan said. "Then we'll make sure the governor makes the right choice."

***

Brennerman placed the folder in the center of his desk. It contained the report Harold Wolfe filed after his investigation in Richeleau. It took Brennerman more than a week to obtain it. Between the Inquisition's byzantine approval process and Krueger's smirking condescension, he almost decided it wasn't worth the effort. But Hoch's insinuations wouldn't allow him to forget it.

A courier delivered a copy that morning, but he waited until his adjutant left for the day so he could read it without interruptions. Back ramrod straight, he took a breath, opened the folder, and began reading.

Half an hour later, he slumped in his seat and stared into space. That it was a pack of lies wasn't surprising. As a fresh-faced plebe in the academy, it came as a shock to Brennerman the extent to which Imperial officials went to cover their own incompetence. But it was usually a simple gilding of the lily. A blurring of sharp edges. It was so common, one learned to read between the lines to distinguish the lies from the truth.

But Brennerman had never been the scapegoat of someone's obfuscations before. What Harold Wolfe submitted to the Inquisition was an outright fabrication that completely obscured the threat *Oss'stera* posed and placed much of the blame for the troubles with the Union mercenaries at Brennerman's door.

He focused on the last line of the report.

It is my conclusion that the group who call themselves Oss'stera are a small-time criminal organization with only local significance. My recommendation is to let the local gendarmes deal with them.

Brennerman wasn't personally aware of all the events Wolfe described, but he conducted his own investigation after the battle at the fort and uncovered enough to follow Wolfe's narrative. If this was their only evidence of what occurred, it was no wonder the local Inquisition commander and Hoch dismissed the rebel threat.

He sat up, straightened the papers, closed the file, and gazed at it. The report made no difference to his plans at a tactical level. His men were already searching the terrain east of Richeleau on foot. Though they found nothing so far, they had only covered a small part of the ground. All the report did was raise the stakes for Brennerman. Left uncontested, it would ruin his career. He was confident the truth would come out. He would be vindicated, and he would be sure everyone knew it was he who defied the doubters and rooted out the rebels.

But the report teased at more fundamental questions for Brennerman. The Inquisition's primary role, the reason it existed, was to root out threats to the Empire, both religious and secular. They had elevated a man to inquisitor who lied to cover up a clear threat.

He stood, retrieved the report, and hid it away in a filing cabinet. Closing the drawer, he gazed, unseeing, at the wall. Wolfe's lies were personally devastating for Brennerman. But from a broader perspective, Wolfe was only one man, one crack in the vast Imperial edifice. Brennerman shook his head. The problem was the inquisitor's perfidy wasn't unique. Not by a long shot. How many cracks were acceptable before the entire structure quivered and fell?

7

Siofra

Alar tugged on the neck of the servant's uniform. The fabric itched, and it was tight across his shoulders.

"Don't fidget like that when you're serving the guests," Ragan said. She plucked a speck of lint from his shoulder and brushed the spot with her fingers.

Alar grinned at the mother in Ragan emerging, then turned his attention to *Alle'oss* men and women dressed in the same uniform he wore entering the governor's mansion through the servant's entrance. He glanced at Ragan and said, "Tell me again what my job is."

Ragan frowned up at him. "It's not that complicated."

"Right. I got that. I'm just having trouble wrapping my head around it."

"You walk around among the dignitaries carrying a tray of canapes —"

"Canapes?"

She pursed her lips and looked up at him. When she saw his grin, her eyes narrowed. "Just follow the other servants to the kitchen, pick up a tray and follow everyone to the ballroom. I'm sure you'll figure it out." She pointed to another group approaching the servant's entrance. "That group's big enough for you to blend in. You got the pass?"

He fished the paper out of a pocket and held it up. "You sure about this guy? Vinton?"

"Absolutely," she said. "He's been catering the governor's affairs for years and he owes me. You remember the story?"

"I'm Aron. I'm Vinton's nephew. He hired me at the last minute as a favor to my mother."

"Right. I doubt you'll need it with the pass, but you never know. You better hurry." She caught his arm and said, "Be careful."

"Always." Alar set off at a jog to join the others as they passed the guard, all of them holding up their passes for him to inspect.

He followed the chattering group to the kitchen, which was a hive of activity. No one paid the slightest attention to him. Following Vinton's other employees, he picked up a small tray and carried it through a set of swinging doors, then up narrow stairs, through another door and found himself in a familiar room. It was the governor's ballroom, the room in which they planned the attack on the Union mercenaries the previous winter. It looked different, illuminated by dozens of candles and full of Richeleau's elite in formal attire arranged around the room in small groups.

He paused, eying the wealthy *Alle'oss* men and women mingling with Imperials and suppressed a flash of anger. It wasn't helpful and might not be fair. Just because they were socializing at the governor's ball didn't mean they supported the Empire. And regardless of their current sentiments, if the *Alle'oss* were going to win their freedom, *Oss'stera* would need these people on their side. Another problem to solve.

Putting that aside for later consideration, he turned his attention to the other servants carrying the trays from group to group, offering the small food items on their trays. He just needed to stick around until he found an opportunity to sneak away. Picking one of the servants, he trailed along behind her, mimicking her actions while keeping an eye out for the Desulti representative. Ragan said her name was Siofra.

He didn't really need to see her to accomplish his task, but he was curious.

"Alar?"

Alar was so absorbed in searching for his quarry, he barely paid attention to the people he was offering the canapes to. He looked up into Gerold's face. The governor's assistant glanced down at Alar's uniform, then he met his eyes with a quizzical frown on his face. Before he could speak, Alar said, "No, sir. I'm afraid you're mistaken. My name is Aron."

"Aron?"

"Yes, sir. Would you like —" Alar froze, mouth open, then glanced down at his tray and noticed for the first time what it contained. Squinting at the small concoctions, he realized he had no idea what they were. "Some food." When he looked up, Gerold was fighting to keep a smile off his face.

"No, thank you," Gerold said. "However, I've been meaning to have a word with the caterer. Perhaps you can show me where Hera Vinton is?"

"Ah," Alar said. "Of course, sir. You can… follow me." He turned and headed back toward the door that led to the kitchens. Just before they exited, Gerold took his arm and steered them behind a large potted fern.

"What are you doing here?" Gerold whispered.

"Finding out what the Desulti want."

Gerold glanced down at his uniform again. "What were you going to do? Ask her while offering her a canape?"

"No. I was going to snoop around her suite, then hide in the room where she meets the governor."

Gerold took a canape from Alar's tray and popped it into his mouth. "Come with me."

Alar followed him through the ballroom, then out a large double doorway into a hallway. He was leading them to the governor's office. When they entered the outer office, Gerold closed the door and said, "Explain."

"We think the Desulti are here to convince the governor to allow them to take part in *Oss'stera's* arrangement with the governor."

"I was thinking the same thing."

"They'll push us out," Alar said. "And you'll be in business with the Desulti, whether you like it or not."

"The Desulti representative is attending the party. Her suite is on the second floor. You'll never get past the guard."

"Is there a guard outside the door to the suite?"

"No. On the stairs to the second floor," Gerold said with a shake of his head. "But —"

"Don't worry. The guard won't be a problem." Alar set the tray on Gerold's desk and fished the key Ragan gave him from his pocket. "Will this work?"

Gerold, who looked about to ask about the guard, focused on the key, then shook his head again, went to his desk and pulled a key ring from a drawer. He selected a key and held it up. "I had the locks changed. Use this." He handed the keys to Alar and said, "And please return them when you're done."

"Of course. The meeting is tomorrow morning?"

"In the governor's office." Gerold considered for a moment. "There's an empty room in the servant's wing on the first floor." He explained to Alar where it was, then gave Alar a speculative look. "Do you think you can get up here unseen by the seventh bell tomorrow morning?"

Alar nodded.

"You can hide in the governor's rooms before the meeting. You should be able to hear. I'll make sure he's up."

"The governor won't mind?"

"The governor is terrified of the Desulti," Gerold said. "It's all I can do to keep him together and get him to this meeting. I'm worried he'll give everything away. We'll tell him you're here to figure out how to foil their plans. It might bolster his courage."

"I've a better idea," Alar said. He lifted the key ring. "Will these get me into the governor's rooms?"

Gerold hesitated. "What did you have in mind?"

"Let him know the Desulti aren't the only ones he should be afraid of," Alar said with a grin.

Gerold gazed at him, then he looked past him and mused, "I wonder, would that work?" He met Alar's eyes. "Might send him over the edge. We need him to be assertive in the meeting."

"I'll bolster his courage. Let him know he has a formidable ally."

Gerold shrugged. "Not sure I have a better idea. In any case, those keys will not work. I'll leave the doors unlocked." He gestured to the door to the governor's office. "His personal rooms are off his office. He won't be going to his bed until late, though."

"Not a problem." Alar plucked up a canape, waved goodbye, and, leaving the tray, he strode through the door into the hall, chewing what turned out to be a miniature mushroom torte. The guard at the base of the staircase studied him suspiciously, but when Alar strode toward the entrance to the ballroom, the guard turned away, dismissing him. Alar stepped into *annen'heim*.

After his near-death experience with the soul spirit the previous spring, his heart raced every time he entered their realm. But the realm of the dead was silent. There were no signs of spirits nearby. He relaxed and made his way down the hall. Though he intended to go straight to the second floor, as he passed the ballroom, he decided to look for Siofra. Time was measured differently in *annen'heim*. So, though he could move about the room unseen by the guests, everyone in the physical realm appeared nearly frozen to him. He wandered through the ballroom studying the guests, wondering if he would recognize a Desulti who wasn't Murtair.

He found her in a small group of women, standing apart from the other guests in one corner of the room. Siofra. Though she wore a dress that was in step with current Imperial fashion, he knew it was her. The giveaway was that among the women accompanying her was a woman who was obviously a murtair. The bald scalp and distinctive black garments were unmistakable. Her stance appeared casual, but there was a tension in her body, as if she would spring into action at a moment's notice. Unlike the other women, whose attention was on Siofra, the murtair gazed at the other guests with the same calm intensity he remembered from Brie.

They were standing beside a painting by Omar, one of the masters of the *Alle'oss* new school. Alar studied Siofra's face. Her manner was as unlike the haughty women in her entourage as it could be. Her head tipped slightly to the side, a half-smile lending her expression a playfulness out of step with his expectations. One hand held a glass of wine and the other gestured toward the painting with splayed fingers, as if she were commenting on it to the other women. The overall effect was disappointing. He wanted to despise her, but she seemed like a woman it would be pleasant to spend an evening with.

After committing the women's faces to memory, he left the ballroom, slipped past the guard at the base of the steps to the second floor, and found his way to Siofra's suite. No one was in the hall, so he returned to the physical realm and unlocked the door. He paused inside, taking in the room. The early evening light coming through a row of tall windows on the opposite wall provided just enough illumination to make out the plush furnishings. Crossing the room to a small desk, he lit a lamp and searched the desk drawers. Nothing.

He held the lamp up and studied the room. Nothing looked promising, so he tried the door next to the desk. It led to a bedroom. He found what he was looking for on the bed; a small satchel. He carried it to a desk tucked beneath the windows and set the lamp down. The satchel was locked.

He considered breaking the lock, but only for a moment. They would suspect the governor, and he didn't know how they would react. They might use the incident as leverage in their negotiations. Disappointed, he searched the pack on the floor at the base of the bed but found nothing else useful.

He was turning to retrieve the satchel from the desk when he caught sight of a small book on the bedside table. Retrieving the lamp, he held it above the book and lifted the cover with one finger. A handwritten inscription on the first page read:

Siofra's Personal Journal

Scooping up the journal, he hurried to the desk, slid the satchel aside and laid the book flat. Flipping through the pages to the last entry, he slid the lamp closer and peered at the cramped runes. The entries appeared to be random thoughts.

I must remember to commend Laoise. She was right about the governor. The man is quite clearly terrified of the Murtair.

Alar chuckled. He couldn't blame the governor for that.

The governor has quite the collection of fine Alle'oss art. Are these the works that he intended to use to pay his debt? If so, what changed his mind? Why does he not pay off his debt rather than incur interest? Remember to ask Brie.

Alar pursed his lips. They would have to find a way to prise those works from the governor's collection before the Desulti got their hands on them. He scanned the entries, moving backward, until he found what he was looking for.

The governor will have to see our offer is preferable to what the Alle'oss can offer. The Order can provide access to larger markets and has the experience to manage the logistics. Though I have to admit we may have underestimated the Alle'oss, they will not be able to exploit this opportunity to the fullest for some time. In the event the governor feels some loyalty to the Alle'oss, we'll offer to come in as partners. The relative advantage the Order offers will become apparent to all before long. As a final argument, we can play on the governor's fears and inform him that the Alle'oss can't protect him in the event Imperial authorities discover the scheme.

Alar stared at the page. The short missive almost had *him* convinced. How was he going to convince the governor he was better off partnering with *Oss'stera?* If Adelbart discovered their first shipment was sitting in a decrepit shack in Lachton because they couldn't find a buyer or a barge to ship it, the negotiation would be over before it started.

Hoping for something he could use, he continued flipping through the pages, until he found:

I'm now convinced that it must be Nessa who is manipulating events surrounding Tove, and I have my suspicions about what she's trying to achieve. Her presence has ignited long simmering —

A key was inserted into the lock of the door in the other room. Alar looked up at the dark windows. He had been in the room much longer than he thought. He blew the lamp out as the door opened.

"Wait here." A woman's voice.

The voice had a tense, clipped quality. Somehow, he knew it was the murtair. He leapt up and had just returned the journal to the bedside table when he glimpsed movement in the darkness in the other room. He stepped into *annen'heim.*

There were spirits about. Their mournful wails reminiscent of the terrifying *sjel'and* Ragan channeled into the physical realm in Kartok. But these were far away, so he relaxed and approached the door. The murtair stood frozen just on the other side of the threshold, leaving him just enough room to squeeze past. A short, wicked blade protruded between the fingers of her clenched fist. The same type of knife Brie used against him when they fought. Alar studied her face. The slightest widening of the eyes suggested she saw him before he crossed the boundary. Whether it was enough for her to recognize him later, he didn't know. Did Brie tell them he was a realm walker? She told him secrets were the basis of relationships, but whose secrets was she talking about?

He turned sideways so he could squeeze past and froze. He left the satchel on the desk. They would know someone searched the room. There wasn't anything he could do about it, so with a sigh, he squeezed past the *murtair*. Fortunately, the door to the hallway was open and the woman he presumed was Siofra was standing aside so he could exit.

He remained in *annen'heim* until he was in Gerold's office again, then crossed the boundary and returned to the physical realm.

8

Persuasion

Alar paced the width of the governor's large bedroom, bathed in moonlight leaking through high windows. It had been hours since he escaped Siofra's room, but his mind was still occupied by what he read in her journal. What was he going to tell the governor to convince him to shut out the Desulti? Unlike most of his fellow rebels, Alar always saw to the center of things, and what he saw now was the governor's best choice was to go into business with the Desulti. They would make him rich, protect him from Imperial authorities, and despite the fact the women in the Desulti escaped the Empire, their interests were aligned with the system they fled. Though a black market arrangement with the Desulti would still be illegal, it wouldn't be treason.

He had no counterargument, and worse, he couldn't focus on the issue because of what he read about Tove. Brie told her it would be difficult for her in the Order. Told Tove she wouldn't be able to protect her. The frustratingly brief snippet he read suggested powerful people in the Desulti were using his friend for their own purposes. The word 'igniting' from Siofra's journal sounded ominous. If he had only been able to read the rest of the passage.

He left the bedroom door ajar, so when the door in the governor's office opened, Adelbart's boisterous drunken slurs gave Alar time to hide behind the door from the office to the bedroom.

The governor entered the bedroom, a lamp in one hand. His other arm encircled the waist of a giggling woman wearing the same uniform Alar wore. The woman looked as if she were not much older than Alar. He peeked around the edge of the door and watched the governor set the lamp down on his bedside table. He bent down to kiss the woman, then said, "Just one moment. Don't go anywhere." He slipped into what Alar discovered earlier was a garderobe.

Moving silently, Alar left his hiding place, slipped his hand around the woman's head, covering her mouth and muting her scream.

"What's that dear?" The governor's muffled voice.

"You should leave," Alar whispered into the woman's ear. "And don't tell anyone I'm here. The governor is perfectly safe. Nod if you agree."

She nodded.

Alar let her go. When she turned and saw he was *Alle'oss*, her already wide eyes opened even wider. Alar put his finger to his lips, motioned to the door, and stepped aside to let her pass. Once she was gone, he positioned himself beside the garderobe door and waited.

The governor appeared, wiping his hands on his dinner jacket. "Now, dear, where were —" He froze, his eyes searching the room. Sagging, he said, "Well, zut. Not again."

"Governor," Alar said quietly.

Moving so fast, Alar startled, Adelbart launched himself into the air, rolled across his bed and landed on his feet on the other side, crouching and staring at Alar with wild eyes.

Suppressing a smile, Alar stepped up to the bed, close enough so the light from the lamp on the bedside table illuminated his face.

The governor squinted at him. "Alar?" He straightened and massaged his chest. "What in Daga's name are you doing here? You nearly gave me a heart attack."

"I think you know why I'm here."

Adelbart's eyes cut to the door. "What do you expect me to do? Say no to the Desulti?" He gave a weak chuckle. "If that's what you came to ask, you're wasting your time." He pointed at the door. "Did you see the murtair?"

Alar came around the bed, forcing Adelbart to shuffle back into the corner. "The Desulti are not going to kill an Imperial governor."

"Well, excuse me, but the assurances of an *Alle'oss* rebel count for little against what I know of the Order." Adelbart rubbed the base of his throat. "It was only a miracle and quick thinking on my part that saved my life when that other murtair, Brie, came looking for their blood money."

"We have a deal."

"Deals can be amended. And show me where it's written down." Adelbart shook his head. "I know I owe you, but I'm sorry Alar, circumstances have changed."

No argument miraculously presented itself to Alar, so he resorted to the one card he had to play. He slowly drew his knife. The governor watched it with wide eyes.

"Governor," Alar said. "There are worse things in the world than the Murtair." He lifted the knife, angling it so it reflected the light from the lamp into the governor's eyes. "When you meet with the Desulti tomorrow, I'll be listening."

A small frown chased the fear from the governor's face. "How —"

Alar angled the tip of the blade toward the governor's throat. "You'll listen to their offer, but no matter how promising they make it sound, you'll tell them you need time to consider."

Ripples from the governor's internal calculations appeared on his face. He was looking for a way out. Alar stepped into *annen'heim*.

Alar's demonstration had its desired effect. When he reappeared on the far side of the room, the governor fainted. After reassuring himself Adelbart wasn't dead, Alar retreated and found the servant's room Gerold directed him to. As it was, he only had to wait an hour before it was time to return to the governor's rooms. When he stepped out of *annen'heim*, Adelbart was finishing dressing for the meeting, the unmistakable marks of a sleepless night on his face.

"Daga! Don't do that," Adelbart said.

Alar grinned. At least the governor didn't leap over his bed this time. "You remember what we talked about?"

"I remember," Adelbart said, mopping at his forehead with a kerchief. "Make no commitments. Tell them I have to consider." He tucked the kerchief into a pocket and eyed Alar. "This is how you…" He waved a hand in the direction of the stairs that led to the dungeon. The previous winter, Alar rescued Adelbart's daughter from a group of mercenaries who held her hostage in the governor's own dungeon, killing a half dozen of the hulking men single-handedly. When Alar smirked, the governor said, "That makes some sense."

Gathering himself, Adelbart straightened his jacket and met Alar's gaze. "You don't need to threaten me. I remember what I owe you. My daughter's life is worth almost any sacrifice to me. However, this is the Desulti we're talking about." When Alar started to speak, Adelbart waved his hand. "One cannot simply say no to the Order." He pointed to himself and Alar. "*We* must find a way past this. If possible." He put his hand on the doorknob and said, "Frankly, I'm not optimistic."

***

Alar had pressed his ear against the door so long it was getting sore by the time the governor's meeting with Siofra was wrapping up. She eloquently presented the case he read in her journal. It sounded even more convincing in her melodic voice. Even through the door, he felt the force of her personality, felt himself drawn in by her charm. He hated her.

The governor, on the other hand, surprised him. He bobbed and weaved so adroitly, Alar wasn't exactly sure what he did or didn't agree to. He was beginning to feel some hope. Then she revealed the iron in her velvet glove.

"Governor, I'm sure you are aware what a dim view Imperial officials would take of this arrangement with rebels."

In the silence that followed, Alar considered whether he would have time to kill both Desulti before the murtair responded. It was only a passing thought. He killed before, but almost always in battle. This would be murder, pure and simple and would only exacerbate the larger problem of what to do about the Desulti.

Finally, the governor found his voice. "Is that a threat?" Alar couldn't help feeling a little proud of how steady his voice was.

"Oh, no," Siofra said with tinkling laughter. "No threat. On the contrary. I only want to point out when you partner with the Order, your interests align with ours, and your safety and reputation become our concern."

Alar's heart sank. He hadn't had a lot of experience with the governor, but already he knew fear of disgrace and prison was the surest way to motivate him. Siofra apparently did her homework. Alar was so preoccupied with his own thoughts, he didn't notice the meeting breaking up until the door opening pushed him back.

Gerold leaned in and said, "You can come out. They've left."

When Alar emerged into the governor's office, they stared at one another in silence.

"She makes good arguments," Gerold said finally.

"Yes, she does," Alar said.

"What we must do," Adelbart said, "is find a way to *partner* with the Order." He held up a hand when Alar grimaced. "The Desulti are nothing if not pragmatic. You must offer them something they value. If you show them you are a worthy partner, and prove trustworthy, they will keep their word." He stood and straightened his jacket. "And as you say; she makes good arguments. I assume you wish to amass wealth with this venture." When Alar nodded numbly, the governor said, "They can help you do that."

Alar stared at Adelbart. Where did this man come from?

"Perhaps," Gerold said, "you should pay this Siofra a visit. You can be quite persuasive. Show her who you are. She seems reasonable."

Adelbart looked Alar up and down and said, "Maybe you should clean up a bit first."

***

Brennerman strode across the plaza toward the governor's mansion, his adjutant, Jan, in his wake. He dreaded meetings with civic authorities. They were small men, too often motivated by infuriating political considerations. But the military was technically subordinate to the Imperial government in Argren, and as the commandant of the fort, Brennerman was required to respond to all their petty concerns. Today, he was meeting with the city planner about an issue with water management in the district around the fort. It was maddening.

He was halfway across the plaza when he glanced to the right at two men emerging from the mansion's servants' entrance and came to a stop. Jan swerved just in time to avoid him.

"Sir?" his adjutant asked.

Brennerman didn't answer. One of the men was Gerold, the governor's assistant. But it was the other man who caught his attention. He was *Alle'oss* and wore a servant's livery, but he looked familiar. The two men talked for a moment, then the *Alle'oss* man turned and strode across the front of the mansion. It was the leader of *Oss'stera*. Alar.

Brennerman pointed and said, "That is the leader of the rebels."

Jan followed his gaze. "Want me to get some men?"

Brennerman hesitated, then shoved his satchel at his adjutant. "No time. You remember what I briefed you on about this meeting?" When Jan nodded, he said, "I'll return as soon as I know where he goes." Without waiting for a reply, he jogged after his quarry.

There were few people on the street in the wealthy neighborhood around the mansion. It was easy to keep Alar in sight, but he couldn't get too close. The rebel was wary, stopping frequently to check whether he was being followed and twice taking unnecessary detours.

Brennerman lost him when they entered the crowded streets of the working-class district on the south side of the city. One moment, he glimpsed the rebel's blond hair, the next moment, he was gone. As if he vanished into thin air. He searched for a time, but he knew it was hopeless. With his uniform, he was instantly recognizable. The farther south he went, the more animosity he attracted. Finally giving up, he headed north, followed by openly hostile glares.

Brennerman wasn't a drinking man and wouldn't normally be caught dead in a tavern in his uniform. But the incident left him troubled and as he entered the friendlier district around the governor's mansion, he found himself entering a tavern to give himself time to try to understand why. In a daze, he ordered brandy and, ignoring the curiosity of the other patrons, he sat at a table in a back corner.

The leader of the rebels emerged from the governor's mansion in disguise with the governor's assistant. It couldn't be that Gerold didn't know who it was. He was there at the fort during the battle. There could only be one explanation. Conspiracy. That Adelbart was treasonous wasn't a surprise. It fit with his assessment of the governor's character, and it would explain his refusal to acknowledge the rebel threat. And it made sense that Gerold was involved. The governor wasn't capable of hiding a conspiracy on his own. No, Brennerman wasn't surprised. But coming so close on the heels of his discovery of Inquisitor Wolfe's lies, it was…

He sighed, settled back in his chair, and let his gaze drift across the customers in the tavern. They all had the black hair of the Volloch caste, the pinnacle of the Empire's rigid caste system. And no wonder. A sign on the tavern's door proudly proclaimed it a Volloch only tavern. *Alle'oss*, Styrians, Tituun, Ferol, Andian — members of the Brochen caste — weren't welcome. The tavern was a haven where he and his fellow Volloch could avoid the riffraff.

He chuckled sourly at how transparently ridiculous it was. Hoch told him, "The next time you raise your voice to one of my men, I'll pull the rank that matters." He didn't need to explain what he meant.

Brennerman and the young lieutenant, watching with glee, understood. Yes, Brennerman was welcome to share this tavern with his fellow Volloch, but even among the Volloch, the circumstances of one's birth mattered. The Volloch had their own castes to ensure everyone knew their place. Hoch, Adelbart, Gerold… they were all of the Gabra caste, descended from the Gabran clan, the clan of the first Seidi sister, Abria. It was her magical gifts that allowed the Vollen people to build an Empire.

Brennerman's forefathers were of the Baird clan, the last Vollen clan to bend the knee to the Gabrans. So, because his ancestors placed a higher value on their independence than other Vollen, he and his fellow Baird paid a daily price over a thousand years later. To Hoch, Brennerman was part of the riffraff. Better than Brochen, but only just.

As a child, Brennerman railed against the injustice. His ever-patient mother would nod, listen and soothe his pique with gentle words. Not his father. He told his son to shut up, face reality and be grateful he wasn't Brochen. It wasn't until years after his death that Brennerman understood his father's anger was rooted in his own frustrations. Though he was a successful merchant, caste continually presented him with obstacles no Gabra would face.

Brennerman enlisted in the cavalry, hoping competence would count for more than caste when men's lives were on the line. His years in the Imperial Military Academy disabused him of that notion. If anything, the peacetime military was more virulently caste conscious than the greater society. Despite his storied career as a cadet, it wasn't long after he graduated that he resigned himself to never rising above lieutenant. Rumors of war with the Kaileuk revived his hopes. Surely, the crucible of war would burn away the fetters of caste.

And at first, his hopes proved prophetic. The Empire expected the momentum of a surprise attack would carry them through the swamps along Kai's northern border to the savannas that opened out to the south. Once on the open plains, the Empire's cavalry and heavy infantry would give them an advantage. Though cavalry was useless in the swamps, Brennerman's men fought their way down the relatively dry strip along the coast on the Southern Sea. They were the first, and as it turned out, the only Imperial unit to glimpse the grassy sea of the savannas. Unfortunately, the Imperial forces became mired in the swamps and there they remained.

Victor Storm promoted him to captain for his triumph. But the promotion wasn't without consequences. Though Storm might be blind to caste, it seemed few others in the cavalry were as open-minded. The colonel who informed him he was being relegated to Argren implied it was to ensure he didn't rise any higher.

Adelbart's treason, Wolfe's perfidy, Hoch's bigotry. These were only the most recent reminders that the Empire didn't deserve his devotion. But long ago, he made a promise, and he would keep it. Even if the one he promised would never know. He would keep his faith to her because, without it, he had nothing left.

He set the empty snifter down, rose and strode toward the exit. Alar's appearance with Gerold proved there was a conspiracy. The rebels would have to have a base nearby. He would find it, eliminate the rebels and uncover the conspiracy. None of that would change the mind of a man like Hoch, but he, and many others, would know in their hearts what kind of man Brennerman was.

9

Allies

"I can't go to Ka'tan," Alar said to Ragan. They shared a table at the Black Husky tavern. He had just finished telling her everything he learned and what Gerold and Adelbart suggested. "I have to get back to Lachton before the wedding."

Ragan sipped her ale, then leaned forward with a conspiratorial smile. "You don't need to go to Ka'tan to meet Siofra. She's on her way to the wedding."

Alar frowned. "That's awfully convenient." He didn't trust coincidences when Ragan was involved.

Ragan shrugged and ladled up a spoonful of soup.

He set his tankard down and picked up his spoon. "What am I supposed to tell this woman?"

"I'm confident you'll think of something." Ragan sat back, the finger of a hand resting on the table tapping absently. "What I know of Siofra is she is a true believer in the Order, but she has her own ideas about what the Order can become."

"What does that mean?"

"The Desulti became strong to offer women an alternative to the stifling paternalism of the Empire. The irony is their prosperity is intimately entangled with that of the Empire. Partly, it's proximity. They are located in the Empire, after all. But more importantly, many of them are still Imperial in their thinking. They understand the Empire. The way business is conducted, the influential players, the legal system. It's all familiar to them."

"How does that help?"

"The Desulti have diversified their business interests under Siofra. Their overseas operations are still not that significant, but it says something about Siofra that she looks beyond the Empire. Maybe she's not shackled to the Imperial way of thinking."

Alar sat back and gazed across the busy tavern. "That *is* interesting. Not sure how it helps. Yet. But it's interesting." He sipped his ale, then cocked his head and decided to try, once again, to pry loose some of Ragan's secrets. "Can't you just, you know, look into the future and tell me what to say to her?"

Ragan gestured with her tankard and said, "Even if I was able to identify a future where you persuade Siofra to partner with *Oss'stera*, I couldn't tell you what to say."

"Why not?"

She focused on him so long, he was thinking she wasn't going to answer. Then she gave her a head a shake, looked out across the tavern and said with a sad smile, "The future turns on such small events. Were I to tell you what to do, then the future I saw would no longer be possible."

Alar stared at her. He let his head fall back and looked up at the rafters hidden in shadow. "Because in the future *you* saw, you didn't tell me what it is I'm supposed to do."

Ragan smiled at him. A ghost of the proud mother smile she used the day he met her. "Very good."

"But you asked me to save Harold Wolfe." She came to him and asked him to keep the Inquisition novice alive through the tumultuous night when Alar rescued Brie and Tove and *Oss'stera* fought Union mercenaries.

She returned her gaze to her bowl. "Sometimes there is no choice. Death eliminates all possibilities."

"And did it work? Keeping him alive?"

Ragan nodded slowly. "Almost. He will need encouragement."

Alar decided he didn't want any part of that, so he stayed silent.

"I did learn something that night," Ragan said. "Something important, I think."

"Should I ask?"

She spoke quietly, as if she were speaking to herself. "I used to think all events are equally likely." She lifted her hands, palms down, and wiggled her fingers. "But there are currents, eddies. Events are tossed about like water in a mountain stream, pulled to and fro by unseen things." She let her hands drop. "What I glimpsed that night was there are people who…" She reached out and clenched her hand into a fist. "Wrest events to their will. People who pull the currents of time one way or another." She let her hand fall again and turned a vague gaze on him. "I've worked so hard to manipulate events. Unsuccessfully, for the most part. What I should be doing is finding the right people and putting them where they need to be to influence the future." She sighed. "Then I must stand back, let events play out, and hope for the best."

Ragan was silent for a long moment, then focused on him. "You and Tove are such people."

"So, you want to use us," Alar said. He let an edge into his voice, expecting Ragan to deny it, but she nodded.

"Yes. But don't worry. Our goals are the same. I would see you — both of you — succeed because it is good for the world." They gazed at one another. "It was you who counseled me to work to destroy the Empire. Did you think you would have no part to play?"

"I told you once before, when your schemes hurt the people I care about, we would have a problem."

"I remember." When Alar started to speak, she raised a hand to silence him. "I can't guarantee your safety or the safety of everyone you care about. What we are trying to do will require great bravery and sacrifice."

"But…"

"But isn't it enough that I will put you in situations in which you know success *is* possible? You only need to find the path yourself. That knowledge is more than most people ever have."

Alar returned her gaze. Did he trust her? Not entirely, but what was he to do about it? She could ask whatever she wished. He could always say no. "I guess that will have to be good enough."

Ragan smiled and leaned her elbows on the table. "I can give you one piece of advice."

"Okay."

"Violette would make a good ally."

Alar stared at her. "Violette?"

"Bergamot. The woman getting married in Lachton."

"Right," Alar said. "I remember. The unhappy bride. Sounds like a perfect candidate for the Desulti. That why Siofra is going to the wedding?"

"Siofra is just going to offer support to a friend. And to conduct business." Ragan shook her head. "No, Violette doesn't want to run away from the Empire. She likes everything her high social standing provides. All except being married off to someone who would eclipse her."

Alar frowned.

"Violette is a formidable woman, and she likes to be in charge."

He nodded slowly, his gaze in the distance. "So, how does that help me?"

Ragan shrugged. "I wouldn't have any idea. You've proven yourself resourceful. Be creative."

***

Ukrit poured a bucket of water into the trough he and Scilla dragged from one of the abandoned buildings for the horses, then set the bucket down. He was tempted to lie down in the tepid water. Lachton was much hotter than the foothills around Richeleau in late spring.

Hand absently patting the horse's rump, he examined the dilapidated building attached to the shack that was their home. It was obviously once a warehouse, but it was mostly old, warped boards and gaping holes now. He and Scilla scavenged some of the straight boards to patch the largest holes in their humble home's roof.

With a sigh, he entered the shack where Scilla waited and hoisted himself up to sit on a crate. Scilla stood still, a hand resting on the crate containing honey, her eyes unfocused. The clang of a barge's brass bell rose above the indistinct murmur of the harbor a hundred paces to the east.

"We've tried every tavern and cafe on this side of town," he said.

His voice bringing her back from her thoughts, she noticed the pot of honey in her hand and returned it to the crate. Sighing, she turned to face him and rested her hands on her hips. "It's not like we really needed the coin. We have enough to get us to the wedding. Just needed to stay busy."

"You worried?"

"Yes. Alar should have been back already." She bit her lip and looked out the door. "What do we do if he isn't back in time?"

Ukrit shrugged. "We show up at the estate the day after tomorrow. He'll know where to find us when he gets back." He looked around at the stacked crates. "Not sure what's going to happen to all this while we're locked up in the estate."

"This your office?"

Ukrit looked up at someone silhouetted in the doorway. At first, he had a hard time putting the gruff voice together with what looked like a child. Then the person came further into the room and the silhouette resolved into a short man. Scilla and Ukrit could only stare as he picked his way over the uneven floor, scowling around at the interior of the shack. His short stature was enhanced by an unruly bush of a beard that spread as it descended to the middle of his chest. The crimson beard and a fringe of matching hair that emerged from a shapeless knit cap showed he was *Alle'oss*.

"Can we help you?" Scilla asked.

"Heard you're shopping Argren honey around."

"We are," Scilla said. "You in the market?"

The man didn't answer. He gazed around at the stacked crates. "Name's Taavi. I captain a barge works the Odun River."

"You're *Alle'oss*," Ukrit said.

"Smarter than you look. What gave it away?" Taavi peered past Ukrit to the crates stacked against the back wall.

"It's just, none of the other barge captains we talked to are *Alle'oss*," Ukrit said, not bothering to hide his annoyance.

"No," Taavi said. "Not since the Imps got interested in Lachton."

"Is it against the law for an *Alle'oss* to captain a barge?"

"No, not officially," Taavi said, lifting the lid of a crate and peering inside. "But they set the rates, levy the taxes. Hard to stay in business unless you're Volloch."

"There's a tax on being *Alle'oss?*" Scilla asked. When Taavi glared at her, she gave Ukrit a small shrug and mumbled, "Sorry."

"How are *you* still in business?" Ukrit asked.

"Stubborn," Taavi said. One brow rose and disappeared beneath the hair protruding from his hat. "And I'm willing to help out them who wish to avoid Imperial attention." He paused for a beat, then returned his scowl to the merchandise.

Scilla cleared her throat and cut her eyes to Ukrit. "You here to make an offer?"

"Considering it," he said, nudging Scilla aside and peering into the crate containing the pots of honey.

"We can't pay you," Ukrit said. "Up front, that is."

"No kidding."

"You'll get yours on the back end," Scilla said.

"I'm guessing these goods don't have an Imperial seal," Taavi said. Documentation with an Imperial seal confirmed merchandise passing through the Empire had been inspected and the taxes paid.

"Oh, yes," Scilla said and hurried over to the stack of crates they used for a desk. She retrieved the documents the governor's assistant, Gerold, provided Ukrit, and handed them to Taavi.

Taavi took the documents, surprise smoothing his scowl. He glanced at the two of them, then carried the papers to the door, and peered at them in the sunlight. After examining each one, paying special attention to the wax seals, he turned back around and said, "These look real."

"They *are* real."

The captain stared at Ukrit, then examined the documents again, holding the seals an inch from his nose. "Where'd you get them?"

"We have a deal with the governor," Scilla said.

Taavi's head came up and both of his eyebrows disappeared beneath the fringe of hair. "Adelbart?"

Scilla and Ukrit nodded.

"To avoid inspections?"

"And taxes," Scilla said.

Taavi went still, then his head pivoted toward Ukrit for confirmation. When he nodded, Taavi licked his lips and looked around the shack again. "How'd you manage that?" Before they could answer, he waved a hand and said, "Never mind." His eyes roved methodically over the crates, glancing down at the bill of lading from time to time, his lips moving as if he were doing a calculation. Then he let his hand with the documents drop to his side and asked, "How were you planning to get this loaded onto a barge in the harbor?"

"We have the documentation," Scilla said, pointing. "And besides, we haven't seen any inspectors in the harbor."

"You don't see any *Alle'oss* captains, either," Taavi said, his ruddy complexion darkening. He waved a hand at their worn clothing. "Bumpkins come down from the hills. Think they're gonna get rich smuggling goods through the heart of the Empire. Think they're smarter than those dumb ole Imps. Waltz into town, stumbling around, *interviewing* Imp barge captains." He waved his free hand and pasted a silly smile on his face. "Hello everyone, we're smugglers." His voice rose as he slipped into a string of *Alle'oss* Ukrit was sure would bring a blush to his cheeks if he understood it.

Then, as if someone flipped a switch, Taavi's face cleared, and he fell silent. "Still, must be something to you. You got this deal with the governor." He wiped his mouth with the palm of his hand. "This the only shipment, or will there be more?"

"As much as we can move," Ukrit said. "The more successful we are, the more we can get."

"Any weapons?"

"You want weapons?" Scilla asked.

"No. They just cause problems." He waved the documents. "These'll pass for most inspections, but if they find contraband, they'll look closer. They find weapons, they hand you off to the inquisitors."

Scilla shook her head. "No. No weapons."

"You got a customer in mind?"

"We were hoping to find a buyer in Hast," Scilla said.

Taavi swore in *Alle'oss* again, but before he could gain momentum, he stopped abruptly. "Only merchants in Hast are Imperial. You got documentation, but it'd be best if we avoid Imps. They'll cheat you if they know you're *Alle'oss.*"

"But there's a big *Alle'oss* community there."

"Can't get licenses to do business outside the *Alle'oss* ghetto."

"Do *you* know anyone who would be interested?" Scilla asked.

"We'll take it to Lubern, the port on the Southern Sea," Taavi said. "There's non-Imp merchants there." When Alar and Scilla just stared at him, he said, "Forty percent's my cut. Of the gross. You got more to ship when I get back, I'll take that too. Same deal."

"Fifteen percent is fair." Scilla said.

"And how would you know what's fair?"

"You shouldn't have told us how difficult the Imps make it for you to stay in business," Scilla said.

Taavi's face went slack for a moment. His laughter was so unexpectedly joyful, Ukrit couldn't help smiling. When his laughter died, a smile crinkled the corners of his eyes and revealed surprisingly white teeth. "Not as hopeless as you appear. Twenty-five percent."

"Done," Scilla said.

Taavi nodded as if they already agreed and handed the documents to Scilla. "This is what you're going to do. You're going to load this onto a wagon. Take the road north to the fishing village at the mouth of the river. It's the only *Alle'oss* fishing operation left. We'll load up there." He glared at them until they nodded.

"You're taking a big risk," Scilla said. "Why would you do this?"

Taavi spit on the floor. "Got no love for Imps. Sides, you two stumbling around Lachton being stupid puts us all at risk. If you're going to stick around, someone needs to take you in hand." He glared a challenge at them. "We load up tomorrow, midday. Don't be late." He spun around and stalked out.

Scilla and Ukrit stared at the door, then looked at one another. "What in the Mother's name was that?" Ukrit asked.

"An answer to our prayers?"

"Do we trust him?"

"He's *Alle'oss*," Scilla said doubtfully.

Ukrit stared at her, then looked at the door again.

"Plus," Scilla said, gesturing toward the door. "If he was trying to con us, I think he would be…" She paused, hand hovering.

"More persuasive? Slicker?"

"Yes," Scilla said. "Or at least less of a jerk."

"What do you think Alar would say?"

"We were interviewing Volloch captains," Scilla said. "At least this one is *Alle'oss*. Besides, it's like you said, what do we do with this stuff while we're at the wedding?"

Ukrit slid off the crate he was sitting on and turned to gaze at the stacks. "Well, I guess we better get started. It's going to take us the rest of the day to get this loaded."

***

The small fishing village was a collection of shacks on a muddy bank of Lake Vitaeshu where it fed the Odun River.

"I can see why the Imps left this place alone," Ukrit said.

"Lucky for us," Scilla said. "I hope."

The village looked as if it was more prosperous at one time, but most of the buildings appeared to be abandoned now. As they neared the docks, a group of men and women tending a fire below a smoke house looked up. Taavi watched them approach from the roof of the cabin on the stern of a barge moored at one of the docks.

When they pulled to a stop at the landward end of the dock, Taavi turned and shouted in *Alle'oss* to a woman with short, gray hair. Moments later, the crew was removing crates from the wagon and loading them onto the barge.

Ukrit made his way down the dock, dodging the crew, and crossed the gangplank. Looking up at Taavi, he offered him the inspection documents.

Taavi scowled and nodded to the gray-haired woman. She took the sheets from Ukrit without a word and examined them.

"Should we trust him?" Ukrit asked her quietly. Despite the gray hair, the woman didn't appear to be as old as he assumed.

She glanced at Ukrit, then looked up at Taavi. "No," she said with a small smile. She folded the documents and stuffed them into a pouch at her belt. "But you can trust me. Name's Sinta." She offered her arm. When Ukrit took her forearm, she said, "Should be back in a month or so." She winked and turned away before Ukrit could respond.

Scilla joined him and said, "What did she say?"

"She said we need to pray to the Mother and Father this is the right thing to do," he said and met her eye. "If it isn't, Alar is going to kill us."

10

Extraordinary Thieves

After leaving Ragan, Alar hurried to *Honutok* to tell Lief about the Desulti's interest in their deal with the governor. He warned him to keep an eye out for Desulti making mischief in the Ishien River Valley. Then he hitched a ride on a caravan traveling from Richeleau to Lachton.

As he neared the abandoned warehouse district in Lachton, his pace quickened. But when he rounded the corner, and the shack came into view, he stopped in his tracks. The wagon was there. The horses looked up when he appeared, but nothing else moved.

"Scilla. Ukrit," he called as he approached the shack. He peered into the dim interior. It was empty. Not only were Scilla and Ukrit not there, the crates were missing as well. Entering cautiously, he set the pack filled with Scilla's pigments down and peered around, muttering, "I'm going to assume this is good news."

"Alar!"

He whirled. Scilla stood in the doorway, Ukrit peering over her shoulder, a wide smile on their faces.

Scilla rushed him and threw her arms around his neck. Alar wrapped his arms around her, lifted her off her feet, and spun her around. He set her down and found her lips, forgetting, for a moment, the Desulti, Siofra, the wedding and even Ukrit's bemused presence.

"Ahem," Ukrit said.

Alar relinquished their kiss and grinned at Ukrit, who leaned on the doorjamb with his arms crossed. Alar stepped back and gestured to the empty room. "What happened?"

"We sold it," Ukrit said. "Everything."

"Actually," Scilla said, "we found a captain who agreed to ship it to Lubern. He's going to sell it for us."

"A captain?" Alar asked. When they nodded, he asked, "Did you get it in writing?"

"Well," Scilla said. "No, but he seemed…" She turned to Ukrit for help.

"He seemed like a jerk," Ukrit said. "But he's *Alle'oss.*"

Alar's furrowed brow smoothed. "An *Alle'oss* captain?"

"Yes," Scilla said. "He said the Imps are making it difficult for the *Alle'oss* in the shipping business. We…" She gestured to herself and Ukrit. "We trust him."

"Or we trust his first mate, anyway," Ukrit said.

"When will he —" Alar started.

"We don't know," Ukrit said. "A month, maybe. But he said when he gets back, if we have more, he'll take that too. He gets twenty-five percent of the gross. We get the rest."

Alar took in their faces and shrugged. "Well, okay." He raised his arms to his sides and grinned. "We've already paid the good citizens of the Ishien River Valley. It's a gamble, but it's our gamble, and what are our options?"

"That's what we thought," Scilla said, sounding relieved.

Noticing their new clothes, Alar said, "You're ready for the wedding, I see." Ukrit wore a short tunic cinched at the waist with a belt and loose woolen pants tucked into his boots. Scilla wore a flowing blue dress, and a fitted bodice that laced up the front over a cream-colored chemise.

"Yes!" Scilla said excitedly. "And…" She scooped up a package she dropped and tore the brown paper that wrapped it. A pair of boots thunked to the floor at her feet. Tossing the paper aside, she held up a bundle of cloth, a wide smile on her face.

Alar looked past Scilla and found Ukrit grinning as well. "What's this?" he asked, taking what turned out to be a pair of pants from Scilla.

"We're presentable," Ukrit said. "We can't have you looking like a vagabond."

Alar took a jacket from Scilla, held the pants and jacket up, and examined them. They were a gray linen cloth with darker gray pinstripes and black velvet trim. "It's…"

"Fancy," Ukrit said, waggling his brows.

Scilla threw a scowl over her shoulder, then grinned at Alar and took the jacket from him. "It's what all the well-to-do young gentlemen are wearing. We have work clothes, but you're our manager. You have to look the part," she said and held the jacket up by the shoulders. "Do you like it?"

Alar tucked the pants under his arm, retrieved a shiny black boot from where it fell and held it up. The leather was a lot stiffer than the moccasins he wore his entire life. He took in Scilla's hopeful smile, trying to think of a response, then Ukrit spoke.

"*Extraordinary* thieves, remember? Might as well start looking the part."

A corner of Alar's lips twitched, then his smile grew. "Right," he said. "You're right. No, this is good."

A light blush colored Scilla's cheeks as she brushed Alar's hands aside, threw the jacket over an arm and held a fine linen shirt to his chest. "You're going to look so good."

"How did you know my size?" Alar asked.

"I… From memory," Scilla said hurriedly, a blush coloring her cheeks. When Alar lifted a brow, she shoved the jacket and shirt into his arms, lifted her hands and held them at shoulder width, palms facing inward. She mimicked running her hands from his arms to his shoulders, squeezing her fingers, then her eyes flicked down.

"It was embarrassing," Ukrit said.

"The boots were a guess," Scilla said. She gathered up the garments in a rush and said, "We better go."

Alar wrapped his arms around her and pulled her against him, squashing the clothes between them. "I missed you." Before she could answer, he pressed his lips to hers. Letting her go, he asked, "Where are we going?"

"Hold on," Ukrit said. "What happened in *Honutok?* You were there a long time."

Alar shook his head. "I've got a lot to explain, but it's a tale best told over a meal. I'm famished."

"We used some of our last coin to get a room at an inn up near the estate," Ukrit said. "We figured showing up well rested, fed and bathed would make a good impression."

"That was an excellent idea."

"It happens," Ukrit said, one brow quirking up.

"We just came by to leave a message for you," Scilla said.

"Let's go," Alar said.

When they emerged from the shack, an *Alle'oss* boy was pouring a bucket of water into a trough for the horses. He let the empty bucket dangle from his hand and eyed Alar.

"This is Fin," Scilla said. "He's agreed to take care of the horses while we're at the wedding."

Ukrit gave the boy a stern look and said, "We've given him enough coin for feed *and* a generous payment."

The boy frowned at his tone. "I won't let nothing happen to them." His hand came up and rested protectively on one of the horse's flanks.

Alar strode forward and extended a hand. "*Lehasa*, Fin. I'm Alar."

The boy stared at the offered hand, then extended his own.

Alar took his forearm and gave it a squeeze. "I'm sure Sigurd and Olafson are in good hands." When the boy frowned, Alar pointed at the horses. "That's Sigurd, and that's Olafson."

The boy looked as if he wasn't sure what to make of Alar, but he mumbled, "I'll take care of them."

Alar nodded. "I have every confidence that you will." He released the boy's forearm and followed Scilla and Ukrit, wondering if he would ever see the horses again. But what option did they have? They couldn't afford to stable them. He glanced back before turning down a side street. Fin was scratching below Sigurd's cheek while letting the horse nuzzle his other hand.

"Where'd you find Fin?" he asked Scilla.

"Came out and found him pouring water into the trough," Ukrit said. "Unbidden. We asked him if he wanted to take care of them."

"Good enough," Alar said. "If you trust him, I do." Relegating his worries about the horses to the background, he turned his attention to what was to come.

⁂

Alar put Scilla's and Ukrit's questions off until they were bathed and seated in the common room of the inn. Faced with their impatient frowns, he said, "I ran into Ragan in Richeleau."

"Uh oh," Ukrit said.

"No. It was lucky I ran into her. Though I wonder how much luck has to do with when Ragan appears. The Desulti are trying to push us out of the deal with the governor."

"That's *not* good," Scilla asked.

"No, it's not," Alar said. "But knowing what they're up to gives us a chance to come up with a plan." He told them about his adventure in the governor's mansion and what he and Ragan discussed.

When he finished, he gazed at the other patrons in the tavern, giving Scilla and Ukrit time to digest what he told them. It was, by far, the nicest establishment he had ever been in. He glanced down at the pewter tankard on the table before him. The ale was no better than at the Black Husky, though.

"Tove is a Desulti," Ukrit said.

Alar returned his gaze. It didn't surprise him the news about Tove was Ukrit's first concern. The two of them became close before she left.

"I don't like that there might be people using her," Scilla said.

"That's what I thought," Alar said. "But Ragan says she's okay. For now." He thought for a minute, then added, "Tove's as tough as anyone I know. If they try to use her, she'll probably make them regret it."

"Right," Ukrit said softly.

They nursed their ales and listened to a woman singing a mournful ballad none of them had heard before.

"So, what *are* you going to tell this Siofra?" Scilla asked.

"I'm still working on that," Alar said. "You two have any suggestions, I'm listening."

"I have full confidence in you, Alar," Ukrit said. "Right now, I'm too nervous about tomorrow to think about anything else."

"I know what you mean," Scilla said. "I doubt I'll be able to sleep a wink tonight."

A server set three plates in front of them and turned away without speaking.

"Friendly," Ukrit said.

"The wrong part of the city," Alar said. He lifted his tankard. "A toast to Taavi, Tove, and another grand adventure." They clinked tankards, then set into servings of roasted quail, bread, potatoes and beans.

***

"How does it feel?" Scilla asked anxiously.

Alar stood in their rented room, awash in early morning sun. He looked down as he worked his toes in the new boots, then took a few tentative steps to the other side of the room and pivoted around on his heel. "These feel incredible," he said. They were stiff, but he kept that to himself.

"They should," Ukrit said. "They cost enough."

"Well, I figured you'd be miserable walking around in cheap boots," Scilla said with a broad smile. She hurried to retrieve the jacket from the back of the desk chair where Alar tossed it the night before. "Here. The last touch."

Alar turned and worked an arm into the jacket which Scilla held up. Once it was on, he noticed Ukrit smiling at him and asked, "What?"

"I have to admit," Ukrit said. "No one will know you are the ragged scoundrel I know you to be."

Scilla was glowing, her hands clasped below her chin. "You look amazing."

The jacket was tight across his shoulders, but he supposed it could be he wasn't used to wearing such a garment. He clasped the bottom of the jacket, which came to his waist, in the front and gave it a tug. "I feel… Dashing. Charming. *Extraordinary*," he said with a wide smile for Scilla.

Scilla let out a small squeal and threw herself at him.

Scilla's high spirits faded as they made the short walk to the estate. The closer they came to their destination, the quieter she became, answering Alar's questions with one-word mumbled responses. By contrast, Ukrit filled the silences with nervous chatter. Olson waited for them outside the servant's gate. When he saw them, he drew up, a wide smile stretching his lips. "Right on time," he said. He looked them up and down. "You look perfect." His fingers alighting on Alar's arm briefly. "Now, follow me."

He led them through the gate, but instead of following the path along the back wall they took the first time, he led them deeper into the estate. The path hugged the border of Violette's garden. In the few weeks since they saw it, spring's magic had transformed it. Some of the flowers Helmut spoke of were blooming, producing a riot of color. The bright green leaves of spring cloaked the trees, and the garden was alive with a variety of songbirds about the business of courting and nesting.

After leaving the garden behind, they entered a stand of oaks, then crossed a wide lawn toward a large pavilion. Olson held the canvas flaps of the door aside and allowed them to enter. The interior was lit only by the light filtering through the fabric. A few people who looked like servants were busy roping off the space along the sides into equal-sized areas that contained easels and worktables.

Olson gestured to the partitioned spaces with a flourish. "These are where you will work. As you are the first to arrive, you may have your choice. Use the rope to close the area you choose." He gave them a small bow and a wide smile, then swept his arm toward two long tables in the center of the space. "Your meals will be served buffet style. Breakfast at the eighth bell, lunch at one and supper at seven."

"Three meals?" Ukrit asked. "We… uh… don't have to pay for them, do we?" When Olson's brows rose, he mumbled, "Right. Sorry." As Olson led them out the other end of the pavilion, Ukrit mumbled to Alar, "That meant no, right?"

They exited the pavilion, then walked along a gravel path to a brick building with multiple chimneys from which smoke was issuing. "This is the kitchen," Olson said. "As there will be no meals served before the reception tonight, you may have a bite in the kitchen for lunch. Ask for Ingrid and tell her Olson sent you."

He led them along the face of the kitchen, then across a narrow yard shaded by more oaks to a long low brick building. Opening the door, he allowed them to enter, then followed. A long hallway extended the length of the building, with doors at intervals on both sides. He stopped at the first door. "As you are the only female artist, I've reserved this room for you," he said to Scilla. He pushed the door open and stepped back to allow Scilla to enter.

Light streamed into the room from windows on the wall opposite the door. A bed extended from beneath the windows. A small desk and armoire were the only other furnishings in the room.

Scilla set her small pack on the bed and said, "It's very nice."

Looking pleased, Olson led Ukrit and Alar to the next door. "I assume you will have no problem sharing a room," he said. Before they could respond, he pushed the door open and stepped back.

The room was similar, except there was no desk and instead of one double bed, there were two twin beds pressed up against the side walls.

When they gathered in the hallway after depositing their belongings, Olson said, "The other artists will be arriving throughout the day today. There will be a reception in the main house this evening at the seventh bell. Someone will arrive to show you the way. You will receive instructions on what is expected of you tonight." He paused, gazing at them expectantly. When no one had a question, his demeanor shifted subtly. No longer the officious manager of the estate, he faced Scilla and Ukrit and spoke in a confidential tone. "You two are the only *Alle'oss* artists to receive invitations."

Scilla's wide eyes stared out from a pale face. Ukrit stood with his hands in his pockets, his shoulders rounded.

"I say this not to put additional pressure on you, but as a warning. As an *Alle'oss* who has held a position of responsibility among Imperials for some time, I can tell you they will underestimate you. They will disparage your work and try to undermine you. Don't listen to them." He straightened, taking on the stiff posture of his position, his voice returning to his official tone. "I have seen their work. You are twice the artists they are. Show them what you are made of." He gave them a brisk nod. "Until this evening."

They watched his back retreating to the door on the far end of the long hall. Noting Scilla and Ukrit's stricken expressions, Alar gave Scilla a wide smile, slapped Ukrit's back and said, "No pressure, though."

11

They're Afraid of You

After unpacking their meager possessions, Alar, Scilla and Ukrit explored the estate. Everywhere they went, men and women wearing the same livery as the gate guards peered at them curiously, but no one questioned them. The estate was immense, with many buildings, but the manor house dominated the grounds. It was large enough to occupy a full city block in Richeleau.

Like all Imperial buildings, everything was square and grandiose. Alar wondered if there was ever an Imperial building of substantial size without a row of columns across a veranda that extended the width of the enormous central building. Wide double doors, flanked by guards, stood open in the center of the veranda. Massive wings extended to either side and behind the central edifice.

Having explored the area around the house, looking for likely ways for Alar to get in at night, they stood in the shadow of one of the ancient elm trees that bordered the cobbled driveway in front of the house, watching servants coming and going.

"Neo-Imperial," Ukrit said. "Very nice."

"Very big, anyway," Scilla said. "We could house all of *Oss'stera* in one wing. How many people you think live here?"

Alar pointed to a row of cottages just visible through a stand of trees beyond the artists' dormitory. "Those look like servant's quarters," he said, then waved a hand at the manor. "So, this must be just the family."

They gazed silently at the building for a time, then Ukrit said, "That's a lot of kids."

"Or a lot of empty rooms," Scilla said. "The only child I've heard about is Violette."

"Finding the chest with the dowry in there may take longer than we thought," Ukrit said.

"Keep your eyes and ears open," Alar said. He eyed a woman in Lord Bergamot's livery descending the steps of the manor. "Get to know the servants. Maybe someone will let something slip." He turned away from the manor and nodded to the artists' pavilion, which occupied a spot on the immense lawn east of the manor. "Let's go claim your stalls."

The workers had finished erecting the partitions that defined the stalls when they arrived. The pavilion was deserted. Scilla walked to the center of the space and turned in place.

"Does it surprise you that you're the only woman artist?" Alar asked.

Scilla shook her head absently, a finger resting on her cheek as she studied the work areas.

"Women don't paint in the Empire?"

"Oh, they paint," Scilla said. "For themselves or their families. The art establishment would never accept them as serious artists." Pointing to one of the stalls near the entrance, she said, "That one." She unhooked one end of a rope attached to one side of the opening and attached it to a hook on the other side. Stepping back, she put her hands on her hips and nodded.

"I'll take this one," Ukrit said, pointing to the adjacent space. After extending the rope across the entrance, he turned around and asked, "Where do you suppose we get supplies?"

"I imagine they'll tell us tonight at the reception," Scilla said. She turned away from her space and said, "Anyone hungry?"

They were heading toward the exit closest to the kitchen when a loud voice outside the entrance on the far end stopped them. A moment later, two men with the black hair of Volloch burst through the flaps. The speaker was tall, stick thin and spoke with an unfamiliar accent. He wore a suit similar to Alar's. Once inside the pavilion, he drew up, forcing the second man to sidestep to avoid colliding with him. The tall man gestured broadly, and said, "The light in here is just atrocious." He turned toward the other man, who was weighed down by a large wooden chest. "How do they expect us to create art in here?"

"You're right, master," the man said, nodding furiously. "Perhaps…" His eyes flicked up to the taller man's face. "Perhaps they will raise the sides. To allow more light."

One hand perched on a hip, the taller man spun around and let his imperious gaze sweep across the interior. "Perhaps —" When he spotted Alar, Scilla and Ukrit, he froze. He flicked a hand toward the stall nearest the door they entered and said, "That one, Heinz."

While Heinz unburdened himself, the man strode across the pavilion. He came to a stop two paces away and peered down his nose at them, lips puckered. After a thorough inspection, he said, "The *Alle'oss* artists." It didn't sound like a question, but when none of them spoke, he grew stern, bent slightly forward and asked, "Correct?!"

Alar smiled, stepped forward, and offered his hand. "Yes, you are indeed correct." The man didn't seem to notice Alar's hand, so Alar lowered it. "I'm Alar." He swept an arm toward Scilla and Ukrit. "May I introduce Scilla and Ukrit Woodsmith, masters of *akana si.*" The man's woolly eyebrows shot up his forehead as if seeking a better angle to peer down at them.

The surprise that Alar's announcement brought to the man's face fled, to be replaced by narrow-eyed speculation. A hand came slowly up until a finger rested on his lips and he muttered, "*Akana si.* Hmmmm. We shall see. We shall see ABOUT THAT." He spat the last two words, prompting the three of them to lean away. He gave them a fierce nod, pivoted around, and strode away.

"Whoa," Scilla whispered.

"Was there something weird about that?" Ukrit asked. "Something weird… About. That."

"There was indeed something weird about that," Alar said, returning his smirk. They watched the man haranguing Heinz for a moment, then Alar said, "Let's go eat."

Smoke was rising from four of the five chimneys when they arrived outside the kitchen. Alar was forced to jump aside when a woman wearing the estate's livery emerged from the open door and crossed a small courtyard to the manor house at a jog. Peeking inside and seeing the coast was clear, he beckoned to Scilla and Ukrit, then slipped inside.

They stood by the entrance, gaping at the army of men and women at work in the enormous kitchen. The heat from fires in four great hearths along the sides would have been unbearable on the warm day, but the heat escaping through vents in the ceiling pulled a breeze through the open doors. They shuffled out of the way of the door and watched what looked like chaos.

"That's a lot of cooks," Scilla said.

"That's a lot of food," Ukrit said.

"For the reception tonight," Alar said. "Maybe. They couldn't eat like this every day, could they?"

"Olson said we should talk to Ingrid," Ukrit said. "Who do you suppose —"

"Ahhhh! *Ertsi kīlata Alle'oss*!"

The cooks parted in front of an enormous *Alle'oss* woman like underbrush in front of a mountain bear. Once she was clear of the throng, she extended her arms and barreled toward Alar. He just managed to root his feet to the spot to meet her onslaught, when she stooped and threw her arms around him, squeezing him in a squishy hug, then gave him a fleshy smack on the cheek. Having escaped, Alar glimpsed Scilla's startled face before the woman engulfed her.

After giving each of them equal attention, she stepped back, beaming and wiping flour dusted hands on her apron. She was taller than even Ukrit. Bright red curls were confined in a loose bun on the back of her head. A sea of freckles obscured the burn scars of a seasoned cook on her arms and hands.

Alar started to introduce them, but she flapped a hand to forestall him. "No introductions necessary." She gestured to the crowd of cooks, whose hands remained busy while they kept an eye on their conversation. "Olson has told us about you." She extended a hand to Alar and said, "You must be Alar." Alar took her forearm in the *Alle'oss* fashion. "And you have to be Scilla and Ukrit. The artists." She offered them her arm, then before any of them could speak, she herded them to an old beat up table in a corner outside the hustle and bustle. "Have a seat, all of you," she said. "You will be wanting lunch." She whirled away and plunged into the maelstrom.

Alar grinned at her disappearing bulk, then turned and found Scilla gazing pensively around the kitchen. "Scilla? Are you okay?" he asked and rested his hand on hers.

Scilla forced a smile onto her face. "I'm fine. It's just all these people expecting so much from us. I don't want to disappoint everyone."

"You won't."

"You don't *know* that." There was a hint of pleading in Scilla's frown.

"No, I don't *know* it, but I have faith. You remember what Olson said about that painting you did at the audition. And you only had four hours to do that one."

"I don't know what you're complaining about," Ukrit said. "I don't know how I'll be able to finish a piece in marble in one week."

Alar leaned in and made sure they were looking at him. "Remember why we're here. We're here for *Oss'stera*. It would be great if you produced masterpieces, but what's important is we find that dowry. And escape, of course."

"You're right," Scilla said, determination firming her frown. "We can't forget the big picture."

Ingrid reappeared carrying an enormous platter. She set it down on the table and said, "Eat as much as you wish." She winked. "But remember the reception tonight. You will want to leave room to try everything."

"*Tok*, Ingrid," Alar said.

"*Aurina sha*," she said and turned away.

"Bless the Father," Ukrit said, gazing at the platter. "This is as much food as we get in a day back in *Honutok*."

"Two days," Scilla said.

"A week," Alar said. "Some weeks."

"And we get to eat again tonight," Ukrit said, his smile growing.

Piled on the platter were two roasted quail, a variety of nuts, two hard cheeses, a soft cheese, sliced bread, a small pot of jam, apple slices, and grapes.

"Shouldn't let it go to waste," Alar said. He took a slice of bread, still warm from the oven, and spread jam on it. Speaking around a mouthful, he said, "No matter what happens with your art, we'll eat better than we ever have for the next couple of weeks."

"Right," Ukrit said. He pulled off a quail leg. "We might as well enjoy it while it lasts."

Scilla watched them eat, then plucked a grape from the bunch and popped it into her mouth.

***

By the time a servant appeared that evening to announce it was time for the reception, most of the rooms were occupied. Many of the artists obviously knew one another as they gathered in small groups in the courtyard outside the dormitory, excitement at being involved in the wedding animating their conversations. Although Alar noticed many of them casting the *Alle'oss* furtive glances, no one introduced themselves. His own attempts to insert himself in their conversations were met with indifference or outright hostility.

"Friendly bunch," Ukrit muttered as they followed the servant toward the manor.

Alar looked back and discovered no one else was following. "You think we're the only ones who will be there?"

The servant glanced back, then slowed until he was walking beside them. "It's considered gauche to arrive at social events on time." He looked up at Alar. "Wasn't expecting anyone to follow me."

"Gauche?" Ukrit asked.

"Unsophisticated," the *Alle'oss* boy said.

"Well," Alar said. "That would be us." The boy gave him an uncertain look, but when he saw Alar's grin, he smiled. "What's your name?" Alar asked.

"Trell. And you're Alar." He twisted around and pointed at Scilla and Ukrit. "Scilla and Ukrit."

"What is it you do, Trell?" Alar asked.

The boy frowned at him.

"What is your job at the estate?" Alar gestured around.

"Oh," Trell said with a nod. "A little of everything. My Ma says I'm a gofer, because I go for things. But I also shine boots, clean the horses' stalls, sweep, polish, clean… Whatever needs doing, really."

"So, You would be the man to come to if you wanted to find out what's what in the estate." When the boy frowned again, Alar said, "You work everywhere, know where everything is, probably know everyone. You know what's going on."

"Yeah," Trell said, his smile returning. "I suppose I do."

"You're a good man to know, Trell."

They climbed the steps to the manor's main entrance, passed between the guards, and entered an immense circular room. Alar paused to take it all in. Two staircases, one on each side, curved along the walls up to a second-floor balcony. Large doorways opened off the right and left walls.

Trell was heading to the doorway on the right when he noticed they were no longer following him. "This is the Entrance Hall," he said, his voice echoing.

They followed when Trell entered a rectangular room nearly as large as the Entrance Hall. The setting sun shone through tall western facing windows. Art adorned every available spot on the other three walls. Alar was about to ask Scilla what she thought of the paintings but stopped when he saw her drawn face. Taking in the statues scattered around the room, he whispered to Ukrit, "These any good?"

"Top shelf," Ukrit said, examining a statue of a woman holding up a cup in two hands, as if in offering. "Olson said Bergamot was into art. He wasn't lying."

"This is the Reception Hall," Trell said. He gestured to tables piled with food near the side of the room opposite the door. "The buffet is for the artists, so help yourselves. The others will probably start showing up in a half hour. I'll leave you to it."

"*Tok,* Trell," Alar said.

Trell hesitated, then said, "If you want anything, ask anyone for me. They'll know where I am."

After Trell left, they glanced at one another. Ukrit shrugged and set off toward the buffet tables. Alar and Scilla followed, the click of Alar's boots on the marble tile echoing in the massive space. The tables were arranged in an arc. They stopped at the center of the arc and stared at the food.

"You think it would be gauche to eat before everyone else arrives?" Ukrit asked softly.

"I can't believe you can eat after that lunch," Scilla said, her hand on her stomach.

"My philosophy is to eat like the bears in the mountains," Ukrit said. "As much as you can, when you can, because lean times are coming."

"You planning on hibernating this winter?" Alar asked.

"Considering it." He gave them a nod, then set off toward the plates stacked on one end of the buffet.

"He does snore like a bear," Alar said to Scilla.

"You ever hear a bear snore?"

"If a bear did snore, it would snore like Ukrit. I'm not that hungry, but I wouldn't mind sampling those pastries. Come on, you can have a bite."

Three hours later, Alar, Scilla and Ukrit stood near the entrance beside the statue of the woman with the cup. Having eaten his fill, Ukrit studied the sculptue, a tankard of ale in his hand.

"Not very friendly," Scilla said, gesturing across the room to where the artists gathered around the buffet.

Almost all the artists brought a second person with them. To Alar they looked as if they were servants, but Ukrit said they were apprentices. Most of the apprentices circulated in small groups around the room, perusing the paintings. The artists were partaking of the buffet. The tall artist they saw in the pavilion, who Ukrit christened About-That, stood in the center of the largest group, speaking animatedly and casting them dirty looks. Heinz, About-That's apprentice, was the only one who deigned to greet them when he arrived.

"They can't all be jerks," Alar said. "Maybe they just need time to —"

"They're afraid of you."

A man appeared from behind the statue. He was nearly Ukrit's height and wore an obviously expensive suit in the Imperial style. He stopped beside Alar and gazed across the room toward the artists. Alar studied his profile, thinking he looked familiar, but he couldn't place where he'd seen him. The man sipped his wine, then offered his other hand to Alar. "I'm Holden."

Glancing at the man's black hair, Alar took a chance and clasped his hand in the Imperial fashion.

The man looked at their hands, then gave Alar a small smile.

"Afraid of us?" Alar prompted.

Holden pointed at Scilla and Ukrit with his wineglass. "Afraid of them."

"Why would they be afraid of us?" Scilla asked.

He swept his glass across the Volloch artists, sloshing wine on the floor. "Everyone has heard of the *Alle'oss* new school. *Akana si.*" His brow furrowed briefly. "Anyone with any knowledge of art, anyway."

Alar looked across the room and noticed Holden's arrival caused a stir. People were openly watching their exchange.

Holden leaned down, close enough that Alar smelled the alcohol on his breath, and whispered, "And everyone has heard what the Inquisition did to the new school artists. Outside the Empire, that is seen as a tragedy of the highest order." He straightened and pointed across the room, his nose wrinkling. "But these men are all Imperial. They were happy to let the Inquisition eliminate the competition." The wine in his glass sloshed dangerously again. "Then *you* show up." He gave them a wide smile and spread his arms to encompass Scilla and Ukrit. He paused for effect, then let his arms drop, sipped his wine and shrugged. "They're terrified you might really be what Olson claims you are." He peered at them, swaying slightly. "Are you?"

"Absolutely!" Alar said. "Olaf himself would weep if he returned from exile to gaze upon Scilla's works."

Holden's gaze swung from Scilla to Alar. Scilla made a small, distressed sound, but Alar, readying himself to catch Holden, whose sudden head movement upset his balance, couldn't check on her.

"Olaf, hmmm?" Holden asked. He took a step toward Scilla, lifted her hand and kissed it. "I hope that is true. It has been long since I wept for beauty."

He was turning away when Alar asked, "Excuse me. Who are you?"

The man's brows knitted. "Holden." He looked at Ukrit. "Didn't I say that already?"

"Yes, you did," Alar said. "I mean, what is your relationship to this event?"

"Ah, yes, quite right." He offered a hand again and said, "I am Lord Holden Mueller. The groom." He dipped his head, then retreated unsteadily across the room toward the other artists.

"Didn't Olson say the bride, Violette, wasn't thrilled about getting married?" Ukrit asked.

"He did," Alar said. "Ragan said something similar. I'm feeling all warm and cozy about this marriage."

"I'm not entirely sure we'll actually have a wedding," Scilla said. "We better find that dowry soon."

"I don't know about you two, but if today is any indication," Ukrit said, "I think Volloch live weird lives."

Scilla snorted, but before she could respond, a large group of people entered the room.

"The lord of the manor," Scilla whispered.

Olson, standing in the back, caught Alar's eye and gave him a small smile. The man, who was obviously the lord, lifted both hands and beckoned the artists to gather around. He was shorter than Olson, and unlike Olson's practiced facial expressions, the wide smile on the lord's face appeared spontaneous and genuine. Yet he projected power. It was his relaxed posture in comparison to the men gathered behind him, his broad shoulders, the cut of his expensive clothes. His black hair was going to gray at the temples, but he moved with a young man's energy. When everyone formed an arc facing him, he gave them a wide smile and introduced himself as the bride's father, Lord Anton Bergamot. "Welcome!" he said and applauded the artists. His entourage joined him, until he lifted his hands out to his sides, palm down, quieting the applause.

As the lord gave his welcome speech, Alar let his gaze drift across the artists, noting who looked bored and who looked eager. The established masters and the up and comers.

Scilla nudged him with her elbow, then nodded to Olson, who had taken the lord's place. Unlike the flowery speech by the lord, Olson was straight to business.

"The wedding guests will arrive in a week. One week from tonight, a banquet will be held." He spread his arms. "Your completed works will be on display in this room from that night for the duration of the festivities."

There was a round of polite applause and murmured comments.

Olson gestured to the lord and said, "As you know, Lord Bergamot has agreed to purchase all of your works." He gave them a sly grin. "But it is possible that one of the guests will outbid his generous offer." The applause was more enthusiastic this time. "So, it would behoove you to make your best impression at the reception. The wedding will be held a week after the opening banquet."

After the applause, Olson asked if there were any questions. When no one spoke, he said, "You may choose any subject as long as it features the happy couple, the wedding, or the estate." He paused again, his eyes flicking to the *Alle'oss.* "And of course you must choose acceptable subjects. Do not forget that brothers of the Inquisition will be in attendance."

Alar glanced at Ukrit and Scilla and found them looking back at him with wide eyes.

Lord Bergamot made some closing remarks, then left to more applause. Alar watched the artists filtering back toward the buffet table.

"I don't know about you," Ukrit said, "but I need another ale. You two want one?"

"I could use one more," Alar said.

"Not me," Scilla said. "I'm not feeling well."

After Ukrit left, Alar asked, "You okay?"

"I think I'm just nervous." They watched the other artists parting at Ukrit's approach. "Ukrit never seems to worry."

"He just hides it better. And the ale helps."

"Alar, Scilla." Alar turned to find Olson approaching. He glanced across the room to Ukrit, making his way back to them, two tankards in his hands, returning the other artist's scowls with a wide smile. Focusing on Scilla, he asked, "How are you settling in?"

"Quite well, thank you," Alar said. "I don't know that I've eaten so much in one day in my life."

Olson gave him a polite smile, then focused on Scilla again. "Scilla, I've been meaning to ask you. Have you thought about the subject for your work?"

Scilla's arms crossed over her stomach. She shook her head and said, "No. I was hoping for inspiration tomorrow morning."

Olson's brows drew down, but before he could speak, Alar said, "Don't worry, you won't be disappointed." He paused and dipped his head. "In any way."

Olson met his gaze, gave him a nod, then smiled. "I have arranged for your supplies to be delivered to the pavilion. I will, of course, be in and out if you need anything, but I must be off now."

Ukrit arrived and handed a tankard to Alar. Taking in Scilla's expression and Olson making his rounds of the room, he sipped his ale and asked, "Did I miss something?"

Scilla turned on Alar. "I wish you would stop speaking for me."

Alar was about to say he would if she would speak for herself, but seeing her expression, he said instead, "I'm supposed to be your manager." She started to respond, but he put a hand on her arm to stop her. "I have absolute faith in you, even if you don't. I will sing your praises without reservation. Both of you. You concentrate on your art and let me handle everything else."

"I just don't like you making promises we… I may not be able to keep," Scilla said.

"All we can do is do our best," Ukrit said. He gestured to the room with his tankard. "None of these twits have helped anyone escape an Inquisition prison or defeated a band of Union mercenaries. I doubt these pampered *nāminu* have had friends butchered by Imps." He looked from Alar to Scilla and sipped his ale. "They don't get to judge me. Or you."

Scilla threw her arms around his neck, sloshing ale onto the marble floor.

12

Lief's Logic

Alar told Lief to bring people with him to the Ishien River Valley, so he brought Zaina and Keth. At thirteen summers, they were the youngest of *Oss'stera's* fighters, but no one was more dangerous with a bow than Zaina, and Zaina never went anywhere without Keth. Plus, Lief enjoyed their company.

As they neared their destination, the prospect of seeing his family eased the fatigue he accumulated during their arduous trek. *Honutok* was Lief's home now, but he grew up in one of the smaller villages in the Valley and his large extended family still lived there. He paused at the top of the hill that was the entrance to the Valley, enjoying the beautiful vista. Then Zaina, growing impatient, interrupted his moment.

"They got an inn in this town?"

Lief grinned. It was the first thing like a complaint from either of his companions. Alar told him to make haste, so he pushed them as they made their way through the rugged terrain. He had taken the grueling hike through the mountains to Lirantok before, but it was an unpleasant revelation for Zaina and Keth. Smoke from cook fires in Lirantok, where Old Jep lived, was visible above the trees, blocking their view of the village. It was only a little farther. He set off down the hill. "I was hoping we could stay with Old Jep tonight," he said. "We'll stay with my family tomorrow night."

"As long as they have a bed," Zaina said.

"I'm going to need days to catch up," Keth said. "Not looking forward to the trip back."

"If all goes well, we'll be driving wagons full of merchandise on the way back."

"Can we have a good meal tonight?" Zaina asked. "In a tavern."

"My treat," Lief said.

***

Lief knocked on Old Jep's door, then stepped back. When the door opened, it wasn't Jep who stood there. He frowned at the woman, pointing at her, trying to bring her name to mind. "I know you." He lifted his hand to his head. "You got hair now." He recognized her from the characteristic black garments of the Murtair, though she had been bald when he saw her last. It was Brie, the Desulti assassin who fought Alar the previous winter. She came to steal the paintings *Oss'stera* found among the goods on an Imperial supply caravan.

The woman's eyes narrowed as she studied his face. "Lief," she said. She looked past Lief and pointed at Keth. "I remember the boy, but I don't know her."

"Zaina," Zaina said. "And the *boy* is Keth."

"You're Brie," Lief said. When she nodded, he asked, "Where's Old Jep?"

"He's in town."

Lief took a step toward the door and said, "We'll wait inside."

Brie hesitated, then shrugged and retreated into the interior.

She sat at the table, a book open in front of her. Lief sat opposite her. Zaina and Keth groaned as they settled into rocking chairs in front of a cold hearth.

Lief gazed at Brie. She ignored him, her attention on the book. Alar warned him the Desulti would try to horn in on the deal *Oss'stera* made with the governor. Told him to keep an eye out for Desulti when he came to the Valley. It couldn't be a coincidence this woman was visiting Old Jep. When she glanced up at him, he asked, "Why are you here?"

"Jep offered me his guest room."

"Great," Zaina said under her breath.

"I mean," Lief said, "why are you in Lirantok?"

Brie closed the book and leveled a gaze at him. "I had business to discuss with Old Jep."

He glanced at her hair again. "What kind of business?"

"That's between Jep and me."

Lief rose, scanned the room, then checked the other rooms. Nothing looked out of place.

Brie watched him, looking amused. "Jep's in town."

"Alar said you're an assassin," Lief said as he returned to his seat. "Why'd they send an assassin to see Jep?"

Brie didn't answer.

Lief had listened to what Ragan told Tove about the Desulti before Tove left to join them. Women who fled the Empire and made themselves wealthy for their own protection. He found it fascinating, but it didn't escape him they hid themselves in Argren. "That Ragan woman told me women ran away from the Empire to become Desulti. That right?"

Brie's eyes narrowed slightly. She hesitated, but then she said, "Mostly."

"So, you have no reason to love the Empire."

"What's your point?"

"You live up near Ka'tan. You've seen the slaves that work the mines."

For the first time, Brie appeared uncomfortable. "Again, what's your point?"

"Do you know why Alar made that deal with the governor? The black market deal?"

"The same reason we would make that deal."

"That's right. He made it for the same reason the Desulti would. To become rich enough to protect ourselves from the Empire. So we can stop the slavers condemning our people to death in the mines, stop the inquisitors kidnapping little girls, stop the Imps riding into a village, killing people just so the governor can take what he wants."

Brie's expression had frozen.

"That's why you make yourselves rich, isn't it?" Lief asked. "To protect yourselves from Imps. But maybe you left the Empire, and you're still Imps. Don't care about anyone but yourselves, especially us Brochen." He paused and said, "You've been living in *our* land for years. No one's complained. What have you done for the *Alle'oss?*"

The door opened, startling everyone in the room.

"Bless the Mother," Zaina mumbled and settled back into her chair.

Jep stood in the door, taking in the scene. "Lief," he said finally. He stepped into the room, closed the door, and looked Keth and Zaina over. "Don't know these two."

Zaina stood and extended an arm. "Zaina," she said. She hooked a thumb at Keth, who remained seated. "Keth."

Jep took her arm, an amused smile on his face. "You two with this *Oss'stera?*"

Zaina nodded. "I have thirteen summers." She released his forearm and returned to her seat. "In case you're wondering."

Jep smiled at her, then turned a speculative gaze on Lief and Brie. "You two getting acquainted?"

Lief stood and fished the pouch of coins Alar gave him from his pack. He shook it, producing a pleasant jingle. "From the first shipment. Alar wanted you to have it."

Jep stared at the pouch and looked up at Lief's face. He took it, worked it open, and peered inside. "Looks to be more than we agreed to," he muttered.

"Alar says it's a show of good faith," Lief said, putting some emphasis on the last two words. His eyes cut to Brie, then he said to Jep, "We're ready for another shipment."

"Well, now," Jep said. "This might change some minds."

***

Brennerman set the file containing his adjutant's weekly reports to the side and glanced up at his window in time to see Schenk, his head scout, hurrying across the fortress's inner ward, a determined set to his expression. It looked like he was heading toward the door to his adjutant's office. Brennerman let hope flare for a moment before tamping it down. It had been weeks, and his patrols had found no sign of the rebels' base.

He listened as the scout entered the outer office and spoke to his adjutant. A moment later, Schenk appeared. He saluted and said, "I found them, sir." When Brennerman stood, Schenk said, "You'd best change your clothes." With Brennerman's approval, his scouts had adopted the buckskins common among some *Alle'oss* who lived up in the mountains. Brennerman swapped out his blue uniform for the more muted colors of his work clothes, then they headed east out of Richeleau on the Ka'tan road, accompanied by his unit's other two scouts. Four leagues east of the city, they dismounted.

"Silence from this point, sir," Schenk said. When Brennerman nodded, Schenk said, "No talking. Watch your step. Follow me closely."

Leaving their horses in the care of the other scouts, Brennerman and Schenk continued on foot. After two hours creeping through the forest, Brennerman was beginning to think Schenk was lost. But then the scout dropped to his hands and knees, crawled to the top of a rise and lay on his stomach behind a rangy elderberry. When Brennerman joined him, he pointed and whispered, "There."

Brennerman wasn't sure what he was seeing. At the bottom of a hill, a granite cliff thrust up. It was thirty paces high. In the center of what he could see, the dark mouths of two openings led into the cliff. "Caves?" he whispered.

"No, not caves. More like slot canyons or ravines. They're open on top."

"Okay, but what am I looking at?" A gust of wind brought the scent of wood smoke. "Smoke. A village?" He looked at the scout, who pointed to the top of the granite wall. Brennerman carefully pulled a branch aside and looked. An *Alle'oss* man standing on the top of the cliff was silhouetted against the sky, a strung bow dangling from one hand. "A sentry."

"Right," Schenk said. "There are more posted in the forest. That's why I took you on such a circuitous route to get here."

"Not typical of an *Alle'oss* village."

"Exactly. That's what caught my attention at first. From the amount of smoke in the evenings, I'd estimate there's maybe two, three hundred back there. It's surrounded by this granite outcrop, so it's hard to be sure." He extracted a spyglass from a pouch at his belt and extended it. After looking through it briefly, he handed it to Brennerman. Pointing to the base of the cliff, he said, "Look just inside the ravine on the right."

Brennerman put the spyglass to his eye. It took him a moment to find the entrance, but when he did, his mouth dropped open. He let the spyglass fall and turned to look at Schenk, who nodded.

"Crates," Brennerman said.

"Can't be sure because of the shadows, but it looks to be an Imperial eagle on the sides of the crates. They must be using the space for storage."

This was it! Brennerman gazed at Schenk for a moment longer, his mind racing, then he returned his attention to the crates. It was hard to be sure, but he thought Schenk might be right; the emblem painted on the sides of the crates looked like an Imperial eagle; the seal of the Imperial military. If he could trace those crates back to the missing supply caravan, he was looking at his vindication.

He handed the spyglass back to Schenk and studied the terrain in front of the cliffs, then looked up at the sentry. "Not going to be easy if they know we're coming."

"Right. If we could get through the ravines unseen, surprise might give us an edge. Still, we can't be sure what's on the other side. We don't know how deep the canyons are or how narrow they are once you get inside. Might end up coming out single file on the other end. If it's just the cavalry, it'll be fifty against three hundred. I'm not fond of those odds." He paused. "Any chance Hoch would join us?"

Brennerman clicked his teeth gently while he thought. The rumors of what happened when he met Hoch spread through the fort like a fire on a dry savanna, raising the tension between his men and the rangers to an alarming level. He would have been proud of the loyalty the troopers showed him, but it complicated the question of gaining Hoch's cooperation. "If we can devise a plan of attack, then get him out here so he can see for himself." He fell silent, then said, "Maybe."

"I could sneak in there at night. Bring back the proof we need. Something with the seal."

It was tempting. The sentry on top of the cliff wouldn't spot him at night, but if it were Brennerman, he would post more sentries in the ravines. "Not yet. Might warn them. If you're right about the numbers, we'll need the element of surprise, even with the rangers."

"Against *Alle'oss?*"

Brennerman heard the same skepticism in his scout's voice he heard from everyone else when it came to the idea of *Alle'oss* rebels. He turned and looked at Schenk. "These *Alle'oss* have already wiped out a ranger company and fought Union mercenaries to a standstill." He held Schenk's gaze for a moment, then looked away. "I'm confident we can handle them, but I will not underestimate them."

"Yes, sir." They watched as the sentry was relieved by a woman. "It would help to know what to expect inside."

"It would. Let's get back and come up with a plan to find out. In the meantime, keep them under observation." As they were turning away, the familiar forest sounds were interrupted by a commotion at the entrance of one of the ravines. Brenneman looked back in time to see a woman leading a gaggle of boisterous children out of the left-most opening. They looked to be between seven and nine years old. Despite their piping voices and laughter, the woman got their attention and had them sit in an arc facing her. Brennerman couldn't hear what she said, but it looked as if it was a school.

"We're in luck," Schenk said. When Brennerman looked at him, he said, "Might be three hundred in there, but they're not all fighters."

Brennerman returned his gaze to the children as the woman said something that sent them into gales of laughter. "Could be messy," he said.

"Hard to avoid. But if they *are* rebels, they accepted the consequences when they turned traitor."

"Right." After one last lingering look, Brennerman backed away from the elderberry bush, rose and followed his scout.

The sudden appearance of the children caught him off guard. Unprepared, memories of the last time he saw his own son escaped from where he confined them. Absently following his scout, he let the memories have their way for the first time in years, surreptitiously brushing away tears before they dampened his cheeks. When Schenk glanced over his shoulder, Brennerman averted his gaze.

Schenk's attitude about killing children wasn't surprising. As the conflict in Styria became ugly, what had been unofficial attitudes within the military toward rebels became official policy. Rebellion was to be rooted out leaf, stem and root. That meant a whiff of suspicion was sufficient justification for massacring entire villages; men, women, and children. As veterans of the Styrian conflict, Hoch's rangers couldn't help being involved with what Brennerman considered indiscriminate murder.

Brennerman wasn't, as most *Alle'oss* thought, an unfeeling monster. He regretted what happened during the cavalry raid on Lirantok the previous autumn. He instructed his men to leave the citizens and buildings intact as long as they encountered no resistance. The *Alle'oss* didn't know how lucky they were. If Hoch's rangers encountered even the feeble resistance the *Alle'oss* in Lirantok offered, they would have massacred everyone and razed the village. Still, though he regretted what happened, the *Alle'oss* had to learn there were consequences for resisting. It was better to squash rebellion in measured ways before it spread. Otherwise Argren would be another Styria.

By the time they made it back to their horses, Brennerman had gained control of his wayward emotions. He knew where the rebels were now. He just needed to find a way to obtain the proof he needed and eliminate the threat to the Empire while avoiding a slaughter.

13

Paint That

By the time Alar entered the pavilion on the day after the welcome reception, the artists were already at work. He'd eschewed his new suit and donned his buckskins. He assumed that was the reason for the attention he garnered at his appearance. Scilla, wearing a paint-stained smock over her dress, stood in her work area, hands on her hips, staring at a blank canvas. He was heading over to her stall when he noticed Ukrit motioning him over, an air of panic about him.

"I have no idea what to do," he whispered when Alar came near.

Alar took in the pile of clay bricks stacked in a small wheelbarrow beside a pedestal. "Sculpt," Alar said with a grin. When Ukrit grimaced, he said, "Like the horse you did before. Right?"

Ukrit's grimace became a scowl. "That lord is supposed to buy what I make. Clay won't last, no matter how careful you are with it." He threw his hands out to his sides. "I can't believe that's what Olson wanted me to do."

Alar gestured to the wheelbarrow. "Well, there's the clay."

Ukrit was about to respond when he saw something over Alar's shoulder and slammed his mouth shut.

Alar turned and found Olson, tall, thin, fastidious, smiling at them. But what drew his eye was the man standing next to him. He was taller than Olson and wider than two Olsons. The thick mat of wiry hair peeking around a leather apron over a bare torso glistened with sweat. From the breadth of his forearms and the charred pivots in this apron, Alar guessed he was a blacksmith. Though wiry, black hair hung down his back in a thick braid, his skin was swarthier than a Volloch. The man glowered at Ukrit as if studying something stuck to the bottom of his shoe.

"Alar," Olson said, a small frown appearing as his eyes flicked down to Alar's clothes. Then he smiled at Ukrit and gestured to the blacksmith. "Ukrit, this is Chekka, the best blacksmith in Lachton, and," he leaned in and said confidentially, "maybe the only blacksmith with any experience casting bronze."

"Bronze," Ukrit murmured. "Of course."

Alar glanced back at him, hoping to see a relieved smile, but found a worried frown instead.

"As you are the sole sculptor here," Olson said, "you have exclusive access to his services." He nodded to Alar, turned and hurried away.

Chekka eyed Alar, then dismissed him and focused on Ukrit. "You never worked in bronze before." Alar guessed it wasn't a question, but it was hard to tell through his odd accent. "Terror in your eyes," he said in answer to their unspoken question. "You sculpt?"

Ukrit nodded. "Marble mostly. Some clay."

Chekka nodded. "Come," he said, turned and stalked toward the exit.

Ukrit gaped at him.

"You better go," Alar said. As Ukrit hurried to follow, Alar called, "Don't make him mad." Ukrit made a rude gesture as he disappeared through the tent flaps.

Grinning, Alar turned to find Scilla staring blankly at him. "You okay?"

She startled, her eyes focused, and she asked, "What?"

Alar came around the partition into her stall and stood next to her, facing the blank canvas. "It's red."

"They already put the grounding on it," she mumbled. "Not how I would have done it, but it saves me a step."

"Grounding, hmmm." Alar nodded. "I asked if you were okay. You seem distracted."

"I don't know what to paint." She threw her hand at the offending canvas. "I had all kinds of ideas yesterday." Casting a furtive glance at the other artists who were busy applying paint to their canvases, she leaned close and whispered, "They all seem so sure of themselves."

"You ever hear the story of the fox and donkey?"

Scilla frowned, one corner of her lips pulling back. She looked at the canvas without answering.

"So, you have," Alar said. "The donkey was so sure of himself, because he was ignorant. The fox," he put an arm around her shoulders and pulled her close, "doubted himself because he knew how difficult the task was." He grinned widely at her frown. "And what happened?"

"The donkey drowned," Scilla said flatly. "But that —"

"Was just a story," Alar finished for her. "Everyone knows the story because of the wisdom it contains."

Scilla's lips twisted. "Maybe. But what do I *paint?*"

Before he could answer, a commotion behind them drew his attention. He turned, leaving Scilla staring at the canvas. The engaged couple, Holden and Violette, entered the pavilion, trailed by what was obviously a gaggle of Volloch elites. Holden caught Alar's eye and gave him a small smile, but the rest of the group looked as if they were trying their best to fulfill Alar's stereotype of their kind. They huddled together and glanced around as if they might soil their expensive clothes just by being there.

The artists' reactions were entirely the opposite. As one, they abandoned their work and flowed toward the couple, exclaiming enthusiastically at the privilege they had been granted. What followed was a scene of contrasts. On one side, the well-dressed elite, their noses firmly in the air, their body language conveying their sense of superiority. On the other, the artists, dressed in work clothes, jostling one another eagerly, hands out in entreaty. They obviously knew how lucrative having Violette and Holden as patrons would be.

Scilla was so focused on her canvas, she hadn't noticed the commotion. Alar took her by the shoulders and turned her around. "Paint that," he said.

Scilla stared at the gathering, her lips parted slightly. The bride and groom stood in the center, facing the artists. The elites gathered in a tight group behind them, pulling back and peering at the artists as if they were wild animals. The artists leaned slightly forward, their adoring eyes on the couple.

It was a moment, then it was gone. Holden said a few words, welcoming the artists and expressing his gratitude to them for contributing to the celebration. Violette didn't speak. Then they all left in much more haste than they arrived, leaving the artists to hover around the buffet table, speculating excitedly about their prospects.

"Go away," Scilla said and turned back to the canvas.

Alar kissed her on the cheek, made his way through the chattering crowd to the buffet table, and plucked up an apple. Returning their disapproving frowns with a grin, he exited the tent and strolled toward the manor house. It really was an enormous building. How was he going to find the chest with the dowry? He could move unseen in *annen'heim* but he couldn't pass through solid objects. He would have to return to the physical realm to open doors, and locked doors remained impassable obstacles. It would take forever to search the entire building. If he could narrow the location down to a single wing, that would help.

"Can I help you?"

Alar turned to find a servant peering uncertainly at his buckskins. "Perhaps. Can you tell me where I might find Trell?"

"Trell?" When Alar nodded, the servant said, "He's in the stables, mucking out the stalls today."

"Thank you," Alar said, and set off across the lawn.

He paused beside the corral to offer the apple core to one of the stable's residents, then made his way inside. He didn't see anyone in the interior, but a wheelbarrow outside an open stall told him where he would find Trell. As he approached the stall, Trell appeared, stripped to the waist, dripping with sweat, a pitchfork full of soiled straw in his hands.

"Trell!"

Trell paused, the pitchfork above the wheelbarrow. When he saw who it was, a grin illuminated his face. He dumped the straw, stuck the tines in the ground and leaned on the handle. "Alar, right?"

"That's right."

"What can I do for you?"

"I was hoping for a tour of the manor house," Alar said.

Trell looked down at his soiled clothes.

"Another day?"

Trell's grin returned. "Sure. They got me working up in the house polishing all the brass tomorrow. You can tag along."

Alar climbed the open stall door, put his back to the column between the stalls and watched Trell work. "I'll come help you polish."

"Truly?" Trell asked skeptically.

"Sure." Alar watched Trell return to the stall, then asked, "What do they do with all that space? They can't live in it all, can they? How many kids do they have?"

Trell laughed. "Violette's got a younger brother. That's all of them." He dumped another load of straw in the wheelbarrow. "The family lives in the north wing on the second floor. Most of the rest of the house is empty, usually. It's all closed off until they have big events like the wedding. Then they need rooms for the guests. Not everyone, of course. Some stay in town, but the most important people stay in the manor."

The north wing. That was helpful. "How often do they have something as big as the wedding?"

Trell shrugged and reentered the stall. "Three, four times a year. The Lord, he's very important. Most of the big social events in Lachton happen here."

"Who comes to those things?"

"All kinds." Trell scooped up another load. "Inquisition brothers, lords and their wives. Generals. We've had some sisters. You know from the Seidi. The governor of Argren comes all the time," Trell said, frowning and shaking his head.

"What?"

"No idea how a man like that became a governor."

Alar chuckled. "His mother is the emperor's sister."

Trell's eyebrows shot up his forehead. "Truely?"

"Yep. So, the governor will be coming to the wedding?"

"I assume so," Trell said, dumping another load into the wheelbarrow.

Siofra and Adelbart would both be at the wedding. Alar wondered if Siofra would take advantage of the opportunity to pressure the governor. He would have to keep an eye on that situation. He hopped down. "Thanks, Trell. I'll come looking for you tomorrow."

Trell waved and disappeared into the stall.

Alar was returning to the pavilion when he saw a familiar figure sitting in the shade of an oak tree. Ukrit was so involved in what he was doing, he didn't notice Alar approaching until he stepped up beside him.

"What's got you so engrossed?" Alar asked.

Ukrit glanced up, then returned his attention to the sheet of paper on top of a board balanced across his knees. "Chekka wants me to sketch my sculpture."

Alar looked more closely at the drawing emerging under a piece of charcoal. "That's pretty good. Why didn't you just paint, like Scilla?"

"It's a long way from drawing to painting. I *can* paint, but I'm nothing like Scilla," Ukrit murmured. "Besides, I like sculpting."

Alar watched him applying shading to his drawing. "It's a horse." Ukrit hummed an acknowledgment. "But not like your other horse."

Ukrit sat up and looked down at his drawing. "All the sculptures of horses I've seen have the horse just standing there. I wanted this to be more dynamic."

"Why does Chekka need a drawing?"

"We have to create the armature. It's like an iron skeleton I apply the clay to."

"And then?" When Ukrit looked up impatiently, Alar asked, "It's still clay, right? You said that's a problem."

Ukrit's face cleared. "Somehow, that clay statue becomes a bronze statue. I don't know how, and I'm afraid to ask. Chekka doesn't have a lot of patience." He looked pointedly up at Alar. "Now, if you have your questions answered, Chekka is waiting." He bent over his drawing without waiting for a response.

Alar wandered away, thrusting his hands into his pockets. He found Scilla busy covering the red canvas with white paint using a wicked-looking knife. When he stepped up beside her, she glanced at him, then ignored him.

"It's white, now," he said.

She sighed and turned to face him, brandishing the knife. "Alar, you're going to have to find some way to occupy yourself. I don't like to be interrupted while I paint."

"Okay, okay," he said, hands in the air, in a warding gesture. He wandered through the pavilion, examining the other artists' works. All of their canvases were a solid white or gray. From the way some of them examined their canvases, he guessed they were waiting for them to dry.

Tearing off a hunk of crusty bread, he drizzled honey on it and stepped out into the sunshine, having to make way for a man in a servant's livery coming the other way. Gazing up at the manor, he chewed thoughtfully. He would visit the manor that night and explore. He wiped his fingers on his shirt and gazed around at the vast estate. Now what?

***

Brother Vint hurried to the pavilion. He only had time for a quick peek before he was missed, but he wanted to know where the *Alle'oss* artists were at work.

The Inquisition routinely planted spies on the estates of important lords. Vint took it as a point of pride when he learned of his assignment on Bergamot's staff. Evidence of malfeasance by a man like Bergamot would provide the Inquisition leverage on one of the most powerful lords in the Empire. Unfortunately, as far as he could tell, the lord was a paragon of virtue. Or unusually clever. Vint worked for Bergamot for a year and found nothing useful to the Inquisition.

Reading between the lines of the last message he received from his superior in the Inquisition, he guessed they were only waiting until after the wedding to reassign him. That would be disappointing. Bergamot was unusually generous with his servants compared to other lords, and Vint had been on the estate long enough to make friends. He needed to find something his superiors valued, and soon.

When he heard about the new school *Alle'oss* artists, he couldn't believe his luck. If they were already on the list of banned artists, that would be all he needed. Even if they weren't, if they were like the other new school artists, they would push the boundaries of what was acceptable, and Bergamot would be responsible.

He pushed past an *Alle'oss* man in buckskins as he entered the pavilion, then stopped and looked around. Only one *Alle'oss* artist was at work. A woman. He moved further into the space so he could see her canvas over her shoulder. She was just applying white paint over a red background.

As he returned to his duties in the garden, he considered his best course of action. He got a good look at all three *Alle'oss* when they arrived. He would forward their names and descriptions to the commandant of the Inquisition house in Lachton. In the meantime, he would keep an eye on the artists' progress.

14

I'm Scrapping It

Alar lay on his bed, hands behind his head, gazing up at a ceiling illuminated by light from a waxing gibbous moon filtering through the open windows. The sounds of the estate going to sleep had ceded the night to the crickets and the owls. He checked on Ukrit, who lay on his back in the bed across the room. Though he couldn't see whether his eyes were open, the absence of his rumbling snores suggested he was awake.

Rolling out of bed, Alar padded to the window and peered up at the early summer constellations. It was past midnight. Time to go.

"Be careful," Ukrit muttered.

"You worried about me?" Alar asked, crossing the room to the door.

Ukrit snorted. "I'm worried about Scilla and me. If you get caught, we'll deny ever knowing you. Plus, you didn't tell her what you were doing. She'll kill me if anything happens to you."

Alar grinned and put his ear to the door. Hearing nothing, he eased the door open and peeked into the empty hall, then stepped through. Once outside the dormitory, he paused and *pulled.* One of the benefits of being a realm walker was the bursts of energy he could pull from the spot in his mind where he heard his spirit's song. The rush swept away his fatigue and left his limbs light and springy. He bounced on his toes a few times, then crouched and stepped into *annen'heim*. Peering up at the moon made wavey by the boundary between the realms, he listened to the distant wails of the *sjel'and.*

The spirits weren't close, so he set off toward the manor house. As he expected, the large double doors at the front entrance were closed and a pair of guards were frozen in the act of patrolling the wide veranda. During his explorations earlier in the day, he noticed a door that led into the rear of the manor across from the kitchen, so he made his way around to the back of the house.

He was surprised to find a light on in the kitchen. When he peeked in, he found Trell and another boy illuminated by a pair of lamps. Trell's arms were submerged in soapy water and the other boy was drying a pot. They appeared frozen, but he could tell Trell was speaking and the other boy was laughing as if Trell was telling a funny story.

Alar crossed the brick courtyard to the manor house. The door was slightly ajar. After glancing around to be sure he didn't miss an observer, he crossed the boundary and returned to the physical realm. As he eased the door open, he listened to Trell telling the other boy an account of how Adelbart became governor. Somehow, he took the simple fact Alar told him about the governor's mother and spun an elaborate tale involving mistaken identity and blackmail.

Grinning, Alar stepped inside, eased the door closed and studied his surroundings. He was in a pantry. Opposite the door he entered, a hallway extended further into the building. He crossed into *annen'heim* and strolled down the hall. After wandering through a maze of rooms and halls, all obviously part of the infrastructure required to stage elaborate social events, he finally found something familiar. The food had been cleared away, but the banquet tables remained. This was the room where they attended the reception the previous evening. Trell called it the Reception Hall. He crossed the room and entered the immense Entrance Hall. There was another guard frozen halfway across the wide marble floor.

Alar sauntered over to stand next to the guard and gazed at the twin staircases that wound up to the second floor. Where to start? He and Ukrit decided they would probably keep the chest containing the dowry in the lord's room, which, according to Trell, should be in the north wing. He took the stairway that hugged the curving wall on the north side of the lobby. On the landing, he paused and gazed at the door. It was closed. To open it, he would have to return to the physical realm. Crouching and pressing himself against the balcony's back wall, he crossed the boundary.

He was greeted by the echoing click of the guard's boots on the marble floor. Creeping forward, he peered down the stairs, ready to retreat into the underworld. Fortunately, the guard didn't look up and his footsteps faded as he entered the Reception Hall.

Alar put his ear to the door to the family's wing. Hearing nothing, he tried the knob. It wasn't locked. "Why would they lock it with so many guards around?" he mumbled as he eased the door open and peeked into a long hallway. Lamps mounted at intervals on the walls, their wicks turned down, provided just enough light to see. Closing the door behind him, he paused to take stock.

Hallways extended straight ahead and to the left. Shrugging, he strolled down the hall ahead of him. With nothing else to go on, he reasoned a lord would want his room to be at the end of the hall so he would have windows on two walls.

After listening at the last door and hearing nothing, he tried the knob and found it unlocked. Cracking the door open, he peeked inside. There was just enough light entering the windows to reveal a room that fit Alar's idea of what a lord's study should be. Floor to ceiling bookshelves lined the two walls without windows. A billiard table occupied the corner between the bookshelves. Chairs and a sofa were arranged around a hearth. As with the Reception Hall, paintings and sculptures were displayed around the room. Alar entered and closed the door behind him.

It only took moments to discover there was no chest. Sighing, he sat on the billiard table and gazed around the room. There were valuables here, but nothing he would know what to do with and nothing that would change *Oss'stera's* fortunes.

"Couldn't get that lucky," he muttered and hopped down from the table.

He left the room, stood in the middle of the hallway, and stared toward the other end. There were a dozen more doors in the long hall. "Better get to it," he murmured.

None of the rooms were locked. There were offices, closets, sitting rooms, a music salon with a harp and grand piano, a sewing room, and a library large enough to warrant two doors. But no chest.

As he was leaving the library, he glanced at the titles of a row of books illuminated by moonlight and came to a stop. He worked one of them free and looked at the cover. The title read, *Tales of Lohkti: The Lovable Rogue.* The idea that Imperials were reading stories about this character was unsettling. Lohkti was an oafish figure in *Alle'oss* folklore, a caricature meant to amuse. The stories were humorous lessons for children. Did Imperials know that? Alar flipped the book open and read a sentence at random.

Lohkti stuffed the honking goose inside his cloak and ran with the gendarmes in hot pursuit.

He replaced the book and ran his finger along the other books on the shelf. *Lohkti's Adventures in Brennan. Lohkti: The Wise Alle'oss. The Amorous Adventures of Balder the Thief.* There was an entire shelf of books in a similar vein. Shaking his head, Alar continued his search.

After leaving the last room, he stood next to the exit and considered the other hall. These were probably the family's personal rooms. He'd been lucky so far that he hadn't encountered anyone, but there would be people in the bedrooms. It would be riskier to search them. Still, he knew that when he started, and since he spent a lot of time in *annen'heim*, it couldn't be much past midnight. He might as well get it over with.

Deciding to start with the last room, he had taken two steps when the first door on the right opened. Surprised, Alar froze rather than retreating into the underworld. Holden, the groom, stood in the doorway, wearing nightclothes and holding a candle.

Alar expected him to shout for the guards, but Holden only stared at him. As the moment dragged out, the corners of Holden's lips curled ever so slightly.

"Alar," he said. "This is a surprise."

"I, uh…" Alar motioned over his shoulder.

"Was just leaving?" Holden asked, his brows lifting.

"Right." Alar turned around and sauntered to the exit. With his hand on the knob, he looked back, nodded and said, "See you in the morning?"

Holden grinned. "I'm sure."

Alar cracked the door, peeked out, then, with a glance back, he eased through the door. As soon as he shut it, he slipped into *annen'heim*.

***

"Find it?" Ukrit asked when Alar returned to their room.

"No," Alar said.

"That's unfortunate."

"Yeah." Alar flopped onto this bed.

"There's always tomorrow night."

"Maybe." Alar put his hands behind his head and stared at the ceiling. He remained in *annen'heim* almost the entire way back to his room, so only a few minutes passed in the physical realm since Holden caught him. Even so, if he was going to sound the alarm, the guards should be pounding on his door by now. His adrenaline ebbed as the minutes dragged by, but he forced himself to lie awake for hours, body taut, listening for the sounds of approaching guards over Ukrit's snores. The sun was making its imminent appearance known when he finally succumbed to his fatigue.

⁂

When Alar's eyes opened, he was surprised to find he was still in his room in the artists' dormitory. The sun was well up and Ukrit was gone. Groaning, he rolled out of bed, stood with his arms out and *pulled.* A rush of invigorating energy poured forth from the spot in his mind, leaving his limbs tingly. It wouldn't completely erase his fatigue, but it left his mind clear and put some spring in his step.

After making himself as presentable as he could, given his lack of sleep, he made his way out of the silent dormitory. Emerging into the bright sunlight, he paused and looked out across the estate. Still no guards. Holden was clearly inebriated when they met him at the reception. He didn't appear drunk the previous night, but while lying in bed waiting to be arrested, Alar decided that was the only explanation for Holden's blase reaction to finding him sneaking around the manor in the middle of the night. He was blind drunk.

The promise of breakfast and seeing Scilla sent him toward the pavilion. When he entered the tent, he glanced at Scilla and froze. She stood with her back to her easel, a palette and brush in her hands. A man standing with his back to Alar gestured to the canvas on Scilla's easel and said something that made her smile. Although Alar couldn't see his face, it was unmistakably Holden.

Alar licked his lips and made his way over to the two of them, forcing himself to appear casual. When Scilla greeted him, Holden turned around.

"Lord Mueller," Alar said with a smile.

"Alar. You're looking surprisingly… fresh… this morning." He grinned. "And please, call me Holden. Although I am technically a lord, my father is *the* lord in the family. Besides, I feel we know enough about one another to be on casual terms."

"Holden, then." Alar glanced around at the other artists who were trying to keep an eye on the exchange without appearing to. "I'm surprised to find you alone." When Holden's eyebrow rose, Alar said, "Without Violette. Or guards."

Understanding chased Holden's frown. "Ah, well, one wouldn't think guards would be necessary on the estate. After all, who would I need protection from?" He winked, and his gaze lingered for a moment, then he said, "As for my fiancée, she has more important matters to attend to than trivialities like art." He turned to Scilla, gestured to the canvas, and said, "I look forward to seeing the finished painting."

As Alar and Scilla watched him making his way around the pavilion, greeting the artists and stopping occasionally to chat, Scilla asked, "What was that about?"

"What?"

Scilla squinted at Alar. "Really? You're going to play innocent?" She gestured to Holden. "You two were talking about something you weren't saying."

"Who knows how his type thinks?"

"He winked."

"He… what?"

"Alar," Scilla said. "Holden shows up, asking all kinds of questions about you. You show up late, looking awful, by the way. Like you didn't sleep last night." Her brows lifted while Alar made vague gestures. "You snuck into the manor house last night, didn't you?"

Alar leaned close and muttered, "You knew I have to find that chest. How else am I supposed to find it?"

"And that business with Holden was because…"

"He caught me." Alar lifted his hands palms out at Scilla's shocked expression. "He didn't do anything. Didn't call the guards." He glanced back at Holden. "Not sure what his game is."

"You didn't tell me what you were going to do."

"Because you've been so worried about the painting." He turned and waved a hand at the canvas, then paused and stared, his hand outstretched. "It's coming along."

Scilla sketched the scene they witnessed the day before. The focus of the drawing was the engaged couple, the snooty elite to one side and the beseeching artists to the other. It wasn't exactly how Alar remembered it, but she managed to convey the dynamics of the scene better than the reality had. She had started applying paint to Violette. Alar stepped up close to the painting and stared at the woman's face. There was something in her expression that he saw the day before without realizing it. It was so fleeting, he dismissed and forgot it. He lifted a finger to point it out to Scilla, then she spoke.

"I'm scrapping it." She turned to her workbench.

He stared at her back, watching her tidying up. "Scrapping it? Why? It's amazing. Already."

Scilla turned around, glanced at Holden, then whispered, "Those two people shouldn't be getting married."

"You going to paint something that…" Casting about, he couldn't imagine what she had in mind. Whatever it was, no one involved in the wedding would appreciate it. Taking a step closer, he glanced over his shoulder at Holden, who was listening to About-That with an uncharacteristically pained expression on his face. "You… um… think that's a good idea?"

"It will be risky, but I'm done worrying about what they'll think." She flung a hand toward the other artists.

"Risky enough to get us arrested?"

"No, not that kind of risky. It's just a different way of painting. More…" She shrugged. "I don't know how to describe it. Don't worry." She flicked her fingers at him. "Now, you —"

"Go away," Alar said. "I know." He gave her a quick kiss and asked, "Where's Ukrit?"

Scilla turned away and said over her shoulder. "That blacksmith, Chekka, came and got him."

Alar watched her mixing more of the white foundation paint. He had no idea what she was planning, but he trusted her. She understood the situation. Turning away, he gathered up some breakfast and went in search of Ukrit.

***

"What's this?" the commander of the Lachton Inquisition house asked his assistant, taking the single sheet of paper.

"Report from Brother Vint."

"Ah," the commander said. "Has he finally found some dirt on Bergamot?" He scanned the document while his assistant answered.

"Maybe. Unusual, anyway."

"New school artists?"

"Yes, sir. None of the names are on the banned list, but it wouldn't hurt to check on the art. Vint hasn't had any luck with anything else." He paused and said, "Isn't Inquisitor Hoerst attending the wedding?"

The commander popped his lips while he thought. The report included detailed descriptions of the three *Alle'oss*. "Hoerst is busy with some business in Argren. Inquisitor Anders is attending the wedding in his stead. Let's have him check out the art and take whatever action he deems appropriate." Handing the report back to his assistant, he said, "Forward this to Richeleau. They may have a better idea who the three artists are."

"They don't yet have a large staff," his assistant said, tucking the report into the bottom of the stack of paper he carried.

"If they want to pursue it, they can let us know." As his assistant turned to leave, he said, "And if they know who they are, tell them to give us more detail."

"Yes, sir."

15

Gossip

Alar thought he would have to track down a servant to locate the smithy on the large estate, but as soon as he stepped out of the pavilion, he caught the familiar scent of hot iron on a gusty breeze. All he had to do was follow his nose. When he drew near, the familiar sound of the blacksmith's hammer drew him on. The open-air shack was located as far from the manor house as possible, tucked behind a stand of maples and hickories. Alar took in the scene while he finished his breakfast.

Ukrit, stripped to the waist, watching Chekka hammering a long, thin iron bar, didn't notice Alar. When the blacksmith thrust the bar into the forge, Ukrit jumped to work the handle of the bellows. Chekka spotted Alar and yelled something to Ukrit. Ukrit barely glanced Alar's way, then returned his attention to the bellows. Not until Chekka pulled the iron from the forge did Ukrit come out to meet Alar. Sweat poured down his torso. He started to speak, but apparently decided a nod was sufficient.

"He's got you working," Alar said.

Ukrit grunted.

"This part of the sculpture?" Alar had to shout over the bright ping of the hammer.

Ukrit nodded. "Armature. It's like a skeleton I sculpt the clay on." He wiped his forehead and flicked the sweat away. "When I showed him my drawing, you would have thought I insulted his mother. Been grumpy ever since."

"What's the problem?"

"Complicated. Now I know why all the bronze horses I've seen are standing still." When Alar lifted a brow, he said, "All the legs and the body are straight. My horse is in motion, so the armature is more complex."

"He try to talk you out of it?"

"For at least an hour," Ukrit said with a grimace. Noticing Chekka returning the iron to the furnace, he hurried back to the bellows.

"You stick to your vision," Alar yelled after him. Returning Chekka's scowl with a wide grin, he turned and walked along the path that took him back to the manor house. He had an appointment with Trell.

One of the guards at the entrance to the manor looked familiar, so Alar stopped and peered at him. When the man grinned, Alar asked, "Helmut?"

Helmut nodded. "We met the day Scilla sold Olson her painting."

"Right," Alar said, joining the guard. "How are things?"

"Doing well." Helmut glanced around and asked, "Scilla here?"

"She is. She's busy with her painting in the pavilion with the other artists."

Helmut nodded. "Maybe I'll drop by and say hello when I get off duty." He was looking out across the broad lawn in front of the estate, but as he spoke, his eyes flicked to Alar.

"She's awfully focused when she's working," Alar said. "Might be best to let her work." Helmut's face fell. "But I'll be sure to tell her you want to say hello."

Helmut perked up and returned Alar's grin.

"You seen Trell?" Alar asked. "I told him I would help polish brass."

"Polish brass? You're a guest. What you want to do something like polish brass for?"

Alar leaned closer and spoke confidentially. "You want to know the real gossip, you get to know the people who do real work. They know what's really going on." He straightened. "Right?"

"Yeah, I suppose that's right. What is it you want to know?"

Alar chuckled. "You should have seen all the other artists falling over themselves when the bride and groom visited the pavilion yesterday."

"Oh, yeah?"

Alar nodded. "You know, of course, that what all artists need is a wealthy patron. A lover of art who has the coin to nurture young promising talents."

"Yeah, I suppose I see that," Helmut said. "Gotta pay the bills while you learn."

"Exactly," Alar said with a knowing smile. "As Scilla's and Ukrit's manager, my job is to find that patron for them. Give them peace of mind so they can create beauty." He smiled, giving Helmut time to follow the path Alar set in front of him. He was thinking he would have to give him another hint when Helmut finally put it together.

"So, you hope to give Scilla an advantage finding this patron by learning something about the bride and groom," Helmut said, speaking slowly.

Alar winked and placed his index finger alongside his nose.

"That's smart. Real smart."

"So, Helmut," Alar said, stepping close and glancing over his shoulder. "What can you tell me about Lady Violette and Lord Mueller?"

Helmut glanced around nervously.

"Scilla would be very grateful if something you told me helped her find a patron." Alar winced inwardly, imagining what Scilla would say if she heard him. But it worked.

A smile grew on the guard's face. He glanced around again and murmured. "I know they don't want to get married."

Alar pulled back and lifted his brows.

"It's true." Helmut waved a hand to encompass the estate. "All us who work here know it."

Alar pasted a confused frown on his face. "So, why the wedding?"

"Business," Helmut said with a knowing nod. "These elites don't treat marriage like the rest of us."

"No?"

"No. It's their daddies who make the deal, and it's the bride and groom who secure the thing."

"Well, I never…"

"It's true," Helmut said. "Violette's a tough case, too. Her daddy's been trying to marry her off for a time. Keeps falling through. Not this time, though."

"No?" When Helmut shook his head, Alar asked, "What's different this time?"

"See, it's always the groom who calls it off. They come to the estate and meet with Lady Violette, then they leave and never come back. I was standing right on this spot when the last one stalked off like the lady offended him."

"So," Alar mused. "It's the lady who sabotages the matches." It confirmed what Ragan told him. Ever since their conversation, he had been trying to figure out what she was hinting at.

Helmut nodded.

"But she must like Holden, or else they would have already called it off."

"Well, now, that's the odd thing," Helmut said. "Word is Violette don't like Holden any more than the others, but Holden's still here. Maybe he likes his women bossy. Who can say?"

"That *is* curious." Alar gazed across the lawn to Violette's garden. "Maybe Violette likes him better than the others, for some reason."

"Could be," Helmut said doubtfully. "I expect it's more she's just tired of the whole thing. Wants to get it over and done with."

"They wore her down, huh?" Alar asked with a wink.

"So, uh," Helmut said. "Does that help?"

"Yes. I think that might help."

"You'll put in a word with Scilla for me, then?"

When Alar clapped him on the shoulder, Helmut frowned at the familiarity, but when Alar said, "I will, indeed," a smile replaced the frown.

"But first, I have an appointment to polish brass," Alar said and winked again.

"Oh, yeah, right," Helmut said, awkwardly returning his wink. "You'll find Trell up in the family's wing."

"They'll let me in?"

"Sure, if anyone stops you, just tell em you're looking for Trell."

"Thank you for everything, Helmut." Alar set off across the entryway. If Helmut was any sort of guard, he should have asked how Alar knew where the family's wing was, but the guard turned away as soon as Alar entered the door.

He found Trell polishing the brass fittings on the wall sconces in the hall where Alar met Holden the night before. The scent of the polishing compound permeated the air in the enclosed space. Most of the doors were closed, but the one from which Holden emerged was open. Alar peeked in and found a servant tidying up. He was considering whether he should explore it when Trell noticed him.

"Alar!" the boy called. "Thought you were joking about helping."

"Never joke when it comes to work," Alar said, approaching Trell with a broad grin.

Trell handed him a cloth and pointed to the sconce across the hall from the one he was working on.

The sconce looked as if it was already polished, but Alar went to work. After a few minutes, he stood back and peered at his reflection in the brass. Turning, he asked, "So, these are the family's bedrooms?"

Trell dropped his cloth into a bucket and crossed the hall to inspect Alar's work. After a moment, he pointed and said, "You missed a spot."

Alar couldn't see what the boy saw, but he rubbed the indicated spot, anyway.

"Most of these are bedrooms," Trell said, picking up his bucket and moving on to the next pair of sconces. He pointed to the doors to his left and right on the same side of the hall. "These are the Lady Violette's rooms." When Alar followed him, Trell pointed down the hall toward the exit. "Lady Violette's brother." He pointed behind Alar. "The lady of the house, Violette's mother." He pointed to the end of the hall. "The lord on that side and his study on this side."

Bergamot had another study. Maybe that would be where he would stash the dowry. Gazing at the door to the study, Alar said, "The mother and father have separate rooms, huh?"

"Vollochs." Trell rolled his eyes.

An hour later, Alar stood back, rubbing his shoulder as Trell inspected the last sconce Alar polished.

"You're getting the hang of it," he said and gave it one last swipe. He turned a wide grin on Alar and said, "*Tok!*" Alar gave him a surprised smile. "That right?"

"That is right," Alar said. "*Aurina sha.* You're welcome."

Trell took the rag Alar offered him. "I have to do the other hallway in the family's wing. You want to help?" He asked it with a hopeful expression on his face.

"Uh, sure," Alar said, digging his fingers into the cramped muscles of his shoulder. Other than the locations of the rooms, he hadn't learned much useful from Trell, but he was good company, and it wasn't like he had anything else to do. When Trell turned away, Alar tried the knob of the lord's study. It was locked. Glancing at Trell's retreating back, he bent over and peered at the keyhole. He could pick simple locks, but he never tried anything as elaborate as this one. With a sigh, he followed the boy.

They were almost to the door at the end of the hall when it opened, revealing Holden. At first, the lord only noticed Trell. He apparently assumed Trell was leaving, because he retreated to give the boy room to pass, then he saw Alar. He paused, a knowing smile playing at the corners of his lips.

"Alar," he said. "What a coincidence." He looked down the hall, past Alar and said more quietly, "Or maybe not."

Trell frowned at Holden.

Before Alar could decide how to respond, Holden spoke again. "A happy coincidence, however, as you are just the man I was looking for."

Alar pointed at his chest.

Holden didn't answer. Alar shrugged at Trell and followed Holden down the stairs and out onto the veranda. While he walked, Alar gazed around, expecting to find guards waiting for him. But only Helmut and the other guard standing watch were evident.

When Holden paused at the top of the steps, hands in his pockets, Alar watched him out of the corner of his eye, trying to get a sense of his mood. Holden gazed across the lawn, expressionless. After a few moments, the groom glanced back at the guards, who hurriedly averted their eyes, then he headed down the steps. Alar followed, sighing in relief. Whatever Holden wanted, he didn't intend to have Alar dragged away in chains. Not yet, at any rate.

The lord strolled across the lawn toward the garden, apparently in no hurry. He glanced at Alar and said lightly, "I don't know much about the *Alle'oss*." He gestured to a man working in the garden. "Beyond the servants who work for us." He stopped at the edge of the garden and said, "I take that back. I do admire your artists. Olaf, Helena." He glanced over his shoulder, leaned close and whispered, "Valdemar." Straightening, he said, "All the new school artists, of course, but the *Alle'oss* have a long and storied artistic tradition."

Alar wasn't sure how to respond when Holden fell silent, but he didn't look as if he was expecting an answer. Still, though he wasn't sure what Holden wanted, he wasn't about to waste this opportunity. He thought about what he could ask that would be useful, but the question that emerged surprised him. "How did you come to be engaged to Lady Violette?"

Holden looked at him and chuckled. "Are all *Alle'oss* so direct?"

"Excuse me?"

"A Volloch would dance around the subject, looking for some conversational subterfuge to glean the truth."

"It's not a polite question?"

Holden entered the garden and strolled along a winding path until it ended at a small pond. It wasn't lost on Alar he took them far enough from the gardeners they wouldn't hear the conversation.

"What's amusing is that Volloch traditions are so rigid everyone already knows how these arrangements are made," Holden said with a confidential smile. "And yet one does not inquire. It's not polite. Besides, the bald truth would eliminate our favorite sport. Gossip."

"Marriage traditions?"

Holden nodded. "Among other things. For example, I am a third son, so I stand to inherit nothing from my father."

"Nothing?"

"Third sons often go into the priesthood, join the military or one of the orders."

"The Inquisition?"

"Or the Dominicans," Holden said with a nod. "Some lords stake their sons with enough coin to get them started in some profession. If you're smart, talented, have the right connections, you can make a decent enough living."

"But not like first sons."

"No, nor second sons."

"What does this have to do with you and Violette?"

"Faced with only unpleasant alternatives, I procrastinated. I have no intention of joining the priesthood. I have no interest in the military or one of the orders. Yet, unfortunately, I'm afraid I would find myself perfectly useless without my father's wealth." Lifting his chin and cocking his head, he said, "My father offered me a demon's bargain; marry Violette, or go out into the world penniless." Grimacing, he said, "Not really a choice, is it?" He looked at Alar. "Not what Violette's parents wished for, of course, marrying their daughter to a third son. However, my father is a powerful man, and they are so anxious to have the issue resolved, they were willing to pay an exorbitant dowry."

"So, Violette doesn't want any part of this marriage and neither do you."

"That's the shape of it," Holden said with a heavy sigh.

"But Violette has sabotaged her other marriages. Why is she going along with this one?"

"We've moved in the same social circles our entire lives. I would not say we are friends, as such, but we know one another. I made her a deal; we treat our marriage as a partnership. Equal in everything. Whatever we decide to use the dowry for, we share the risks and rewards equally. It's not ideal, but frankly, she's so ready to be out from beneath her mother's influence…" He shrugged. "She agreed."

"A marriage made in heaven," Alar said.

"More like the least objectionable option. For both of us."

Alar studied his profile. Despite his woeful tale, Alar didn't see any trace of it in his expression. "Why are you telling me this?"

Holden shrugged and gave Alar a lopsided grin. "Because everyone else already knows." He nodded to the gardeners, who had made their way to the far shore of the pond. They feigned nonchalance, but they were clearly trying to listen. "Everyone." He met Alar's gaze and said, "I suppose I just wanted someone to hear my confession. Someone who didn't already know the sordid details." One corner of his mouth twitched up. "Plus, I wanted you to know how important the dowry is to our future. Violette's and mine."

His eyes held Alar's for a long moment, then he focused on something across the pond. Alar followed his gaze and found Holden's fiancée berating one of the gardeners.

"Ah, the lovely bride," Holden said with a smile. He rested a hand on Alar's shoulder, gave it a squeeze and said, "Tell Scilla I'm very much looking forward to seeing her finished work. I could tell from the one she abandoned, she is a special talent."

"I will." Alar watched Holden making his way to the bridge that arched over the stream that left the pond on the northern end. The one on which he and Scilla saw the couple for the first time when they came for the audition. The bride and groom greeted one another politely. There didn't seem to be any animosity between them, but neither was there any affection. They turned and walked along the path, Violette pointing out plants and Holden listening.

Alar wasn't sure what to feel. Holden and Violette were Volloch. The great wealth Holden said he couldn't live without was undoubtedly amassed on the backs of many Brochen. Being forced into a loveless marriage didn't rise to the level of tragedy for Alar, whose family was massacred by the Inquisition when he had eight summers. Having been destitute for years, living hand to mouth until very recently, Alar was having trouble mustering any sympathy for either of them.

Still, he found himself liking Holden.

He watched them leave the garden and part ways with barely a wave. The question was what was he to do with what he learned? It fit with what Ragan told him about Violette, and the former novice rarely offered information that didn't serve her agenda. She told him she couldn't tell him what future she saw, couldn't tell him what she needed him to do, but she was obviously hoping he did something. Whatever it was, it wasn't clear to him. Yet.

16

Beauty

When Alar woke on the fifth morning since they arrived, he was alone as usual. Ukrit arrived in their shared room late every night and left before Alar rose in the morning. Despite his grumbling stomach, he lay on his back and stared at the ceiling. He returned to the manor house each of the last three nights. The only good thing he could say about his efforts was no one caught him like Holden did the first night. The location of the dowry was still a mystery. One night, he wasn't able to enter the house as the door across from the kitchen was locked. On the occasions he got in, he had no luck picking the locks to any of the rooms in the family's wing. He was out of ideas, and the week was almost over. Once the guests arrived, it would be much riskier to wander at night.

He was also no closer to understanding what Ragan had in mind. He tilted his head back and looked out the window at a cloudless blue sky. It had to be after the eighth bell. Returning his gaze to the ceiling, he considered how he might corner Holden. Though he saw the lord from a distance on multiple occasions, he had no luck getting close enough to speak to him. Not that Alar had any idea what the groom could say that might help him. He considered talking to Violette, but she was even more impossible to get close to. She was always surrounded by other Volloch women and the obvious disdain she showed the *Alle'oss* servants was a deterrent.

With little to keep himself occupied during the day, he joined Trell in a variety of chores, hoping to learn something he could use. The boy was a font of gossip. None of it useful. Remembering the convoluted story he made of Adelbart being the nephew of the emperor, Alar wasn't sure how much to believe, anyway. Still, Trell had a way with a story, and Alar was getting to know other servants. It helped pass the time while Scilla and Ukrit were occupied.

As they neared the end of the week, his companions had grown increasingly anxious, eating little and barking at him anytime he came near. Alar had taken to having his meals in the kitchen, where the cooks were always happy to see him. But with only one day remaining before the opening ball, he rolled out of bed, determined to check on their progress. With little hope of finding the dowry, they needed the coin Bergamot would pay for their works. After putting himself in order, he *pulled* for a burst of energy and headed to the pavilion.

Just as he arrived, Ukrit burst through the exit, his arms full of items from the breakfast buffet. He froze when he saw Alar, the same panicked expression on his face Alar had seen for days.

"Ukrit." Alar nodded to the food and asked, "You taking breakfast to go?"

"These are for Chekka," he said, twisting away when Alar reached for one of the small rolls filled with cinnamon and raisins, which had come as a revelation to the *Alle'oss.* "You can have one of the barley rolls."

Alar plucked the roll from Ukrit's arms, took a bite and followed Ukrit. "Where are you going in such a hurry?"

"We're pouring the bronze," Ukrit said over his shoulder.

Alar had watched worriedly as Ukrit modeled a horse devoid of any detail on the armature in clay earlier in the week. When he carefully suggested it didn't look like his drawing, Ukrit stopped, straightened, and glared at Alar with an expression that promised violence. Ever since, Alar kept track of his progress from a distance.

On one of his nighttime forays, Alar visited Chekka's shop and found Ukrit tending a kiln used to fire the clay horse. The next day, he watched Ukrit pacing anxiously around the hardened sculpture, tapping it with his finger, waiting for it to cool. When he deemed it cool enough, he applied tinted wax to the clay. What emerged was Ukrit's beautiful drawing brought to life. Alar was only slightly ashamed at the relief he felt.

The only time Ukrit spoke to him, or to anyone other than Chekka, was one evening when he was struggling with the horse's windblown mane. Frustrated, he threw his tool to the ground and whirled around. Catching sight of Alar, he pointed an accusing finger.

"This is your fault! Getting us into this situation. It's impossible!" he shouted, throwing his arms out to his sides. "It can't be done." He jabbed his finger toward Alar and growled, "And if I have to listen to Chekka complain one more minute, I'm going to do something unpleasant!"

Alar only smiled, gestured to the nearly completed sculpture, and said, "What do you mean? It's coming along great."

Ukrit stared at him, his chest rising and falling. Letting his hand drop, he turned back to the sculpture. After a moment, he retrieved his tool and set to work.

The completed wax sculpture was remarkable. Everything Ukrit's drawing promised. The two-foot tall horse was in motion, head down, mane and tail flying, nostrils flaring. The subtle hint of straining muscles beneath the skin gave it life. This was not the stiff horses in the sculptures Imperials were so fond of. Those animals were dominated by their human masters. This was a stallion, wild and free, claiming its herd.

Once the wax sculpture was complete, Alar watched Ukrit insert iron pins through the wax until it bristled like a porcupine. Fascinated, he watched Ukrit enmesh the statue in a scaffolding of wax rods, using small hot spatulas to melt the rods in place. Finally, Ukrit encased the entire construction in a clay cube, and returned it to the kiln. Throughout the process, Chekka swooped in, peering over Ukrit's shoulder, offering advice, cursing and grumbling under his breath.

Now that the process was drawing to a close, Alar studied Ukrit as he carried Chekka's breakfast to the blacksmith's shop. Regardless how the sculpture turned out, Alar was glad it was almost over. Ukrit looked as if he was at the end of his rope. His red hair hung lank, his skin had waxen pallor, and dark circles cradled his blue eyes.

While Ukrit deposited the food in the small brick house, which Alar presumed was Chekka's home, Alar watched the big man tending a forge in an open-air shed. He wasn't surprised to find Trell working the bellows. When the boy saw Alar, he threw him a quick smile, then bent to his task.

Ukrit joined Alar and stood quietly. "Where's the sculpture?" Alar asked.

Ukrit pointed to a hole in the ground. "If the investment isn't sound, it could explode, so you bury it in sand."

Hearing the fear in Ukrit's voice, Alar tore his eyes away from the bright forge and studied his profile. "Investment?" he asked carefully.

"The clay mold that encases it," Ukrit said. "When you fire the investment, the wax melts away and leaves a thin space you pour the bronze into."

Taking advantage of Ukrit's willingness to talk, Alar asked, "What were all those things you attached to it? The iron and wax rods."

"The iron pins hold the core in place when the wax melts. The wax rods are called sprues. When they melt, it leaves channels that let the bronze in and let gasses out." Despite his obvious anxiety and fatigue, Alar could hear the pride in his voice. But then he hesitated and sighed heavily. "If it fails, I won't have time to start over. This is it."

Alar lifted a hand, but before he could rest it on his friend's shoulder, Chekka shouted.

"Ukrit! Come. We pour."

Ukrit jumped and rushed over. Together, he and Chekka lifted what looked like a tall ceramic pot from the furnace, set it on a device with two long handles, and secure it. At a nod from Chekka, they lifted the handles, tipped the pot, and poured the bronze into the hole in the sandpit.

Not knowing what to expect, Alar held his breath. But it was anticlimactic. He couldn't tell whether it worked or not. They set the pot down and backed away. Ukrit, drenched in sweat, trudged over and stood beside him. When he didn't speak, Alar asked, "Now what?"

"In a minute, we'll remove the sand and expose the investment to let it cool. Once it's cool, I'll chip the clay away and see what's what. If it worked, I'll still have to clean it up a bit, fill the holes left by the pins." He shrugged and gave Alar a weak grin. "Won't have time to get it perfect, but as long as the casting worked, I'll have something, anyway."

They watched in silence as Chekka disappeared into his house. Trell waved to Alar as he headed off. Ukrit looked deflated, like a pillow with the stuffing removed. He stared hollow-eyed at the hole from which wisps of vapor rose.

"It's all over tomorrow," Alar said. "One way or another. No matter what comes out of there, you should be proud. You didn't know any of this stuff a week ago, and the wax statue was amazing."

Ukrit let out a small chuckle. "I *will* feel proud when I have enough energy to feel anything." He shrugged. "We'll see."

Alar gestured to Chekka standing in his doorway, scowling around a mouthful of cinnamon roll. "No matter what comes out of that hole, you have to be proud of surviving a week with the grumpiest man alive."

Alar left Ukrit staring at the hole in the ground and returned to the pavilion. When he entered, he came to a stop. Scilla was nowhere to be seen, and standing in front of her nearly completed painting was About-That and two other artists. They were looking at the canvas and gesticulating. Alar crept up behind them so he could hear what they were saying.

"It's an abomination," one of them said. "The paint is just slopped on."

"Look how thick the paint is," another one said. He leaned forward and pointed at the mountain roses depicted near the edge of the canvas. "And you can actually see the brush strokes here."

Alar listened to them disparaging the painting for a few more moments, anger rising to a boil. He was about to speak up when About-That, who had been silent, surprised him.

"You fools!" He threw his hand toward the canvas. "You let your insecurities blind you, focusing on insignificant details and missing the whole." He whirled around and froze.

Noting the glisten in the artist's eyes, Alar smiled and gave him a shallow bow.

About-That sniffed, tossed his head, brushed past him and strode across the pavilion.

The other artists glowered after him, then headed back to their work areas without acknowledging Alar's presence.

Alar watched them go, then taking advantage of Scilla's absence, he turned his attention to her painting. She had been tight-lipped about it and shooed him away whenever he got too close. He had only been able to keep an eye on its progress from a safe distance, pretending to wander around the pavilion while stealing glances when she moved aside.

He knew almost nothing about art, but even he could tell this was something entirely different from the other artists' works. What the two critical artists said was true. The paint was applied in thicker layers. The brush strokes were visible in some spots and the details disappeared if you stood close to the canvas. But when you stood back, taking in the whole, the effect was stunning.

He remembered the scene from the day they came for the audition. Violette and Holden stood on the bridge that crossed the stream in the garden. Unlike the drab garden on that spring day, Scilla depicted an imagining of a garden in its summer glory. One could almost smell the perfume of flowers depicted in brilliant *Alle'oss* pigments. Light shimmered and danced on the water in the pond among the lily pads.

The drooping branches of a weeping willow, tossed by a gentle breeze, balanced the couple standing on the bridge.

But the focus of the painting was the couple. They were depicted with great care. There was no doubt who they were. But Alar didn't have to know what Holden confessed to him to see their sadness. In part, it was the way they held themselves. They stood side by side, their hands lifted slightly, close but not touching. The way their bodies turned slightly away from one another suggested a distance that was more than physical. But it was their expressions that watered Alar's eyes. There was resignation and sadness, but only if you knew what to look for. Scilla managed to convey the truth of this unhappy union, but she had done it so subtly it might be missed on casual inspection.

Motion at his side drew his eye. Olson was standing next to him, gazing at the canvas, an uncharacteristically pensive frown on his face.

"Olson," Alar said. "What do you think?"

Olson glanced at him. He didn't answer at first, then he lifted a hand, as if he would touch the canvas. "It's…" His frown deepened and he let his hand drop.

"Don't think about it. Forget what you know about proper technique," Alar said. "Feel it."

Olson turned his frown on Alar, then returned his gaze to the painting. After a moment, his expression cleared. "I've never seen anything like it." He shook his head and glanced over his shoulder at the other artists before returning his attention to the canvas. "I don't know what the Lord will think."

"What do *you* think?"

His mouth opened, he hesitated, then he whispered, "It's beautiful."

***

Brennerman stood next to the map table in his office, gazing at the area east of Richeleau on the map. It had been three days since his head scout showed him the *Alle'oss* rebel village, but he was no closer to knowing what to do about it than when he returned to the fort that day.

He could attack the village with his dismounted cavalry, hoping surprise would carry the day. But so much could go wrong. If they were indeed rebels, they would fight back, and the outcome of that confrontation was in doubt. There may be a hundred or more rebels who could fight, and they would be on their own ground. Ground that Brennerman didn't know. They already proved themselves formidable during the battle with the mercenaries, and he couldn't believe they hadn't planned for an attack on their base. Fifty troopers weren't enough to guarantee the outcome. His career, such as it was, would be over if he were to lose that battle.

And there would almost surely be collateral casualties.

He had almost decided to follow his head scout's plan. Schenk could sneak into the ravine at night and find evidence of the attack on the supply caravan. But then what? To obtain the vindication he sought, he would have to inform the Inquisition and Hoch. Hoch wouldn't agonize over the proper course to follow.

He lifted his gaze to the wall behind the table and let his eyes lose focus. The *Alle'oss* were rebels. Rebels who already proved they were a threat to the Empire. It was unfortunate the children's parents chose such a course, but it was their choice, not his.

That decided it. He would send in Schenk. Have a squad of troopers nearby in case Schenk ran into trouble. Once he had the proof he needed, he would take it to the Inquisition. His eyes focused and drifted to the portrait of Emperor Ludweig II near the door of his office. He would let the Inquisition decide what was to be done. After all, treason was within the Inquisition's purview, not the cavalry's.

The door opening in his adjutant's office got his attention.

"Can I help you, sir?" his adjutant said. "Excuse me, sir, you can't —"

A moment later, Hoch's bulk appeared in the door.

"Captain Hoch," Brennerman said before Hoch could speak. "You finally came to pay your respects." He turned to face Hoch as the ranger came further into the room.

Hoch's lips twitched. He opened his mouth, then gave his head a small shake and said, "I've heard rumors you found the rebels' camp."

Brennerman kept his face composed. He swore his scouts to secrecy, but Brennerman had been in the cavalry long enough to know that only bought him a day or two before the news got out. To give himself time, he rounded his desk and sat. Folding his hands together on his desk, he looked up at Hoch and said, "I have no proof the village is a rebel camp." He had his mouth open, ready to mention the children, but Hoch would only interpret that to mean the village was more vulnerable.

Hoch eyed him, waiting for him to continue. "The last time we spoke," Brennerman said, "you laughed when I mentioned *Alle'oss* rebels. Now, the mere whisper of a rumor has you convinced? I thought you had orders that would keep your rangers busy."

Ignoring everything Brennerman said, Hoch's eyes flicked to the side. "What kind of proof do you need?"

"Evidence of the supplies from the caravan that disappeared would do."

Hoch frowned, then threw out a hand and said, "Just enter the camp in force. Get whatever evidence you need. If they resist, punish them."

Brennerman should have explained the tactical difficulties with that plan, but what he said was, "Argren is not Styria. A bloodbath would be —"

"If you're worried your cavalry aren't up to the task, my rangers have experience with this type of operation."

Brennerman shot to his feet. "I apparently didn't make myself clear in regards to the chain of command the last time we met. Whether you like it or not, you are under my command. *I* will decide how we uproot these rebels. You have your orders to tend to, for —"

"We found the bodies."

Brennerman paused, mouth open, then asked, "Bodies?"

"The last ranger company," Hoch said. "On the road to Ka'tan. There were signs of an ambush. The bodies were hidden in the forest. The entire company."

Brennerman stared at him, trying to decide what the implication of this news was. "Is there any evidence that would point to who was responsible?"

"Nothing definite," Hoch said. "The local intelligence apparatus is investigating. Their initial finding is that it was the Union mercenaries. I have my doubts." He waved a hand. "But, in any case, my rangers are available to… investigate this rebel camp."

Suddenly, it was clear why Hoch was in Brennerman's office. He was looking for a means to vent his anger and the *Alle'oss* village was a convenient target. If Brennerman allowed him to *investigate* the village, there would be a massacre, regardless what evidence he found. A whiff of rebellion was all he needed. Brennerman let his eyes drop to this desk. "I will apprise you of the course of action I decide on when the appropriate time comes." He looked up and locked eyes with Hoch. From the tension in Hoch's clenched fists and the ruddy tint that rose on his cheeks, Brennerman wasn't entirely sure he wouldn't launch himself across the desk to get at him. But to his relief, the ranger turned away and stalked out the door. Brennerman called after him, "The next time you ignore my adjutant, *I* will pull the rank that matters." Hoch didn't hear the end of the threat as he had already slammed the door on his way out. Not that Brennerman could carry it out. He would have to go as high as Victor Storm to find support in the military and none of the layers of command between him and Storm would allow that to happen. Still, it felt good to say it.

His adjutant appeared. "Sir, I'm sorry."

Breath coming fast and shallow, Brennerman lowered his head to hide the sweat slicking his brow. Wiping his palm across his forehead, he waved his hand. "Not your fault." Dropping into his chair, he pulled a stack of reports from recent patrols to the center of his desk, then had to stop and squeeze his eyes shut.

"Sir?"

Brennerman opened his eyes and looked up. His adjutant held out a single sheet of paper. "Yes?"

"I received a message from the Inquisition commander just before Hoch arrived. I was about to bring it to your attention before…" He held the paper out to Brennerman.

Brennerman took the offered sheet and scanned it.

Captain Brennerman,

We may have a hit on some of the Alle'oss you believe are involved with rebels. Please come to my office at your earliest convenience.

Commander Krueger

Brennerman stared at the words, sensing it held a way out of his dilemma, though he wasn't sure how. Standing, he dropped the message on his desk and retrieved his coat. "I'll return shortly."

Before he was out the door, his adjutant said, "Sir." When Brennerman turned back, he said, "Thank you. For what you said to Hoch. I appreciate it."

"Oh, well. Yes, of course," Brennerman said. "You deserve his respect, regardless of your relative ranks." He gave him a brisk nod and swept out the door.

***

When he was ushered into Krueger's office, the man looked up and said, "Yes, Captain Brennerman, have a seat." He gestured to a chair in front of his desk.

Brennerman remained standing. "Your message said you have information on the *Alle'oss* rebels."

Krueger glanced at the chair, then sighed and rummaged through the many stacks of documents piled on his desk. Pulling a file from the top of one of the stacks, he opened the cover, peered at the top sheet, then handed the file to Brennerman.

"It seems a spy on Lord Bergamot's estate in Lachton informed the local Inquisition house there are three new school *Alle'oss* artists performing at the wedding of the lord's daughter."

Brennerman looked up from the document. Artists performing? He almost asked what that involved, but decided it wasn't relevant. The information in the document added some additional detail about the wedding and the role of the artists. But Brennerman found what he was looking for on the second page. The names and descriptions of the three *Alle'oss*. "Alar," he said.

"You recognize him?"

"Yes. This Alar is the leader of *Oss'stera*," Brennerman said absently while he scanned the rest of the document. When he was done, he looked at Krueger. "They were reported to the Inquisition for the art?"

"Yes, some of the new school artists have chosen heretical or treasonous subjects for their art." Krueger sat back and interlaced his fingers across his stomach. "The Inquisition commander in Lachton is asking an Inquisitor attending the wedding to investigate, but he asked us if we have anyone who would know the three *Alle'oss*." He gestured to Brennerman. "I thought of you, of course."

Brennerman looked down at the document, closed the file, and laid it on Krueger's desk. "You wish me to go to Lachton and… what exactly? There is nothing in that document about rebellion."

"Wellll," the commander said and shrugged. "If the art doesn't rise to the level of outright heresy or treason, an arrest on Bergamot's estate might be problematic. But if someone could also accuse the artists of being rebels…" He shrugged again. "You get the point. Not even a man as powerful as Bergamot could object."

Brennerman stared at him. He couldn't have hoped for a better scenario. The Inquisition would arrest the three *Alle'oss* as rebels, which would vindicate Brennerman. And with the rebel leader in custody, he might find a way to avoid being party to a massacre. But there was something in Krueger's tone which caught at him. "You don't believe the artists are rebels." When Krueger only returned his gaze, he said, "You only want to ensure you can arrest them regardless what they paint."

The commander shrugged again. "The official reasons for the arrest will be for inciting rebellion and carrying out rebellious acts." He stared flatly at Brennerman. "Whether the art they create for this wedding represents a threat to the Empire is immaterial. They will create more art away from observation. Might as well eliminate them while we can." He studied Brennerman, then his head tilted to the side, and he said, "What you or I think is hardly relevant. What matters is a likely threat to the Empire is eliminated. Right?"

"Of course," Brennerman said after a pause.

"Inquisitor Anders is attending the wedding. My assistant has letters of introduction for you." He bent over his desk and said, "Good luck, Captain."

17

Da, Da, Da

Alar watched Ukrit step back from his sculpture, the precision chisel he used to fine tune the mane and tail held aloft. The ever-present Chekka watched him with a flat expression that was as close as he got to a smile.

The previous day, Alar watched Ukrit and Chekka remove the investment from the sand. Though Alar couldn't tell whether the casting worked or not, Uktit was nearly giddy when he found the investment intact. Alar watched anxiously as Ukrit hammered away the investment to reveal the statue. To Alar's eyes, it looked as if something had gone wrong. The sprues filled with bronze and between them and the pins, it was difficult to see the horse. But Ukrit was overjoyed, and even Chekka nodded his approval. Over the next day, Ukrit worked with chisel and pliers to remove the sprues and pins, then plug the holes with molten bronze.

Now, two hours before the family viewing, time had run out. Ukrit let his hand drop, then carefully set his tools on the pedestal on which the horse sat.

"Is finished?" Chekka asked.

Ukrit nodded.

"No polish?"

"No," Ukrit said. "It's wild. It shouldn't look all bright and clean."

Chekka gave a single nod, bouncing his coarse mane, which was free of its confining braid. "Good." He held out his hand.

Ukrit glanced down at the hand, then took Chekka's forearm in the *Alle'oss* fashion. "*Tok,* Chekka."

"*Aurina sha,*" Chekka said with a wide smile.

Ukrit's eyes opened wide as he watched Chekka disappear into his house.

Alar approached Ukrit, grinning at the sound of the blacksmith's deep laughter coming from inside the house.

"*Lehasa,*" Ukrit said.

"*Hasa,*" Alar said. They gazed at the sculpture. "It's amazing."

"*Tok.*" They were silent for a moment or two, then Ukrit said, "You know Chekka's from the Union?"

"Really?" Alar studied Ukrit's pale face. "You okay?"

Ukrit nodded. After another moment, he looked up at the sun dipping toward the horizon and said, "I'm going to get some food, then an hour of sleep."

"You don't want to bring it over to the pavilion?"

"Chekka's going to bring it before the viewing." He gave Alar a weak smile, then trudged down the path toward the pavilion.

Alar watched him go, then gazed at the statue, tears welling in his eyes.

"For someone never work in bronze, is something to be proud of."

Alar glanced up at Chekka, who stood with one hand tucked in his apron and the other holding a cinnamon roll. He bent down and studied the mane. "Some small details could be better." He straightened and popped the rest of the roll in his mouth and shrugged. "Maybe. In case, you should be proud of your friend. He worked hard and made beautiful horse."

"I am," Alar said. "Thank you, Chekka."

Chekka grunted and wandered into his shop.

Alar returned to his room an hour later. After bathing and rousting Ukrit from his bed, he donned the suit Scilla bought him. Then he brushed out his hair and took his time creating the thin braid beside his left hair. It held a bead for Richeleau and a downy screech owl feather *Oss'stera* adopted for themselves. When he was finished, he stared at his reflection. On impulse, he undid the end of the braid and added the octagonal blue bead he had been saving for the right occasion. It meant he was promised. When he finished, he closed his fist around the matching bead, the one he hoped Scilla would wear, then shoved it into his pocket. With one last look at his reflection, he left the room.

He could feel the excitement as soon as he entered the pavilion. Paints, brushes and the other tools of the artists' craft had been stowed away, and the easels moved to the front of the work areas. Artists and apprentices dressed in their finest strolled through the pavilion, sipping wine, chatting and examining each other's works.

The buffet tables were covered with fine white cloth. Small morsels on silver platters were laid out along with crystal glasses and carafes of wine. Ukrit, looking more relaxed than he had in days, despite a face puffy with sleep, stood beside his horse. He lifted his wineglass toward Alar.

Scilla's painting in the neighboring work area, with its vivid colors, drew his eye, but Scilla was nowhere to be seen. He scanned the crowd more carefully and ventured further into the room.

"Alar!" someone whispered.

Alar stopped.

"Back here."

He turned and found Scilla beside one of the large ferns which had been brought in to flank the entrance. She beckoned him over.

"Why are you hiding?" he asked.

Her frown deepened. "I'm not hiding, I'm…"

"Hiding." Alar glanced at a group of highborn Volloch entering the pavilion. "The guests are arriving. You should be over there by your painting."

"I know," Scilla said. "It's just…"

"You don't believe me or Ukrit when we tell you how good it is?"

"I believe *you* like it —"

"But you think we're biased because we love you."

"Well, yes," Scilla said and put a hand on his chest to interrupt his response. "But also, because you're *Alle'oss.*"

"Scilla, you may not have noticed, because you've been so involved in your work, but every time you're not in the pavilion, the other artists sneak over to take a look."

"Really?"

Alar nodded. "I caught About-That staring at it yesterday with tears in his eyes."

Scilla looked across the room to where About-That, excited by the presence of the wealthy Volloch, animatedly lectured the usual sycophants. Heinz, standing outside the group, noticing them looking, smiled and gave them a small wave with a hand below his waist.

Alar waved, prompting Heinz to cast a nervous glance at About-That.

"Maybe I'll go over," Scilla said. "But I'd like a glass of wine first. Come with me?"

"Of course." He gave her a small bow and offered his arm, turning his head slightly, giving her the best view of his braid. Nervously watching the elites gathering around the buffet table, she didn't notice the blue bead.

Scilla glanced at his arm and smiled. "My, what a gentleman." She rested her hand on his arm, and they made their way to the buffet table. Alar recognized Holden, Violette, and Violette's father, Lord Bergamot. He guessed the pinched woman standing beside Violette was her mother. There were other older men and women. As this was supposed to be a family viewing, Alar presumed they included Holden's parents and assorted aunts and uncles. A group of younger men and women stood off to the side with wineglasses in their hands. They must be cousins, siblings, and their spouses.

Holden met his eye and gave him a brief nod before turning away to begin his circuit of the pavilion. They started on the side opposite Scilla's and Ukrit's works.

Alar was pouring wine when the woman he presumed was Violette's mother said, "So, you are the female *Alle'oss* artist."

"Yes," Scilla said, taking the glass Alar offered her.

"We've heard remarkable things about your painting," the woman said. She threw a sour smile at her husband. "From Holden, anyway."

Scilla's lips pursed slightly. Alar was about to intervene when she said, "*Tok.*" Small frowns appeared on the elites' faces and they glanced at one another. "You must be happy your daughter is marrying a man with such discerning tastes."

"Yes. Quite," Violette's mother said, looking as if she didn't know how to interpret that statement, then the group turned away and followed Holden and Violette.

"*Nā minu,*" Scilla whispered, investing as much scorn as she could in the insult.

The parents following Violette and Holden must have been a signal the younger elites were waiting for, because as soon as the older group turned their backs, they made a beeline to Scilla's painting.

"Holden must have told them," Alar whispered.

Scilla watched, open-mouthed. "What? What did he tell them?"

"Let's go find out. Come on, they'll want to talk to the artist." He nudged her forward with his elbow.

"Right." Scilla gulped her wine, set the glass down, sucked in a breath, and blew it out. "Don't go too far." When he nodded, she said, "Here I go."

Noticing Ukrit peering into his empty glass, Alar poured another glass of wine and carried it over to him.

"*Tok,*" Ukrit said.

They watched Scilla chatting and gesturing to her painting. Alar had learned not to take Volloch's reactions at face value. In fact, only in private did they seem to reveal their true thoughts. But if this young group were hiding disapproval, they were master mummers. They appeared genuinely interested and impressed.

"About–That came by," Ukrit said.

"Oh, yeah?"

"Gave my horse his seal of approval."

"What did he say?"

"Nothing," Ukrit said. "Just looked it over, nodded and strutted off like he does."

"Well, then," Alar said. "I guess he *did* see about that."

"I'm going to see what they have to eat. You want something?"

"No, I'm good." In fact, Alar was starving. He had a quick bite with Ingrid in the kitchen at lunch. It was wearing off, but he was too nervous for Scilla to eat.

After the younger elites broke the ice, others, eager to see the painting they heard so much about, bypassed the other paintings and came straight to Scilla's work area. Alar's eyes watered as he watched her grow more relaxed and animated.

Ukrit appeared, mouth full and two glasses of wine in his hands. He handed one to Alar.

"You picked the wrong spot," Alar said.

"Huh?"

"Next to Scilla." Alar gestured to her with his glass. "No one has come to look at your horse."

Ukrit shrugged. "It was me who used to get all the attention back home."

"You?"

"Yeah. Scilla was always this scrawny, awkward kid tagging along." Alar stared at him. Ukrit gestured with the hand holding the glass. "She deserves it. My horse is pretty good, but Scilla created something brand new. I didn't really look at it until I got here tonight. Been too busy." He met Alar's eyes. "No one paints like that. Valdemar would weep if he saw it."

"Valdemar?" Ukrit shrugged and returned his attention to Scilla. "You're a good brother."

Ukrit grunted. "That's what I keep telling her." He nudged Alar and pointed at Holden and Violette, who were nearing the crowd in front of Scilla's painting.

Alar hadn't seen Holden in the pavilion since Scilla discarded her first attempt. Curious about whether the couple would see what he saw in Scilla's depiction of them, he studied their faces as the small crowd quieted and parted to make space in front of the canvas.

They gave Scilla polite greetings, then turned their attention to the canvas.

Their eyes roved the painting, then they found the same spot, and they stilled. A moment later, there was a subtle shift in their bodies. Subtle, but not unnoticed by some of their relatives watching them. Glances were exchanged. A low murmur rose.

Violette's lips parted. "Oh, dear," she breathed. A furrow appeared between her brows. Her fingers came up to rest on her lips. She and Holden looked at one another. She gave him a small shake of her head, said, "I'm sorry," then she turned away, pushed her way through the crowd and fled the pavilion.

Amid the exclamations, Holden's resigned eyes found Alar. He took a step toward Scilla, took her hand and said, "I told you it has been long since I wept for beauty." He kissed her hand and said, "You have given me reason to weep." Then he followed Violette.

Their relatives watched him go, then crowded around the painting.

"What happened?" Violette's mother asked. She frowned at Scilla and asked, "What did you do?"

"Nothing," Scilla said firmly.

"She saw something in this… painting," Violette's father said.

When he reached toward the canvas, Alar reacted. Ducking under the rope that divided Ukrit's and Scilla's work area, he inserted himself between Bergamot and the canvas. The lord startled and froze.

"I'm afraid the paint might not be quite dry," Alar said with an apologetic smile. A dangerous silence fell as everyone waited to see how the lord responded.

Bergamot hesitated, then his hand fell to his side. He looked past Alar and searched the painting. Finally, his frown fell away, and he stepped back. "Yes, of course." He turned to his wife and said, "Go talk to your daughter. Find out what has happened."

The parents left, leaving others to gather around, studying the painting and speculating about what caused Violette's reaction.

Once he was sure no one was going to destroy the painting, Alar looked at Scilla and was surprised to see a small smile on her face. "You did that on purpose," he murmured.

She nodded.

"You realize the lord might not be willing to buy your painting now." She nodded again, but the smile remained. "And if they call the wedding off, we'll have no chance to…" He cut his eyes to the elites who were still discussing the painting.

"All I did was depict the truth," Scilla said. "It's not my fault if they can't handle it." She waved a hand. "As for the wedding, they can't cancel it now. Did you see all the guests arriving? It would be the scandal of the century." She put a hand on her chest and whispered in an affected accent, "Can you imagine the gossip —" She froze, her wide eyes locked on Alar's braid.

Alar reached into his pocket and retrieved the bead that matched the one Scilla noticed. Holding it in the palm of his hand, he asked, "Scilla, will you marry me?"

She launched herself at him, eliciting startled exclamations. They fell into the rope that divided Scilla and Ukrit's work area and sprawled at the base of the pedestal on which Ukrit's horse sat.

Ukrit made a grab for the sculpture and managed to steady it.

"*Da, da, da,*" Scilla said, planting kisses on Alar's face.

"Scilla — *Sheoda,*" Alar said. "I dropped the bead."

18

Clarity

After the family viewing in the pavilion, servants moved the artists' works to a familiar room. Not only had Alar been in the Reception Hall for the artists' opening event, he passed through it three times in his nightly wanderings. The main ball for the wedding guests was held in a grander Ballroom across the Entrance Hall. The guests could leave the ball to peruse the artists' works and return to the ball at their leisure. It wasn't lost on Alar, the arrangement served to separate the scruffy artists from the elite guests.

He paused in the door to the Reception Hall and surveyed the space. Buffet tables piled high with the usual cornucopia of refreshments occupied the center of the room. The artists' works were arranged around the perimeter. It was early and only a few guests were circulating, so most of the artists were talking to one another, holding plates and beverages. Ukrit stood beside his sculpture, a tankard in his hand. Chekka stood next to him, looking uncomfortable in what must have been his dress overalls.

Alar left Scilla in her room, still getting dressed. He wanted to wait for her, but she insisted he go ahead without her. He wasn't fooled. She wanted to slip into the room when the ball was in full swing, hoping she would go unnoticed. Between their engagement and the response to her painting, it was all he could do to get her to sit still long enough to add the blue bead to her braid. It was a joyful moment, full of the laughter and flirting he missed while she worked. Afterwards, they'd spent a few precious moments celebrating.

Hands in his pockets, Alar strolled across the room to stand beside Ukrit. The big blacksmith nodded to him and wandered off in search of an ale.

Ukrit leaned toward Alar and said, "I told Chekka about our disagreement with the Union mercenaries."

"And?"

"He asked me if we won. I told him we did. After he got over his surprise, all he said was 'good'."

"That's it?"

"Yeah. Apparently, Chagan, the mercs' commander, is some kind of warlord in the Union. Chekka crossed him somehow. That's why he's here."

"Crossed him?"

Ukrit shrugged. "Wouldn't say how."

They fell silent and watched guests arriving. Alar was considering following Chekka to the bar when Ukrit spoke again.

"They look different."

Alar followed his gaze to five women standing just inside the entrance. It was Siofra and the other Desulti he saw in Richeleau. Siofra stood alone with the murtair hovering nearby. The murtair wore clothes normally worn by Volloch men rather than the Murtair's usual black garments. The other three Desulti gathered in a small group a few feet away. The glances they threw Siofra gave him the same impression he had when he saw them in the governor's mansion in Richeleau; there was some tension between them.

"Desulti," Alar said. "Wonder if they bring a murtair everywhere they go?"

Ukrit's eyes widened. "Murtair? You mean like Brie?"

Alar nodded and pointed. "The one in pants."

"And no hair. Got an aura about them, don't they? Like they'd snatch the heart out of anyone comes too close. Which one is Siofra?"

"The one in the red gown." The five women moved further into the room, Siofra and the murtair in one direction and the others in another. They wore similar fashions to everyone else. Their hair was coiffed the same. Yet, the other guests obviously knew what they were. Alar scanned the room and noticed others casting furtive glances at the women and whispering. Would they know who these women were without the murtair's threatening presence? Did the Desulti announce themselves when they arrived? How well known were powerful Desulti like Siofra? There was too much he didn't know about them.

Siofra strolled languidly, the short train of her red velvet gown trailing behind her. Her eyes slid past the hopeful artists, casually dismissing their works. A small grin lifted Alar's lips, watching the artists' hopeful faces fall as she passed.

She was beautiful, but that wasn't the most striking thing about her. It was her casual dismissal of the attention she attracted. She had none of the affectations of someone pretending not to notice. She simply didn't care. Even among the elite Volloch, Siofra projected power and privilege. And her power wasn't the borrowed power of other Volloch women. Her power was her own. She knew it, and Alar guessed she was unfazed by it.

She was passing behind the crowd gathered in front of Scilla's painting when they noticed her and parted. She glanced at the painting and stopped abruptly. When she turned to face the canvas, the crowd hurriedly dispersed, leaving Siofra and the murtair alone to approach the easel.

"Whoa," Ukrit said. "Did you see them scatter?"

Alar hurried to the bar, bypassing the line to retrieve two glasses of wine from a servant he knew through Trell. The murtair eyed him as he drew near, but he merely grinned, nodded a greeting and stepped up beside Siofra.

She stared dreamily at the painting, twisting slowly back and forth. One arm crossed her stomach, the hand cupping her elbow, an index finger of the other hand caressing her lower lip.

"Wine?" he asked.

She glanced at him, dismissed him, then her face froze. Pivoting smoothly to face him, her eyes roved his face, lingered on his braid, then found his eyes. He had the distinct impression he was being measured and forced himself to hold her gaze. After a long moment, one corner of her mouth turned up, and she took the offered wineglass by the stem. Her eyes on his, she sipped the wine, then her nose wrinkled. She held the glass up and peered at the golden liquid.

"Not to your liking?" Alar asked.

A delicate eyebrow arched, and her sly smile returned. "The wine or the painting?"

"Either, both."

Her eyes flicked to the painting, then she held up the glass. "The wine is serviceable. It's just that being offered wine by an *Alle'oss* man, I was expecting *Alle'oss* wine."

Alar gave her a small smile. "I agree with your assessment of the wine. However, as we are only guests, we have little say in the menu." He turned to face Scilla's painting. "And the painting? Is it serviceable?"

He watched her from the corner of his eye as she sipped her wine and studied his profile. When she turned to face the painting, she shifted her weight, putting her shoulder close enough to his arm so he felt her heat.

"Unlike the wine, the painting is exquisite." She paused, then asked, "Are you the artist?"

"No, I am but the artist's manager."

"Manager," Siofra said softly. She met his eyes when he looked at her, then she turned back to the painting. "I've never seen the like. The technique is revolutionary. Not even Valdemar or Omar produced such... emotion. Even in their best works." The words were effusive, but her tone conveyed the authority of someone who knew what she spoke of.

"You're an aficionado of the new school?"

Siofra nodded slowly, but didn't speak.

Alar glanced over his shoulder. Seeing only the murtair watching him suspiciously, he leaned close enough to Siofra to catch her delicate scent and said, "I heard the Inquisition destroyed Valdemar's works."

"I heard that as well. But I know for a fact, some survived."

The murtair leaned close to Siofra and whispered in her ear. Siofra's eyes widened slightly, and her gaze lost its dreamy quality. After a pause, she turned, inviting Alar to face her.

"And you?" she asked. "An *Alle'oss*. A manager of artists. You must have seen Valdemar's works?"

Alar glanced at the murtair and saw recognition in her expression. He gave Siofra a small grin and said, "I have, indeed. Including his greatest work, which I won't name. The one for which he was executed."

"So, the rumors are true. It survived."

Alar lifted his glass in toast and sipped.

"Where do you suppose such masterpieces are hidden?" Siofra asked. "Surely, whoever possesses them understands the Inquisition would go to any length to find them."

"I assume, wherever they are, they are safe from... Imperial depredations."

Siofra's lips twisted. She swirled her wine and said, "It's a pity someone hid them away where they can't be appreciated."

"Appreciated by whom?"

She cocked her head, pursed her lips and gave a small shrug with one shoulder. Then she faced the painting again. "I wish to purchase this painting."

"You are free to make an offer."

One eyebrow rose, and the sly grin returned. "Then perhaps we should wait a week. After the wedding, when all offers are on the table. Then we can meet. You and I, away from all these distractions." She turned back to him, gave him a wide smile and said, "To negotiate."

Alar gave her a slight bow. "I look forward to it." He returned her smile and said, "I'm sure we can come to a *mutually* beneficial arrangement."

"Hmmm," she said, then she turned and made her way down the line of easels, the artists eagerly watching her approach.

The murtair's eyes narrowed slightly, then she turned and followed Siofra.

Alar watched her go, then pushed his way through the crowd that filled the void left by the Desultis' departure. Music from across the Entrance Hall underscored the murmur of conversation and signaled the ball was underway. The Reception Hall was filling with guests who wanted to view the art before entering the ballroom. They formed a queue that wandered along the line of easels and gathered in small groups in the middle of the room, partaking of the refreshments. He meandered through the crowd, looking for Scilla. He finally spotted her near the entrance, talking to a familiar figure. Holden.

Alar watched her laughing at something the lord said. Her dress was a simple frock. Her hair fell in loose curls around her shoulders. No makeup enhanced her appearance. Yet, there was a radiance, a vibrancy to her that drew the eyes of every Volloch in the room.

"Good to see Scilla relaxed," someone said at his elbow.

Alar turned to find Ukrit, two ales in his hand. He handed one to Alar. Alar took it, glanced at the wineglass in his other hand and discarded it.

"She's been tight as a bowstring for days," Ukrit said. "Then there was the incident at the viewing."

"Yeah, I thought Bergamot was going to destroy the painting," Alar said absently, his attention on Scilla.

"I was talking about some reprobate asking my sister for her hand."

"Yeah…" Realizing what Ukrit said, Alar smirked. "Reprobate? I expected a bit more respect from my future brother."

Ukrit gestured toward Holden and Scilla. "That Holden must have put her at ease," he said, a sly note entering his voice.

Alar snorted and returned his gaze to his promised. "It's seeing all her dreams of wedded bliss coming true that's put the rose in her cheeks. Not the company."

Scilla took Holden's offered arm and crossed the room toward her painting. As they passed Alar and Ukrit, Scilla whispered, "Holden wants to see the painting again." She smiled and tossed her braid, flashing the blue bead.

"You would think once was enough," Ukrit said. "You know, after…"

Alar watched Holden introducing Scilla to the Volloch, who were admiring her painting.

"Sold my horse," Ukrit said.

"Sold your…" Alar turned to face Ukrit. "You did? That's great! How much?"

"Enough. Olson told me what Bergamot was going to offer, and this was much better. We'll not be sleeping in an abandoned shack anymore. Not for a while, anyway."

"Who'd you sell it to?"

"Someone you know." Ukrit spun around, searching the room, then pointed. "Her?"

Alar followed his pointing finger and found Siofra looking back at him. She lifted her wineglass and smiled.

***

Four hours later, Alar and Ukrit stood by his sculpture, watching the guests come and go. Scilla was still the center of attention beside her painting. Chekka had long since left. Alar idly watched the guests filing past the easels. Curious about the works of the other artists, he made the rounds earlier.

What he saw mostly confirmed what he learned from Sune, Scilla's and Ukrit's teacher, about Imperial art. The paintings were flat, and the artists confined themselves to muted colors. However, he was surprised to find a few artists attempted to produce the perspective effect invented by the new school artists. Unfortunately, most of them applied the technique inexpertly. The viewer was left with a vague sense of wrongness when background objects seemed to violate expectations. To his surprise, the artist who applied the technique most successfully was About-That. His depiction of the bride and groom dancing was much more dynamic than the other works, and the artist used a more adventurous color palette. He caught About-That watching him examining the painting and had the impression he was waiting to see Alar's reaction. When Alar gave him a wide smile and bowed, About-That turned away without acknowledging the compliment. But Alar could see he was pleased.

"How late you think this thing goes to?" Ukrit asked, bringing Alar back from his thoughts.

"Doesn't appear to be slowing down." Alar looked down at the small tag on the sculpture that showed it was sold. "No reason for you to stay."

"Enjoying the disappointment in their faces when they see the tag," Ukrit said. "I can sleep all day tomorrow."

Alar smirked, then looked toward a chattering group that just entered. It was Violette, surrounded by a covey of Volloch women of the same age. He nudged Ukrit. "Hey, look who just came in."

"Violette. No sign of the groom."

"No. I haven't seen Holden since early on. But look closer. The man standing next to Violette."

Ukrit squinted at the party as they joined the queue circulating around the room. "That Adelbart?"

"It is, indeed. And what else is odd about that scene?"

While Ukrit sipped his ale, Adelbart leaned toward Violette and said something, prompting Violette to laugh.

"Hmmm," Ukrit said. "What do you think that's about? Only seen her at a distance, mostly, but I haven't seen that woman so much as crack a smile since we got here."

"No, me either. Seems our governor is full of surprises."

Curious how the bride would react to Scilla's painting after the incident at the viewing, Alar watched them approach it. When Adelbart paused, Violette took his arm and pulled him past it.

"Huh," Ukrit said. "What do you suppose her problem with Scilla's painting is?"

"Too much truth," Alar said vaguely. He had just noticed the three Desulti who accompanied Siofra heading to the exit. "Be right back," he said and pushed his tankard into Ukrit's hand.

Hurrying across the room, he made it to the Entrance Hall in time to see the three women passing through the exit into the warm night. He followed, stopping on the veranda to watch them strolling across the lawn toward a set of benches arranged beneath a willow tree at the edge of the garden. There were guards and guests on the veranda, so he hurried down the steps, intending to find a place he could enter *annen'heim.* As he stepped onto the ground, a person wearing the clothes of a laborer appeared. It was Brie, the murtair he fought the previous winter.

"Alar," she said. Before he could answer, she took his arm and pulled him into motion past the watchful gaze of the guards at the entrance. "Should I ask why you're attending an event like this?" She looked back to ensure they weren't observed.

"I wouldn't advise it," he said, shaking her grip off. They stopped at the corner of the veranda in the shadow of a large arborvitae. "How about you —" Glancing over his shoulder, he turned a worried frown on her and asked, "Someone here in trouble?"

"Not that kind of visit. I'm here to speak to another Desulti."

"Siofra?"

Brie, who was looking toward the three women who were ducking beneath the drooping branches of the willow tree, looked back at Alar. "You know Siofra?"

"We've met."

"She know who you are?"

"I suspect she was aware," Alar said with a grin. "She invited me to *negotiate.*" He waggled his brows suggestively.

"You should take that invitation. She is fair and a woman of her word." Before he could reply, she pointed to the willow tree. "In the meantime, I very much want to know what those three women are talking about."

"I had the same thought. Why don't you use your mysterious Murtair skills and sneak over there for us?"

She narrowed her eyes at his teasing tone. "Because I have a friend who can literally disappear."

"A friend?" he asked, one brow rising.

"Yes. A friend. For my part."

Alar's smile widened and an instant later, he stepped into *annen'heim.* He froze when the eerie moans of the *sjel'and* greeted him. They were close, but it didn't sound as if they detected his intrusion into their realm. It was worth the risk. Keeping an eye on the shadows, he crossed the lawn, slipped around the willow tree, and returned to the physical realm.

A half hour later, Alar peeked around the tree. Seeing the women crossing the lawn toward the manor, he emerged, leaned his shoulder on the trunk, and watched their silhouettes retreating through the swaying branches of the willow. He didn't understand a lot of what they said. It involved internal Desulti politics and women he didn't know. But it was clear there was an ongoing power struggle for the future of the Desulti, and it was also clear that his friend Tove was at the center of it. She was in danger. The question was, what could he do about it?

His impulse was to leave for Ka'tan immediately. But his days of running off on his own were over. He couldn't think only of Tove. He had to think of what was best for *Oss'stera* and the *Alle'oss.* He peered toward the arborvitae at the end of the veranda, where Brie was waiting in the shadows.

From what he read in Siofra's journal in Richeleau, she was aware something was afoot, but she didn't know the full shape of the thing.

How grateful would she and Brie be to learn what he heard? He could demand concessions. He was sure they would willingly pay for what he heard. But that didn't feel right. He couldn't negotiate with Tove's life and, if Siofra was the woman Brie implied she was, she would appreciate the favor he did her.

When he returned to the physical realm two paces in front of Brie, she startled, though she tried to hide it.

She eyed him while he studied her speculatively. "Well?"

"We need to talk to Siofra." He told her what he heard and watched her becoming increasingly concerned.

When he was done, she said, "Siofra will be in the first room on the guest wing on the south side of the manor."

"How do you know that?"

"This isn't our first visit. A man as powerful as Bergamot attracts a lot of attention from the Desulti." She looked back at the steps to the veranda. When she turned back, she said, "I assume you can be in the guest wing at the third bell."

"See you there," Alar said.

He watched Brie disappear around the corner of the veranda, then headed toward the entrance of the manor. He had three hours before he had to meet Brie. It was time to rescue his fiancée from her admirers, take her back to their rooms, and celebrate their engagement. He was mounting the steps to the porch when someone spoke.

"Alar!" It was Holden, sitting on the steps. He lifted his wineglass in toast. "Join me."

Alar didn't hesitate. He had been waiting for a chance to get Holden alone. He sat beside the lord and studied his profile as he stared glumly into the night. The tickle of an idea played at the back of Alar's mind, but he needed time to let it reveal itself. "You're missing your party."

Holden chuckled softly. "Couldn't take the suspense any longer."

"Suspense?"

"News of what happened at the viewing spread fast, even for this crowd. The wagers started not long after. If you have any coin, I'd get in on the action. I'll even give you an inside tip." He leaned toward Alar and whispered. "We have no choice but to go through with it." He leaned away, cast a sidelong look at Alar and said, "By the way, Scilla told me what the blue bead means. At least one of us is to be congratulated."

"*Tok*," Alar said. Holden lifted the glass again, let it drop, and gazed across the lawn. "I saw Violette earlier."

"And?"

"She was with Adelbart."

Holden nodded. "They're childhood friends." He gestured toward the west with his glass. "His parent's estate is a few leagues that way." He lifted his arms and gestured around. "Makes this place seem a hovel."

Alar couldn't imagine it. Bergamot's estate was already larger than most *Alle'oss* villages. "She was laughing." Alar watched Holden's face for his reaction.

The lord's head swiveled around to look at him.

"At something Adelbart said."

"Ah." Holden sat back, extended his legs, and rested his elbows on a higher step. "That *is* an odd thing. Adelbart always seemed to me a bit of a boob, but he's the only man Violette has ever taken to. In a friendly way." He chuckled. "I suppose she doesn't see him as much of a threat."

Alar stared at him, then looked out over the lawn, Ragan's hint suddenly snapping into focus. "Holden," he said, a smile growing on his face. "I may have a solution to your problem. Yours and Violette's."

"Our problem?"

"Would it be possible to meet with you two tomorrow? In private?"

***

Even in the wee hours, guests roamed the estate and lounged in various nooks in the manor house. The one advantage to all this activity was the doors were always open. As long as he encountered no spirits, Alar could remain in *annen'heim* and come and go wherever he pleased.

Arriving in the guest wing ten minutes before the third bell, and finding the hallway empty, he returned to the physical realm and was greeted by muted sounds of revelry. He wasn't sure how Brie would make her way inside the manor, but he headed to the window at the end of the hall. If a guest arrived, they would see only his silhouette against the moonlit window and leave him alone. Hopefully.

He glanced over his shoulder as the voices in the Entrance Hall rose momentarily. When he turned back, he was startled to see someone peering through the bottom corner of the window. It was Brie. She pointed to the latch and mimed lifting the window. Alar frowned and shook his head, tsking and wagging his finger. Brie's eyes narrowed. She produced a long, thin strip of metal, but before she could use it to flip the latch, Alar twisted the latch and lifted the window. He stepped back, allowing her room to enter the hall.

She brushed past him. "Come with me."

She stopped in front of the last door before the exit, lifted a hand to tap on the door, then hesitated. "What I have to say to Siofra won't make much sense to you. Just listen until I ask you to tell her what you heard." When Alar nodded, she knocked on the door. A moment later, it opened to reveal the murtair who accompanied Siofra. Recognition, but no surprise, lit her eyes when she saw Brie, then she saw Alar, and a guarded mask slid across her face.

"Brie," she murmured.

"Eirin," Brie responded. "This is Alar. He's a friend. We need to speak to Siofra."

Eirin stepped back and pulled the door open. Siofra, wearing an elaborately embroidered night dress, sat at a desk set against the opposite wall between two tall windows. The room wasn't as lavishly decorated as her chambers in the governor's mansion, but the Bergamots had obviously acknowledged her status by assigning her this room.

When she saw who entered, she rose, an astonished expression on her face. "Brie. What has happened? Why is Alar here?"

"I have a confession," Brie said. "And Alar has information for you."

Alar tried to follow the conversation. They mentioned some of the same names he heard from the three Desulti, and it was apparent he was right about the power struggle in the Order. But he was nearly out of patience when Siofra looked at him and spoke.

"And what information do you have for me?"

"I saw the women who came with you heading out to the garden, so I decided to eavesdrop."

"And?"

"They said something about Lyssa moving the Council to Kartok." Kartok was the largest city in Argren and had largely been taken over by the Volloch. While the news didn't mean anything to Alar, it had a profound effect on Siofra.

She gaped at him. "You must have misheard."

"No, I'm quite sure I heard them clearly. They said the Volloch were taking over Kartok and the Desulti could be part of *polite society* there. They're tired of being outsiders."

"The Order would never stand for that," Eirin said.

"They said there's no one left to oppose it," Alar said. "Except Nessa and Siofra." He caught Brie's eye and said, "They also said Lyssa would take care of the *I'oss,* so they wouldn't have to see her scarred face anymore." That would have to refer to Tove, who wore scars inflicted during her stay with the Inquisition.

Ignoring his last comment, Eirin asked Siofra, "What does it mean?"

"Lyssa and the Ruling Council want to bring the Desulti into the Empire. It will destroy the Order," Siofra said. "Eirin, saddle our horses. We leave immediately."

Eirin nodded, retrieved a pack from the corner and left.

"Alar, I appreciate what you have done for us. I won't forget it."

"Just take care of my friend," Alar said.

"We will," Siofra said. "Brie, I have a task for you."

19

Adi and Vi

Early in the morning after the opening ball, Alar took the steps to the veranda of the manor house two at a time. He breezed past Helmut with a wave and joined Holden in the Entrance Hall. The lord looked as if he hadn't slept a wink the night before. He wore the same suit he had at the ball and dark circles underlined bloodshot eyes above unshaven cheeks.

"*Lorna*, Holden," Alar said. "Late night?"

Holden scowled. "Do all *Alle'oss* have ironclad constitutions?"

"Just the lucky ones." In truth, Alar had only fallen asleep two hours earlier, but a few *pulls* had washed away much of his fatigue, and he wasn't going to allow Holden or Violette to see how tired he really was. "Is Violette awake?" With their busy pre-nuptials schedule, early morning was the only time the engaged couple could meet with him.

"She is awake." Holden led Alar toward the staircase on the right side of the Entrance Hall. "But she is not happy about it. She will test you. I advise you not to rise to it." In the family's wing, Holden rapped on the door to what Trell told Alar were Violette's chambers. When a muffled voice bade them enter, he led Alar into a sitting room.

Violette, dressed in a simple morning dress, was draped across a divan, a slim book in her hand. She looked as wan as Holden, though she carried it better.

"Lady Violette," Holden said with a shallow bow. He gestured to Alar. "I present to you, Alar."

She let the book fall to her lap and studied Alar. "*The* Alar. The man with a solution to our *problem*." Her gaze traveled slowly down his body, taking in his buckskins and moccasin boots, then rose again to his face. Her eyes flicked to the braid beside his left ear, then found his eyes. "A *real Alle'oss*, right out of the stories. How extraordinary."

Remembering the stories of Lohkti he found in the library, Alar fought to keep his expression neutral.

"As I described to you," Holden said. "Not like the tame *Alle'oss* who live in Lachton. Alar is as authentic as can be." He turned a wide smile on Alar and asked, "Tell her what the… decorations in your braid mean?"

"They mean I'm from Richeleau," Alar said, his voice controlled. "And that I'm promised to Scilla. Among other things."

"Ah," Holden said. "Among other things." His smile softened. "No need to take offense, Alar." He gestured to Violette. "Lady Violette has developed a passionate interest in the *Alle'oss* people." When Alar's gaze went to Violette, the lord continued. "Your culture, your customs, your music, your cuisine. She's particularly interested in your festivals, and your…" He leaned close and whispered, "Language."

Alar met Holden's gaze, and the lord winked.

"*Kisa Alle'oss da?*" Violette purred.

Alar resisted the urge to slap the smug grin from her face. "*Da*," he said. He lifted a finger to forestall her next utterance. "However, it's *kisu*, not *kisa*. Second person." He pronounced the sentence correctly and gave her a wide smile.

A petulant frown appeared on her face. "Well, I've never had a native speaker to listen to."

"And how could you, since speaking our language is illegal?"

"And yet," Holden said. "*You* speak *Alle'oss*."

"After a fashion," Alar said.

"That makes you an outlaw," Violette said. "Doesn't it?"

"Only if I speak *Alle'oss.*" Alar rested a hand on his chest. "But I am a law-abiding citizen of the Empire. A humble manager of talented artists."

"And how would a humble manager of artists know what *our* problem is?" Violette asked archly.

"Your problem, Violette, is that you value your independence. Your parents wish to sell you to a man for their own gain and aren't interested in your desires. You enjoy the privileges of wealth and real power, not the mere trappings of power. But as a Volloch woman, you're unlikely to find both in marriage. You could hold out, continue to reject potential matches, but your parents are growing increasingly frustrated with your intransigence, and you find living with their disapproval intolerable. You could join the Desulti, but for reasons known only to you, that doesn't appeal. So, your only recourse is to marry Holden, who you don't love and who is unlikely to provide for you in the manner you desire."

Violette stared at him.

"Holden," Alar continued, "your problem is that you are a third son and stand to inherit nothing. You aren't satisfied with the options Volloch society offers third sons, and your father has told you he is unwilling to provide any others. So, you're forced into a loveless marriage with Violette to acquire the dowry in order to avoid penury. Yet, as you told me yourself, you have no skills, and I suspect you have no inclination to acquire the wealth and power that would satisfy Violette. Which means the two of you will grow increasingly estranged and bitter as the years pass."

Alar looked from Holden to Violette in the silent room. "Is that about it?"

Violette sighed, tossed the book on a side table and sat on the edge of the divan. "So, you have dissected our miserable predicament. Not that it is difficult to do. It is quite evident everyone is aware of the situation."

"But you say you have a solution?" Holden asked, with little hope in his voice.

"I do, but you must hear me out before rejecting it. All of it."

Violette and Holden exchanged a look, then nodded.

"Violette should marry Governor Adelbart," Alar said. He raised a hand to forestall her protest. "Adelbart has the status that would satisfy your parents. He's an Imperial Governor and the nephew of the emperor. The district he governs is Argren, the home of the *Alle'oss*, and you and the governor admire much about my people." He tilted his head and twisted his lips. "After a fashion." The disbelief in Violette's expression had given way to speculation. "And despite his position, Adelbart has no interest in governing, nor in growing what promises to be a lucrative business relationship with the *Alle'oss*. Frankly, I would prefer to deal with someone more reliable than the governor."

"*You* would prefer?" Holden asked.

Alar waved a hand. "You only need details if you agree to the solution." He turned to face the lord. "Holden, my colleagues and I have begun to export products from Argren, but we are finding the Volloch unwilling to do business with *Alle'oss*. It would be beneficial to have a Volloch man, especially one from a powerful family, to serve as our representative. The pay would be modest to start but would grow rapidly." Holden looked skeptical. "And as you know, one thing the *Alle'oss* can offer the world no one else can is our art." Holden's expression shifted. "After the response to Scilla's and Ukrit's works last night, I suspect a gallery specializing in *Alle'oss* art would do quite well. I would suggest the neighborhood north of the Harbor District and I can guarantee exclusive access to the works of two of the most promising young *Alle'oss* artists. We will be able to name our price for Scilla's works after this week." Alar paused, letting Holden consider. "You won't be as rich or as powerful as your father. Not soon, anyway. But you would be comfortable, and you would be your own man."

Holden dropped into a chair beside the hearth. After a moment, he looked at Violette and said, "What do you think?"

She stood, crossed to the door, then turned around. "The wedding. Can you imagine the storm that will break if we announced this…" She paused, mouth open, a hand making vague gestures. "And my mother despises Adelbart's mother. She would explode."

"Don't announce anything," Alar said.

"What are you talking about?" Violette asked.

"Just leave. We'll sneak you out with Adelbart before the wedding. After a suitable period, there will be a grand wedding in the governor's mansion in Richeleau. It's true, people will talk about the scandal for years. I know that's not ideal, but the alternative is much worse. And besides, what will you care? You'll be married to an Imperial Governor and…" He paused for effect, "you, Lady Violette, will be the governor of Argren in all but name."

Violette's parted lips closed. She straightened, let her hand fall to her side, and turned toward Holden.

"It's about the best deal you'll get," Holden said with a small grin. "You know how Adelbart is. He'll have no problem letting you take the lead. Will welcome it, I suspect."

Violette returned to her seat on the divan. "But we don't even know if Adi would agree to this?"

Alar blinked. *Adi?* He gave his head a shake and said, "Adelbart has been adrift without his mother's influence. If you were willing to indulge his less egregious whims, I think he would be quite happy to call you his wife." Alar had no idea if that was true, but one problem at a time.

"We can, at least, broach the topic with him," Holden said. "No need to decide now."

Violette met his eyes. "And are you happy with this?"

Holden sat back and looked up at Alar. "I think I am. In fact, I find myself quite taken with this idea of a gallery. It may be the only venture for which I have any aptitude."

"Okay," Violette said, the corners of her lips quivering before lifting. "Let's meet with Adi."

Alar raised a finger. "I have but one request." When they looked at him, he said, "We will need coin to get our venture off the ground. I would like to steal the dowry."

***

Alar looked up at the sound of Scilla's laughter. A moment later, she and Ukrit pushed through the flaps of the pavilion's door. It had been two hours since he spoke to Violette and Holden, so they couldn't have had more than four hours of sleep, and it showed. He popped the last of a cinnamon roll into his mouth, licked his fingers, and lifted his hands in applause. "The artists returning to the site of their triumphant debut."

Scilla curtsied and threw her arms around his neck, cutting off his next words with a kiss.

Ukrit picked up a plate at the end of the buffet table. "Pickings are slim this morning," he grumbled.

"It's late for breakfast," Alar said. "The locusts have already come and gone."

Scilla followed Ukrit's example and retrieved a plate. "You talked to Violette and Holden?"

Ukrit paused, a spoon full of eggs suspended above his plate.

Alar glanced at the small group of artists and apprentices gathered around the far end of the buffet table. "I did," he said in a low voice.

"And?" Scilla asked.

"They're in. All we have to do is convince Adelbart."

Ukrit dumped the eggs on his plate.

"You're kidding!" Scilla said. "Violette and Adelbart? I thought you were crazy when you told us what you had in mind." She stared into space for a moment. "She *must* be desperate. I feel so bad for Holden."

"Believe me, he's thrilled. He's quite taken with the idea of an art gallery. I, uh, made promises about your art." Scilla and Ukrit shrugged. "As for Violette and Adelbart… I don't see it either, but Violette is all about power and status. Adelbart has both and doesn't know what to do with either. And believe it or not, she seems to like him. Called him Adi."

"Adi?" Scilla asked.

Piling the last of the bacon on his plate, Ukrit murmured, "What about our deal with the governor? Is she going to honor it?"

"She says yes."

"And you believe her?" Scilla asked.

"You remember why Adelbart was so eager to be part of the deal in the first place."

"He's broke," Ukrit said.

"I may have misstated Adelbart's financial position," Alar said with a grin. "I think when she discovers the truth, she'll be just as eager to work with us as the governor."

"You hope," Ukrit said.

"It's a gamble," Alar said with a shrug. "But she seemed quite keen on running the Imperial side of the operation. Had some suggestions already. Plus, I'm pretty sure this is what Ragan had in mind. She told me Violette would be a good ally."

"If you say so," Ukrit said. "Just saw Adelbart and a couple of other Volloch in the garden a minute ago." He picked up one of the last cinnamon rolls and took a bite. "Might be your only chance to get him alone."

Scilla set her plate down. "Let's go."

"You coming?" Alar asked Ukrit.

"No. I promised Chekka I'd come by when I woke up. He's going to show me how to make horseshoes," he said loudly, then leaned in and whispered, "Arrowheads." He winked and headed for the exit, his plate piled high.

"Ukrit's made a friend," Alar said.

Scilla plucked up a bunch of grapes. "Let's go."

They found the governor in the garden, strolling a path that ran along the shore of the pond, chatting with a man and woman. He looked as if he were telling a story the other two found amusing. When he caught sight of Alar and Scilla, panic momentarily flickered across his face before he recovered his smile. Alar pointed to the benches beneath the tree where he listened to the Desulti the night before. Adelbart gave him a small nod and continued along the path.

Scilla ducked under the branches of the willow and sat cross-legged on a bench. Smoothing her dress across her knees, she set the grapes in her lap, popped one into her mouth and grinned. "So, when is the wedding?"

"Ours?" When Scilla nodded, he motioned to the manor house. "I have it on good authority this wedding will soon be short a bride and groom."

"Not a chance," Scilla said, one brow arching. "We're getting married in *Honutok.* A traditional *Alle'oss* wedding with all our friends present."

Before Alar could respond, Adelbart slipped into the shadow of the tree. Looking as furtive as a thief in a Styrian melodrama, he sat on the edge of a bench across from Scilla and peered back through the branches.

"You ashamed to be seen with *Alle'oss?*" Scilla asked, softening the question with a teasing tone.

"More like partners in crime." Adelbart swiveled around to look at them. "I am the governor of Argren, after all. No one would find it out of place for me to talk to some of my constituents." He smiled at Scilla and leaned toward her. "Especially after your triumph last night. Your painting was on everyone's lips."

"*Tok,*" Scilla said, languidly stretching her arms along the back of the bench.

"Now, I don't know why you wish to speak to me. But before we get to that, I wish to inquire whether I can purchase the painting. After all, I have many spaces on my walls to fill after…" He waved a hand. "The events of last winter."

"Siofra expressed an interest in acquiring it," Alar said.

"Oh, well, yes, I suppose that would be a way to build a bridge." Adelbart grinned at Scilla. "But I get first option on your next work."

"Of course."

"Good." He sat primly and looked at Alar. "Now, what is it you wanted?"

"We have a proposal."

"For me?" Adelbart asked cautiously.

Alar nodded. "Holden told me you and Violette are fast friends."

"That's true," the governor said, perking up. "We've been close most of our lives. The Bergamots were frequent visitors to our estate when we were children." He pulled a handkerchief from his coat pocket and dabbed at his forehead. "She was always happy to visit because she could get away from her mother. For a time."

"So, I know you are aware how unhappy Violette is with this marriage to Holden," Scilla said.

Adelbart nodded. "Yes. Everyone knows, though few have heard it from her lips." He looked from Alar to Scilla, dabbing at his cheeks with the handkerchief. "Why?"

"I spoke to Violette and Holden this morning and they both agreed the solution to her problem is that she marry you," Alar said.

Adelbart gaped at him, the handkerchief forgotten. He blinked, let his hand fall into his lap and looked at Scilla, who nodded.

"Now, think through the advantages before you dismiss it," Alar said. "As you mentioned, you have been lifelong friends. As far as I can tell, you are her only real friend. She comes from wealth and power. She is as fascinated with *Alle'oss* culture as you are."

Adelbart closed his mouth, sat up straight, and cupped his hands on his knees.

"She's beautiful," Scilla said. "She loves the trappings of Volloch society. Imagine you and Violette, standing together, the center of attention at one of your balls."

Adelbart cocked his head, his eyes staring into the vision.

"And Violette is smart and ambitious. She will be a worthy partner in your political and business endeavors," Alar said.

Adelbart's eyes focused and cut to Alar. "Business endeavors? Does she know about our arrangement?"

"She does, and she's keen to maximize the possibilities." Alar sat beside the governor, who turned to face him. "But most important, once she got over her initial shock, she seemed quite eager." Eager was a bit of an exaggeration, but it wasn't a lie to say Violette was not reluctant when Alar left her.

"Violette was eager?" Adelbart asked doubtfully. "To marry."

Alar nodded.

Adelbart looked through the branches of the willow to a group of guests descending the steps of the veranda. "But the wedding, the guests." He turned back to Alar.

"There will be no announcement. You will whisk her away in the middle of the night. When everyone wakes, the bride will be on her way to Richeleau," Scilla said. "How romantic."

Adelbart pointed to his chest, brows rising.

"Yes, tomorrow night," Alar said. "You will say there has been an emergency in Richeleau that you must attend to. You will call for your carriage and we will sneak Violette into it. It will be late, so no one will see."

"There will be such a scandal —"

"Which you and Violette will weather, together," Scilla said.

"She knows what will happen," Alar said. "In three months, there will be a wedding in Richeleau. When the Volloch elite see how in love you are, they will understand how you swept the reluctant bride off her feet. They will be so taken with the story that Violette finally found love, the scandal will be but a memory."

"In love?" Adelbart breathed. "Does Vi love me?"

Alar caught Scilla staring open-mouthed at Adelbart. When she met Alar's eye, he could tell she was thinking the same thing. Adelbart and Violette, Adi and Vi, were in love. The truth had been trapped beneath the layers of Volloch social strictures and Violette's parents' desire to use her for their own gain.

Alar waited until Adelbart's eyes focused and said, "I think she might." He rested a hand on the governor's shoulder but met Scilla's eyes. "You can do far worse than to marry your best friend."

"I must speak to Vi," Adelbart said and stood.

"She will be in her chambers alone at the sixteenth bell," Alar said. "She only has a few moments, but she will be waiting for you."

"Vi expects me?"

"Holden will meet you in the Entrance Hall," Alar said. "He'll have Violette's chambermaid escort you to her chambers."

"Yes, yes. The sixteenth bell." Adelbart straightened, suddenly the picture of an Imperial Governor. "I will inform you what we decide before the banquet tonight. Meet me in the Reception Hall." He was turning away, then paused and said, "I'll bring Gerold. He will need to hear this." And then he was gone, striding in an Adelbart way across the lawn.

Scilla sat up and laughed. "Can you believe it?"

"They're in love. At least Adi is, and if I had to guess, I'd say Vi is at least fond of Adi."

"Why didn't Violette's father make this match already?" Scilla said with a scowl.

"Violette says their mothers had some falling out years ago. They hate one another."

"You're a genius."

"Don't look at me." Alar offered his hand and pulled her to her feet. "This is Ragan's doing."

"Ragan only hinted. It was you who saw the truth." She took his arm as they crossed the lawn. "I need breakfast."

"It's time for lunch." Alar looked up at the sun. "Let's go see if Gerold is hungry, then we can go to the kitchen for a real lunch."

***

Alar watched Scilla interacting with a group of Volloch in front of her painting. It was still early evening and only a few guests were about, but most of them were gathered around her easel. Still busy with Chekka, Ukrit hadn't arrived in the Reception Hall yet. Alar was considering whether he should wait for him before starting on the buffet, when he heard his name. He spun around and found Adelbart, beaming from ear to ear, approaching, a pensive Gerold in his wake.

Adelbart stopped and leaned close, his smile twisting into a mischievous smirk. "We're on!" He put his fingers to his mouth and glanced furtively at a passing couple.

"Excellent!" Alar whispered. "Congratulations."

"Yes," Adelbart said, the smile returning. "I suppose congratulations are in order." He reached back, put his hand on Gerold's shoulder and ushered him forward. "Now, we must work out the details of the caper."

Alar looked from his expectant expression to Gerold's grimace. "Yes, of course. I suggest that I work out those details with Holden and Violette."

"Oh?" Adelbart asked, his eyebrows rising.

"They will have more knowledge of the grounds, the schedule, and such."

"Yes. I suppose that makes sense."

"I've arranged to meet them tomorrow after the midday meal."

"That doesn't leave much time," Gerold said, cutting off Adelbart's response. "Are you sure the… thing must happen tomorrow night?"

"I'm afraid so," Alar said. "After tomorrow, the couple's schedule becomes much more crowded, and we wanted to make sure we have time to reschedule if something goes wrong."

Gerold frowned, his lips pursing. "I suppose I will have to rely on your judgment. You have much more experience with this sort of thing."

That was true, although Alar hoped to avoid the kind of violence and mayhem that usually accompanied *Oss'stera's* ventures. He had no idea how they were going to pull it off, but in his experience, the period before the plan was finalized was the most enjoyable part of the caper. All anticipation and no worry. "Trust me," he said, and winked.

20

Sneaky Stuff

The night of Violette's escape, Alar, Scilla and Ukrit arrived in the Reception Hall early and nurtured their nerves by descending on the buffet even while the servants were laying out the dishes. They greeted the servants, and Alar traded quips with the ones he knew. Once they had full plates, they stood near the entrance, watching artists and apprentices following in their wake.

"Gonna miss this," Ukrit said and gestured to the buffet.

"If all goes well tonight," Alar said. "We may still have a few days, and if the bit with the dowry goes well, we won't have to worry where our meals come from. For a while anyway."

"So, this is my last meal," Ukrit said with a chuckle.

"Don't be so pessimistic," Alar said. "The plan is simple. What could go wrong?"

"Seems like I heard that before," Scilla said. "Besides, in the unlikely event everything does go to plan, there's no guarantee Bergamot won't decide to send everyone home tomorrow. You know, since the bride has gone missing."

"Always so gloomy."

"Okay," Scilla said and gestured to the gathering crowd. "Here we are, hours before we kidnap the daughter of one of the most powerful lords in the Empire. From under the noses of hundreds of Volloch, I might add. And we…" She gestured to herself and Ukrit. "Haven't heard a whisper of a plan. Allay our pessimism."

Alar grinned at the two of them. "Okay, I will —"

"Alar!"

Ukrit spit out a mouthful of quail.

"Bless the mother!" Scilla blurted.

They whirled around and took a step back when they found Gerold standing so close Alar nearly dumped his plate down his front when he turned.

"Gerold!" Alar said. "Don't sneak up on us that way."

"Sorry." Gerold glanced nervously around. "Not used to this sneaky stuff."

"Sneaky stuff?" Alar exchanged a grin with Scilla.

Gerold frowned. "You know what I mean."

"Indeed," Alar said and waggled his brows.

Gerold's eyes flicked up to Alar's brows, his frown deepening. "Adelbart is in a fit state. Walking around, grinning like a madman, talking too loud, sweating like a farm animal. I've gotta give him something. Something to focus his mind. What, exactly, is the plan?"

Alar glanced up at About-That, who entered with Heinz in tow. The artist nodded to Scilla and Ukrit as he passed. Alar took Gerold's arm and led him away from the door and waited for everyone to gather around. "Adelbart's part couldn't be simpler. You bring Adelbart a message just after the twelfth bell —"

"Where?"

Alar blinked.

"Where will the governor be when I bring him the message?"

"It's a good point," Ukrit said around a mouthful of pumpkin puree.

"Right." Alar glanced around the room. "We want a lot of people to hear."

"At the twelfth bell, the Reception Hall will be busy," Gerold said. "I'll ask the governor to be standing near the queue at the bar."

"Good idea," Alar said. Before he could continue, Gerold interrupted him again.

"What does the message say? What emergency would be so important that it would require the governor's presence in Richeleau?"

Alar hesitated. "Is that important?"

"Well, someone might ask. And believe me, you don't want the governor thinking on his feet."

"I'm beginning to see the problem," Ukrit said and popped a stuffed mushroom into his mouth. When everyone looked at him, he said, "You know, why our plans always go awry."

"When has one of our plans failed?" Alar asked, giving Ukrit a significant look and nodding toward Gerold. Gerold's frown showed he hadn't missed the exchange.

"Anyway!" Scilla said. She rested her fingers on Gerold's arm and said, "What would require the governor's attention in Richeleau?"

Gerold stared at her, then looked across the room, his brow furrowing. His mouth dropped open, then closed. He cocked his head, then gave it a shake. He shifted his weight onto one foot, then the other, and brought an index finger up to tap his lips.

Scilla, Alar and Ukrit watched him in silence.

"I'm at a loss," Gerold said and threw his hands up.

"Tell him to say it's a personal matter," Alar said. "Everyone will believe that."

"Well, that's true, but it *is* a little embarrassing," Gerold said.

"Yes, but it has the benefit of being true, which is always better than a lie," Alar said. "And in a week, everyone will know the real reason, anyway."

"I suppose that's true."

"So, we're good with that?" Alar waited while Gerold considered.

"Yes."

"Good. I'll make sure a servant I know is nearby. Adelbart will make a show of telling him to call for his carriage."

"His carriage isn't at the estate," Gerold said, a note of panic in his voice.

"Hah!" Ukrit said. "The plan comes together."

Alar scowled at Ukrit. "I *knew* that. Trell already told me. The carriages of the guests staying at the estate are parked in a field a league from the estate."

Ukrit shrugged and picked up a carrot.

Alar glared at him, then returned his attention to Gerold. "That's why you give him the message at the twelfth bell. We'll make sure it takes an hour and a half to bring his carriage around. The crowd will have thinned out."

"Not that much," Scilla said, watching a pair of early arrivals strolling along the line of easels. "When we left last night, it was still pretty busy."

Alar had noticed there seemed to be as many people out and about in the wee hours as there were in the afternoon. At first, he wondered how they did it, partying all day and all night. But then he realized they tended to party in shifts. One shift ended around midnight, and another ended as dawn broke. What changed as the night wore on was where people congregated.

"Yes," he said, frowning at Scilla. "The Reception Hall stays busy because of the art. But we can't very well have her walking out the front door, anyway." When Gerold opened his mouth, Alar held up a hand. "Just let me get through the whole thing, then we can address any complaints." When Gerold nodded, Alar took a breath, thought for a moment, then started. "Violette will make a show of introducing Scilla around all night. A half hour before the carriage arrives, Adelbart will ask Violette to accompany him to his room to say goodbye. Violette will ask Scilla and a friend who is in on the plan to accompany them for propriety's sake. If any of the women who flock around her try to go along, Ukrit will intervene."

Scilla coughed.

"Me?"

"Ukrit?!" Scilla said when she could.

"It was you who told me he was always in demand at festivals back home," Alar said to Scilla.

"Well… yes, but…"

"Those were *Alle'oss girls,*" Ukrit said. "Girls. We had thirteen, fourteen summers."

"Listen." Alar rested a hand on his shoulder. "These Volloch women are fascinated by roguish types." He lifted a hand and rotated his wrist. "You know, something different from these prancy Volloch men."

"Roguish?"

"Prancy?" Scilla added.

"Yeah." Alar returned Scilla's grin. "They think all men from Argren are rogues. Wear your buckskins, add another braid and some more beads. Be mysterious and, you know…"

"Roguish," Scilla said, her grin widening.

Ukrit looked from one to the other. "Gonna need a few ales for this."

Alar clapped him on the shoulder. "That's the spirit. Violette will bring attention to your charms, so try to look desirable tonight."

"Desirable. Right."

Scilla started to speak, but when she saw Alar's frown, she closed her mouth and gestured for him to continue.

"Anyway, after Violette leaves, people will be so inebriated they won't notice when she doesn't return, at least long enough for her to escape." He pointed at Gerold. "You will be waiting for them in Adelbart's room with a spare suit."

"A suit?"

"Yes, something subdued." Alar glanced down at Gerold's dark gray suit and rested a hand on his shoulder. "Calm down, Gerold. We aren't at the hard part yet."

"Hard part?" Gerold asked, his voice rising an octave.

Ignoring him, Alar said, "Violette will change into the suit."

"Her hair?" Scilla asked.

"She's agreed to let you cut it."

"Me?!"

"Yeah. Something simple," Alar said, gesturing to Gerold's hair.

"Why would I know about cutting hair?" Scilla asked.

"I may have hinted you've had some experience."

"But…" She gestured helplessly to Ukrit's and Alar's long hair. Then she shrugged and made her way around Gerold and studied his hair.

Alar continued. "Violette hides when servants arrive to take Adelbart's baggage. Violette's friend, wearing Violette's dress, allows the servants to see her from behind. Adelbart follows the servants with Scilla. Violette's friend crosses the balcony and goes into Violette's room."

"Risky," Scilla said.

"Yes, but we have to let people see what they think is Violette after you return to the Entrance Hall, otherwise they might think you had something to do with her disappearance. Laugh and make a scene, like Adelbart said something really funny. That will draw everyone's attention away from the fake Violette."

"Funny. Right."

"Adelbart waits for his carriage on the veranda." He pointed at Gerold. "You appear and say you have something to discuss out of earshot. Take him out to where the drive forks into the circle that comes around in front of the manor."

"And Violette?"

"Violette and I will go down the servants' stairs and out the back, next to the kitchens —"

"Ah!" Scilla said. "Food service ends at the first bell, so there won't be as much traffic to and from the kitchen at the second bell."

Alar grinned and gave her a small bow. "Ukrit will be waiting outside the entrance to the stairs so he can let us know when the coast is clear —"

Ukrit swallowed and asked, "What if I'm involved?"

Alar hesitated, mouth open, then asked, "Involved?"

"With a Volloch woman attracted to my roguish charm."

Alar hesitated. Started to speak, then gave his head a shake. "Well, in that *unlikely* event… Just tell her you have to visit the privy." After taking a moment to remember where he was, he continued. "Then Violette and I come around and approach Gerold and Adelbart from the direction of the stables. From a distance in the dark, we'll look like two men. We mingle so anyone watching will lose track of who is you and who is Violette. You flag down the carriage and Adelbart and Violette get in. You and I stroll toward the garden. They keep the shades down while the servants load the baggage on the roof. Then they're off." He held his arms out and grinned. "Ta da!"

They stared at him until Ukrit said, "You're right. It's an airtight plan. I'm getting an ale. Anyone else?"

Alar scowled at his retreating back.

"I'll go apprise the governor of the plan, and… choose a suit." Gerold lips twisted. "Then I'm going to find something stronger than ale." Nodding to them, he spun on his heel and strode away.

"We've had worse plans," Scilla said. "Maybe. You realize if anyone is watching them get into the carriage, they'll be a bit surprised when Gerold turns up at breakfast."

"They'll be long gone by then." He considered. "We'll tell Gerold to stay in his room until the afternoon."

Scilla shrugged. "You came up with this plan on your own?"

Hearing the faint note of rebuke in her tone, he turned to face her. "Violette, Holden and I came up with the plan together. They know the terrain. Besides, you and Ukrit were busy fending off all your admirers this afternoon. If you have any suggestions, I'm listening."

"With Adelbart involved, I don't think changes at this point are wise." She patted him on the arm and said, "It's a good plan. Hopefully." When Ukrit returned, she glanced over her shoulder and whispered, "What about the dowry?"

"Violette says the chest is in Lord Bergamot's room." Alar patted his pocket. "Got a key that opens every door in the manor and the key to the chest."

"And there are no guards?" Scilla asked.

"Violette says there aren't," Alar said with a shrug. "I'll do it after they're gone. They agreed to let me take ten gold Imperials to help Holden get the art gallery going and for our startup expenses."

"Ten gold Imperials," Ukrit said, a touch of awe in his voice. Raising his tankard. "Now, that's the kind of haul extraordinary thieves take."

"Yeah," Alar said. "When you add that to what we get for your works, we'll be in good shape."

"As long as we're not in prison," Scilla said.

***

Captain Brennerman reined up at the front gate of Bergamot's estate and looked down at the guards from atop his horse. It took him nearly two days to ride from Richeleau to Lachton. Before he was posted to Argren, riding two days would have been easy, but it had been many months since he spent an extended time in the saddle. He was weary and didn't have the energy to be polite to these men.

"Captain," one of the guards greeted him. "I'm afraid this is an invitation only affair."

"I'm here on Inquisition business," Brennerman said and handed down the letter Commander Krueger's assistant gave him.

The guard held it up so he could see it in the light of a lantern held by the other guard. Glancing up, he asked, "You Brennerman?" When Brennerman only frowned, the guard smirked and returned his attention to the letter. After a moment, he handed it back. "No weapons."

Brennerman hesitated, then unbuckled the belt that held his cavalry saber, wrapped the belt around the saber, and handed it down.

Taking the saber, the guard said, "Try not to cause a ruckus."

Brennerman urged his horse into a walk, biting back an angry retort. One of the guards jogged ahead of him, no doubt alerting the lord of the manor to his arrival.

It wasn't the first time he encountered that self-important attitude from guards in the service of powerful Volloch lords. Before the recent conflict with the Kaileuk, the Empire enjoyed a hundred years of peace. One of the unfortunate results was men who used to seek glory defending the Empire, now found it more prestigious to serve in the lords' private armies. The size of their security forces was one way the lords measured themselves against one another. Bergamot was a perfect example of the problem. Between his estate, his other properties, and many commercial ventures, he had over a thousand men under arms.

There was a deep-seated animosity between the Imperial military and the lords' private armies. From the military's point of view, those men were cowards, arrogantly smirking at those paying the price to defend the Empire. In the unlikely event the Kaileuk ever broke into the interior of the Empire, the barbarian hordes would swat the lords' fragmented, poorly trained forces aside like so many gnats.

And the worst insult was the pretend soldiers were paid far more for their cushy positions.

Dismissing those vexing thoughts, he looked down the long drive to the manor house, where his vindication waited. The Inquisition commander in Richeleau, Krueger, assured him the arrest warrant would cite rebellion and treasonous acts as their crimes, regardless of the real reason. He gave his head a hard shake, banishing unwelcome doubts that nagged at him since he left the commander's office, and turned his attention to the carriages lining the drive. These would be for the wedding guests staying in the city. Various attendants and the carriage drivers gathered in small groups, barely glanced at him as he passed. As he neared the spot where the drive forked into a wide circle in front of the manor, the stables became visible behind a stand of oaks, across a broad lawn. He veered in that direction.

The process of checking his horse into the stables was frustratingly inefficient. When he was finally free, he set off across the lawn to the manor house. Krueger's assistant told him the wedding involved lavish balls and banquets every night, and it appeared as if tonight's festivities were still in full swing, even though it was near midnight. A lilting tune from a string quartet floated on a soft breeze. Guests gathered in small groups on the wide veranda and strolled the lawn and gardens. Bergamot would only have invited Volloch of the highest castes. A Baird like him would never hope to attend such an event unless he was a servant. Or on Inquisition business.

Having opted for his standard cavalry uniform rather than his dress uniform, he felt distinctly underdressed as he approached the steps to the veranda. Self-consciously giving his jacket a tug, he pulled his shoulders back and mounted the steps. He could only assume the guard from the gate warned the guards at the front entrance to the manor as they only eyed his uniform as he swept past them into an enormous room with twin staircases.

He paused and studied the guests moving through the room. Not seeing anyone with the white uniform of an Inquisition brother, he turned slowly, getting his bearings. The music came from what appeared to be a ballroom through a door on the left. On the opposite side, a door opened into a smaller room. Deciding it would be easier to spot his contact there, he approached the doorway. A quick scan of the room revealed only the drab garments that were typical for Volloch men. No white.

He was turning to search the ballroom when he noticed guests parading along lines of easels arranged around the perimeter of the room. Pursing his lips, he glanced over his shoulder, clasped his hands behind his back, and joined the parade. Not knowing much about art, his initial impressions were that all the paintings look essentially the same. The settings varied, but they all depicted a couple who he assumed were the bride and groom in a staid, formal style with muted colors. He didn't know if he would recognize a painting from an *Alle'oss* artist, but when he saw people gathered around an easel halfway down the back wall, he suspected he found it.

He had to push his way through the crowd to see it but, when it came into view, he stopped dead. His gaze drifted over the canvas, taking in the man and woman standing on a bridge in a vividly rendered garden. His hand came up unbidden, as if he would reach in and pluck a flower. Then he came to himself, glanced furtively around, and let his hand fall to his side. This was it. There could be no mistake. Despite his ignorance of art, he could tell this was qualitatively different from everything else he saw. And he heard his conclusion reflected in the comments of the Volloch standing around him.

But was it heretical or treasonous? He searched the painting, looking for anything the Inquisition might condemn. Some hidden message, perhaps. There was nothing. Perhaps it was something the artist omitted. Some religious message the Inquisition expected. He listened to the conversations around him, hoping he was missing something. Maybe, despite its benign appearance, it inspired heretical thoughts in the observer. But there was no hint of anything untoward.

Turning, he pushed his way through the crowd and paused once he was in the clear. There was nothing in this painting that warranted arresting the artist. Krueger said they would arrest them for what they might paint in the future. He looked over his shoulder at the people who continued to queue up to view the painting. If the artist wanted to, they would certainly attract attention. That made them *potentially* dangerous. It justified keeping an eye on them, perhaps, but was the mere potential of a crime enough for the Inquisition to condemn someone?

His eyes focused on a familiar figure appearing through the door across the room. It was Gerold, Adelbart's assistant. His stride suggested a suppressed urgency. Brennerman's gaze followed him until he disappeared behind a line of guests waiting at the bar. Weaving his way around people, he found an angle which allowed him to see Gerold talking to Adelbart.

"Oh, dear!" Adelbart exclaimed, the volume of his voice rising above the general murmur and drawing attention from all over the room. "Gerold, something of a… personal nature has occurred. I must return to Richeleau."

Brennerman had seen better mummers in the small, unlicensed companies that put on shows in the streets of Richeleau. He took in the faces of others watching the governor and saw his own disbelief in their expressions.

The governor waved a small piece of paper in the air and said to a boy wearing a servant's livery, "Bring my carriage around. I must leave immediately." When he spun around, he locked eyes with Brennerman.

Adelbart froze, his mouth hanging open stupidly. There was a moment when Brennerman was sure the governor was going to turn and flee from the room. Then Gerold looked back to see what the governor had seen. He spotted Brennerman, then whispered something to Adelbart, took his arm and got him moving toward the exit. Gerold watched him for a moment, then turned toward Brennerman, hesitated, and strode purposefully toward him.

"Captain Brennerman," Gerold said. "Can I ask why you have abandoned your post?"

"I'm here on Inquisition business," Brennerman said icily, enjoying the change in Gerold's expression.

"Inquisition?"

"Yes. I've been directed by Commander Krueger to instruct Inquisitor Anders to arrest the *Alle'oss* rebels posing as artists."

Gerold's face drained of color, but he recovered quickly. "Captain, the only *Alle'oss* at the estate, besides the servants, are, in fact, artists. They aren't *posing* as artists." He gestured to the painting Brennerman had already seen. "As you can see for yourself."

"They are rebels," Brennerman said coolly. "And after they are arrested, your conspiracy will be exposed."

Gerold pressed his lips into a tight line, then turned and strode toward the exit.

21

The Caper

Governor Adelbart wasn't seeing any of the people he passed as he left the Reception Hall. He stopped just inside the Entrance Hall, brought to a halt by Violette's tittering laughter. She was just leaving the ballroom, the usual covey of Volloch women flocking around her. He was wondering how he could extract her from that crowd when he noticed a head of dusky blond curls among the architected black hairdos. Scilla.

Flapping a hand at someone trying to get his attention, he crossed the Entrance Hall, reached into the perfumed cloud and extracted Scilla by her sleeve.

"Governor?" she asked when she saw who it was.

"May I have a moment of your time," he said. He glanced around, then pulled her toward the wall beside the exit. Once they were alone, he glanced over his shoulder, leaned in and said, "Brennerman's here. We'll have to call it off."

"Brennerman? Captain Brennerman?" she asked and frowned. "What is he doing here?"

"I couldn't know, but he knows who you and your companions are. Has been quite insistent that you are rebels. This can't be good."

She gazed past him, her brow furrowed in thought for a moment. Then she rested a hand on his arm and said, "Have you called for your carriage?"

"Yes, but —"

"I'll let Alar know Brennerman is here. He'll know what to do." She gave him a reassuring smile. "You keep following the plan. If something changes, we'll let you know."

"Follow the plan," he said, focusing on her blue eyes. When she nodded, he straightened, tugged on the lapels of his jacket, and gave her a brisk nod. Extending his arm, he allowed Scilla to lay her hand on his forearm and smiled down at her. "Let's get you back to Vi."

As they walked across the Entrance Hall, Gerold emerged from the Reception Hall, appearing as panicked as Adelbart. When he drew near, Scilla whispered to him, "Tell Alar."

***

Alar and Ukrit were standing next to Ukrit's sculpture, anxiously waiting for the show to start. When Adelbart's stilted voice rang out across the Reception Hall, Ukrit looked at Alar and lifted a brow.

Alar shrugged. "Maybe no one will notice. It is Adelbart, after all."

"Let's hope so."

They watched Adelbart fairly flee from the room. When they looked back, Gerold had disappeared.

"Now we wait," Ukrit said.

"Yeah. Now we wait." Alar glanced down at Ukrit's buckskins. "You should go let Violette's entourage see you."

Ukrit swallowed.

"You probably won't have to do anything. It's only if someone wants to follow her upstairs."

"You want me to what… just hang around them? Kind of creepy, don't you think?"

"Yeah. It is. Tell you what, we'll both go. We'll just be two men having a conversation."

With a nod, Ukrit set off toward the exit, Alar trailing behind him. While they walked, Alar studied the guests gathered in small groups viewing the paintings. Several days of festivities looked as if it was finally taking a toll on them. The conversations were less animated than the first two nights and many of them wore their fatigue on their faces.

As they drew near the door, Gerold appeared with an expression that sent a cold shiver through Alar.

"Alar!" he said, then drew him and Ukrit away from the flow of people at the exit.

"What's the matter?" Alar asked him as he glanced around.

"Brennerman is here." Gerold held up a hand when Alar started to respond. "He said he's here on Inquisition business. They're going to arrest you tonight."

"Arrest us for what? Scilla's painting?"

"No, he's going to accuse you of being rebels." When Alar didn't answer right away, he asked, "What should we do? Do we call it off?"

"What exactly did he say?"

"He said he was supposed to instruct Inquisitor Anders to make the arrest."

"Anders?"

"Yes, he's the Inquisitor attending the wedding."

"I've seen him," Ukrit said. "Not often, but he's around."

"He spends most of his time in the ballroom," Gerold said. "Or he's closeted with important people. Should we call it off?"

"No, not yet. Anders hasn't seemed interested in us before tonight. We just have to keep him and Brennerman apart," Alar said. "We have over an hour before Violette and Adelbart head upstairs." He scanned the room and spotted Brennerman watching the three of them. He held his gaze for a moment, then turned back to Gerold. "Let me talk to Holden. See what he thinks. You stay close to Adelbart, in case we have to abort. Ukrit, change of plan. You keep an eye on Brennerman."

"And if I see him talking to Anders?"

"Kill them," Alar said and waited in vain for Ukrit's face to show his shock. Ukrit only nodded. "Joking, Ukrit. If you see them getting together, find me or Scilla and we'll… we'll figure out what to do."

Gerold's face was rigid. "I'll go find the governor." He slipped between Alar and Ukrit and headed off.

Ukrit gave Alar a grim smile. "Now, *this* feels like an *Oss'stera* plan."

"Right. We got this. I'll… You see Brennerman?" When Ukrit nodded, he said, "I'll find Holden."

Though he hadn't seen the groom since he left Violette's room that afternoon, he had a hunch where he would be. He found the lord sitting on the steps to the veranda in the same spot he found him two nights before. Holden stared across the lawn, a snifter containing an amber liquid dangling from his hand. Dropping onto the step next to him, Alar said, "Don't you have any friends?"

Holden startled and turned his head to look at Alar. "Many. However, my friends wouldn't be allowed at such a fancy event as this." He returned his gaze to the lawn and asked, "The plan off to a good start?"

"Well, Adelbart won't win any awards for his acting, but that part worked. However, we have run into a tiny snag."

Holden shifted around to look at him.

"There is a cavalry captain, Brennerman, from Richeleau here and he says he's here to accuse Scilla, Ukrit and me of being rebels. He is going to have Inquisitor Anders arrest us."

Holden stared at him. "Tiny snag?"

"Brennerman can't arrest us himself, so we just need to keep him away from Anders."

"Ah," Holden said and settled himself again. "There we might be in luck. Anders is with Lord Bergamot and a few others of their ilk in Bergamot's library."

"Would you be welcome at that meeting?"

"Me?" When Alar nodded, he said, "I suppose. My father is among the privileged few. I think they're just shooting billiards and swapping lies."

"Okay, this is what we do. You go, keep Anders there until after the second bell. Once Adelbart and Violette are gone, we'll… Well, we'll figure that out when we have to."

"Your show." Holden stood, tossed the contents of his snifter into the shrubbery beside the steps, and climbed the stairs.

***

Brennerman watched Alar, Gerold and another *Alle'oss* man speaking urgently. He recognized the third man from the night of the battle at the fort. He only learned his name when he read the report from the Inquisition's spy on Bergamot's estate. His name was Ukrit. The way they huddled together, their tense posture, the way Alar looked at him… It was suspicious. He glanced at the door, where Adelbart disappeared. Something was up.

When Alar left the room, Brennerman watched him go, then returned his gaze to Ukrit. The red-headed man grinned and raised his tankard in toast. Scowling, Brennerman set off after Alar. By the time he made it to the lobby, Alar had disappeared. Adelbart, looking as if he were on tenterhooks, stood next to a Volloch woman Brennerman recognized from the painting. Standing on the edge of the gaggle was the third rebel. Scilla. He relaxed. Alar wasn't going anywhere without the other two rebels.

He glanced back and found Ukrit doing a poor job of looking nonchalant a few paces behind him. There was still no sign of the Inquisitor, so he crossed the lobby and entered the ballroom.

***

Alar twisted around on the step and watched Holden disappear into the manor, then he turned back and gazed across the lawn. If

Holden could keep Anders busy for a couple of hours, they could get Violette and Adelbart safely off. The bigger issue was whether they should even bother. What Alar, Scilla and Ukrit should do is take advantage of Ander's temporary absence to escape.

Then what? They couldn't take the art, so any coin they hoped to make from it would be lost. He could go find the dowry now, then leave right away. That would be the smart thing to do. But it didn't feel right.

Somehow, abandoning Holden and Violette felt wrong. As they concocted the escape plan that afternoon, he could see Holden's and Violette's mood lighten as they realized they might escape their predicament. He left them chatting like old friends. It was probably foolish, but Alar didn't want to leave them to their fate.

But there was a much more important reason to stick it out. Holden could have had him arrested the night he caught him wandering the estate in the middle of the night. Ever since then, Alar wondered why he hadn't. That afternoon, he saw something in Holden that might explain it. Despite being the beneficiary of the Imperial social hierarchy, he despised everything about it. His sympathies lay more with those of the Brochen caste than his own. Alar was sure that was what he meant when he said his friends wouldn't be welcome at the wedding.

That there were privileged Volloch with those attitudes had come as a bit of a shock to Alar, but it didn't take him long to recognize the implications. If there were more Volloch like Holden, people dissatisfied with the state of the Empire, they represented cracks in what appeared from the outside to be an impervious edifice. If he was right about Holden, it was an opportunity he wouldn't abandon easily.

He looked up as the first bell sounded. Rising, he entered the manor and paused to take in the scene. Violette was leading Adelbart, Scilla and another Volloch woman up the stairs. Adelbart's expression reflected his efforts to keep panic at bay. Violette looked as cool as always. As he watched, she rested her fingertips on the governor's arm and whispered something in his ear. Scilla caught Alar's eye and lifted a brow. He nodded, then went in search of Captain Brennerman, his mind searching for a way out for the three of them.

***

The ballroom was a much bigger space than the room with the art, so even though there might have been the same number of people, it appeared emptier. Brennerman paused in the entrance. He didn't see the inquisitor, but he made his way around the perimeter of the room anyway, glancing back from time to time at his red-headed shadow. Each time, the *Alle'oss* man acknowledged him.

When he finished his circuit of the room, he turned abruptly and closed the distance with his pursuer. Ukrit looked for a moment as if he would turn away, but he remained and even gave Brennerman a smile.

"Captain. What brings you to Lachton?"

"Where did Alar go?" Brennerman asked.

Ukrit looked over Brennerman's shoulder toward the exit and pointed.

Brennerman spun around and found Alar standing in the door. He grinned, waved, then turned and disappeared into the lobby.

Brennerman followed. Alar walked leisurely across the lobby. The rebel paused in the entrance to the room with the art, glanced back at Brennerman, then disappeared into the room.

Brennerman found him waiting at a doorway in the center of the wall opposite the windows. He wanted Brennerman to follow him. He waited until Brennerman was half-way across the room, then he slipped through the door, leaving it ajar. Brennerman hesitated. The rebel was obviously baiting him. He shouldn't follow. His hand rested on his hip where he would normally find his saber. Alar wouldn't have a weapon either.

Curiosity finally getting the better of him, Brennerman cautiously pushed the door open. He had to wait for a line of servants who were breaking down the buffet to pass, then he slipped through the door and crept down a dimly lit hallway.

"Can I help you, sir?" a servant coming toward him asked.

Spotting Alar, looking impatient, leaning against the wall farther down the hall, Brennerman ignored the servant. When the rebel saw Brennerman, he grinned, then disappeared around a corner. Brennerman hurried after him, shoving past a cursing man balancing multiple serving platters. He rounded the corner in time to spot Alar disappearing through a doorway ten paces down the hall. Brennerman sprinted after him and skidded to a stop outside the open door. He peered through the door at what appeared to be a storeroom. The rebel wasn't there. He crept into the room. It was lit only by the low light coming through the open door, but even so, he could tell there was no other exit. He peeked behind the door, then moved deeper into the room, peering into the shadows. The door closed behind him, leaving the room pitch black.

***

Alar slammed the door shut and slipped back into *annen'heim*. Unfortunately, the door didn't have a lock, but the puzzle of what happened might keep the captain occupied long enough for Violette to escape. In the meantime, he needed to get up to Adelbart's room. If all was going according to plan, it was almost time for Adelbart's carriage to arrive.

As soon as he found an empty stretch of hallway, he returned to the physical realm and set off at a run, then slowed to a hurried walk as he crossed the Reception Hall. He was mounting the stairs in the Entrance Hall when he came to a stop. Ukrit stood in the middle of the room, surrounded by several of Violette's friends. As Alar watched, he said something that elicited titters and blushes. One of the women reached up and ran her fingertips along Ukrit's braid.

Shaking his head, Alar headed up the stairs, then entered the guest wing and tapped on Adelbart's door. A moment later, the door cracked open and Gerold's wide eyes peered out. He pulled the door open and stepped back to allow Alar to enter. Violette, hair already short and wearing Gerold's suit, minus the jacket, sat in a chair in the middle of the room. She sat on her hands, lips between her teeth, one knee bouncing. Scilla, a pair of shears in one hand and a comb in the other, stood behind her. She gave Alar a smile and returned to her task. Adelbart stood beside them, a small smile on his face as he watched his soon-to-be fiancée being shorn.

"What about Brennerman?" Gerold asked, wringing his hands at his waist.

Alar glanced at the pendulum clock on the mantle. They had ten minutes before they could expect the carriage to arrive. "I think I've given us enough time. But we need to go now. Where is Violette's friend?"

The door to what Alar presumed was the bedroom opened and the woman he saw earlier with Violette and Scilla appeared, wearing Violette's dress. Her face was long and narrow, where Violette's was round, but the advantage to all Volloch having black hair was that they were nearly indistinguishable from a distance. At least they were to Alar.

"Scilla?" Alar asked.

"Done." Scilla set the comb and shears aside, then brushed stray hairs from Violette's shoulders. "That's the best I can do."

"It'll be good enough from a distance," Alar said. "Everyone ready?"

Violette rose and allowed Adelbart to help her into her jacket. When it was on, she turned and studied herself in a full-length mirror, turning this way and that and brushing at her hair with her fingers. Alar had seen her smile as they came up with the escape plan, but the smile that appeared as she bent forward and examined her hair was luminous. Turning to Adelbart, she asked, "What do you think?"

"Very daring," Adelbart said, returning her smile.

A knock on the door brought a yelp from Adelbart.

"Don't worry," Gerold said. "That should be the servants for the luggage."

"Alright," Alar said. "Places everyone."

Violette's friend moved with Adelbart to stand in front of the fireplace, her back to the door. Scilla returned the chair to the desk and sat. Alar and Violette entered the bedroom, closed the door, and pressed their ears to the door. A giggle escaped Violette's lips. She pressed her hand to her mouth, her eyes opening wide.

A moment later, Gerold opened the door. "They're gone."

Alar entered the sitting room and looked around at everyone. "Let's go."

***

Brennerman stumbled blindly toward the exit in the dark, hands out. Finding the door, he yanked it open and stepped into the hall. No one was there. He sprinted back to the intersection and looked in both directions. Only a pair of startled servants looked back at him. Alar was nowhere to be seen. He returned to the storage room and peered inside. Hand on the door to ensure it didn't close, he stepped across the threshold and searched the shadowy corners. The walls were lined with shelves piled high with serving dishes, gravy boats, plates, crystal goblets, teacups, and silverware. There was nowhere a man could hide. Stepping further into the room, he peered behind the door and examined the walls. There didn't appear to be any hidden doors. How did the rebel get past him?

Returning to the main hallway, he followed the servants carrying dishes until he exited onto a small patio between the manor house and the kitchen. If Alar came this way, he was long gone. The rebels knew he was here, and he foolishly told Gerold why he was here. And he allowed Alar to lead him on a wild goose chase to give them time to escape.

Turning around, he hurried down the hall until he arrived in the room with the art. It was as crowded as before, and there was no sign of the *Alle'oss* or the inquisitor. Walking as fast as he could without attracting attention, he entered the lobby in time to see Adelbart leaving through the front door. He was about to follow when Gerold appeared at the top of the stairs on the balcony. Brennerman watched him run down the stairs and stride across the lobby after Adelbart.

By the time Brennerman made it to the exit, Adelbart and Gerold were descending the stairs of the veranda together. He stepped onto the veranda and hesitated. He didn't know where the rebels were, but if he was right about the conspiracy, Gerold almost certainly would. He was about to set off in pursuit when he glanced back into the manor and caught a glimpse of a blue cavalry uniform.

***

Alar and Violette followed Adelbart and Scilla into the hall of the guest wing but turned in the opposite direction and made their way to the door to the servants' staircase at the end of the hall. "Are these stairs used often?" he whispered.

"Yes. But probably not tonight."

She reached for the doorknob, but Alar caught her wrist, shook his head, and pressed his ear to the door. Hearing nothing, he eased the door open and peeked inside.

"I told you they wouldn't be used tonight."

Ignoring her rebuke, Alar took the lamp from her and led her down the dark staircase. The stairs descended to a narrow hallway that extended the length of the manor between the ballroom and the exterior wall.

They were halfway down, the bottom of the stairs lost in the shadows outside the light from their lamp, when Alar heard them. It was the hiss of someone shushing someone else. He stopped so fast, Violette stepped on his heel and pushed him, so he nearly tumbled down the steep stairs. With a yelp, he spun around, took Violette's arm, and shoved her back up the stairs.

"What?" she asked and resisted. But then the thud of feet climbing the steps melted her resistance. She turned and ran, with Alar right behind her.

"Violette!" a man called, the voice sounding as if he were right behind them. Not a guard. A guard would have used her title.

The thud of their pursuers' footsteps were right behind them as they neared the top. Just before Violette reached the top of the steps, Alar stumbled and dropped the lamp. It didn't shatter, but he heard a cry of surprise behind him. It gave him enough time to burst through the door and throw his shoulder against it. He fished in his pocket for the key Violette gave him. There was a thud on the door, but the stairs were steep and whoever was on the other side couldn't get enough leverage.

"Violette! Listen to reason," said a man's muffled voice.

Alar finally retrieved the key and locked the door.

"That witch!" Violette blurted.

Ignoring her, Alar asked, "Are there stairs in the family wing?"

Violette glared at him, then understanding penetrated her anger. "Yes."

Another thud sounded on the door and a muffled voice shouted, "Violette!"

Alar took Violette's hand and pulled her into motion toward the exit. They paused at the door that was open to the balcony and peeked through. No one was on the balcony, but the Entrance Hall was busy.

"They'll see me." Now that Violette's anger had subsided, panic rushed in to take its place.

Alar glanced past her when whoever was locked on the servants' stairs began to hammer on the door. What worried him was what was waiting for them on the other side of the balcony.

He pulled her around to his side. "Stay against the wall and keep your head down. Don't run. Stay even with me."

"Right. Right," she said, nodding.

"Let's go." He peeked onto the balcony one more time, then led them into the open. He strode purposefully, staying close to the wall. Violette pressed herself against his shoulder, her eyes on the floor. Just before they entered the family wing, he glanced down into the entrance hall and glimpsed Brennerman standing in the door to the veranda, looking stunned at something he saw in the Entrance Hall.

Alar peeked back through the door as he shut it, but before he could turn away, Violette shouted.

"You!"

Alar whirled around. Violette's friend, the one wearing her dress, stood frozen, five paces down the hall. Her mouth worked beneath wide eyes, but no sound emerged. Violette strode forward, fists clenched at her side. The woman turned to flee, but Violette caught her by one of her puffy sleeves. When the woman turned back, Violette slapped her, producing a resounding crack.

Stunned, Alar froze until Violette looked back at him and said, "Get the key."

Alar nodded, his hand going to his pocket. Violette took hold of the woman's arm and hauled her down the hall. She glanced over her shoulder at Alar and said, "Come on." Stopping in front of the door to her rooms, she nodded to the lock. "Unlock it."

Alar unlocked the door, pushed it open, and stepped out of the way.

Violette shoved the woman inside. She stumbled on the edge of a rug and fell. "If you keep quiet, I won't ruin your father," Violette said, her voice steely. "You know what I know about him."

"We were just worried about your reputation, Violette!" the woman said, tears streaking her face. "I'm sorry!"

Violette yanked the door close. "Lock it." She turned without waiting and strode toward the servants' stairs.

Alar caught up with her as she reached for the doorknob. "So, the people waiting for us back —"

"Her brothers." Violette met his eyes. "We can only hope she didn't tell anyone else."

"We have to hurry." Alar cracked the door open, and they peered down steep stairs that disappeared into inky darkness. He dropped their lamp in the other stairs. "Leave the door open," Alar said and led her down.

Despite his thumping heart urging him to hurry, after the first ten steps, they were forced to move slowly, hands on the railing, feeling for the narrow treads with their toes. Violette rested her hand on his back. Alar expected someone to appear at any moment, but when they arrived at the bottom, no one waited for them. They were in a hallway. Light from one end of the hall provided just enough light for their pale faces to appear ghostlike.

"Which way?" he murmured.

She nudged him to the right. "This ends in the hall that leads from the Reception Hall to the kitchen."

Alar knew where they were. It was the hall he led Brennerman into. He eased her behind him. Noticing her frown, he whispered, "If anyone is at the end of the hall, it would be better if they saw me instead of you."

Her frown smoothed.

He led her down the hall, noting the open door to the storage room where he confined Brennerman. He peeked into the main hallway as a servant passed. Seeing no one else, he led Violette after the servant toward the exit. When the man glanced over his shoulder, Alar gave him a wide smile. Violette followed so closely, she bumped his back and stepped on his heels.

When they entered a familiar pantry, three chattering servants entered through the door that exited out onto the courtyard before the kitchen. Alar turned sideways, allowing Violette to slide between him and shelves stacked with clay pots and casks.

"Alar?"

Alar froze. "Trell?" He tried a grin and nodded to the others whose names he couldn't bring to mind.

Trell grinned and leaned over, trying to see who was hiding behind him. He felt Violette turning around to face the shelves. "What are you up to, Alar?" His brows bobbed.

Alar opened his mouth, but nothing came to mind. With the servants staring expectantly at him, he leaned forward and whispered to Trell, "Tell you about it tomorrow. Quite the story. But at the moment, I'm in a bit of a hurry." He winked and gave Trell a conspiratorial smile.

The grin which fell away when Alar whispered returned slowly to Trell's face. Finally, he nodded and said, "Okay." He turned to his companions. "Let's go. Just a few more dishes to go." He winked at Alar as he disappeared down the hall.

"Dear Daga," Violette whispered as she shoved her way past Alar to get to the exit.

Lights blazed in the kitchen across the patio, but only Ukrit standing against a door on the far side of the patio was visible. When they burst out of the door, Ukrit startled. He pointed at Violette, who had taken off at a run, then pointed the other way.

"That's the wrong way," Alar shouted as he took off after her.

She led him around the exterior of the family's wing, then paused and gazed across the lawn at the gardens.

"We're so close," she said. "It'll take too long to go around the stables. We can't be too late. We just can't."

Alar edged out into the yard until he saw Adelbart and Gerold waiting where the drive forked. A carriage was approaching on the drive. They were supposed to get far enough from the manor that no one would recognize Violette, but they were out of time. "Let's go," he said and set off across the lawn. Reaching back, he took her arm and pulled her around to his side, away from the veranda. "Keep your head down. Hurry, but don't run."

"I know!"

The veranda was full of people. They passed within five paces of a couple strolling toward the garden. Fortunately, no one paid more than a passing interest in them. As they neared their destination, Alar was forced to clamp a hand on Violette's arm to keep her from running.

While Gerold flagged down the carriage, Adelbart gazed in the opposite direction, toward the stables where he expected Violette to arrive from.

"Governor," Alar called.

Adelbart startled and spun around. Violette almost leapt through the open carriage door before Alar caught her. She gave him a panicked look, but Alar only took Gerold's arm and pulled him around so that he blocked Alar's view of the veranda. "Get in," he said to Violette. With the view of the door blocked by Gerold and Adelbart, Violette launched herself through the door. A giddy smile on his sweaty face, Adelbart followed. Alar looked up at the driver and put his finger to his lips. The man hesitated, then shrugged, looked forward and flicked the reins. Adi's and Vi's giggles emerged from the carriage as it pulled away.

"Hope they pull it together long enough to get his baggage loaded," Gerold said with a worried frown.

Alar watched the carriage, heart thrumming. He had a feeling Violette would make sure they did. "Come on." He set off across the lawn toward the gardens.

22

Common Causes

Brennerman caught up to the man wearing cavalry blue as he was entering the ballroom. He was with another man in a suit, but Brennerman didn't look at him as he tapped on the trooper's shoulder. When the man turned toward him, the greeting Brennerman was about to offer stuck in his throat.

It was Belden Brucker. Brennerman's eyes went automatically to the insignia of rank on Belden's collar and was stunned to find the Imperial Eagle. It meant Brucker was a general, and not just any general. He was in overall command of the Imperial Cavalry, the position held by Victor Storm.

"Ah," Belden said. "*Captain* Brennerman. Where is your salute?"

Brennerman's hand came up mechanically, relying on years of conditioning in the absence of conscious direction. Belden let him hold the salute for a long moment, then released him with a lazy return salute.

"Brennerman?" the man standing beside Belden asked in a booming voice.

Brennerman's head swiveled toward him and felt his heart lurch. Lord Brucker, Belden's father. The man who destroyed Brennerman's life.

The two men waited, but when Brennerman only gaped at them, they scoffed and started to turn away.

"You're a general," Brennerman blurted stupidly.

"Yes," Belden said, turning back to face Brennerman. "As usual, your grasp of the obvious is astounding."

Brennerman made a vague gesture. "How?"

Lord Brucker guffawed and clapped his son on the back. "I'm beginning to see what you mean about him." Then he bent toward Brennerman and spoke loud enough for bystanders to hear. "The emperor recognized my son's worth. That's how."

Belden smirked. "Serving in Argren, you probably haven't heard the emperor promoted Victor Storm to Marshal of the Armed Forces for the duration of this business with the Kaileuk. That left a vacancy at the top of the cavalry arm." He shrugged.

"But… *you*?!" Brennerman asked, knowing he was flirting dangerously with insubordination but unable to stop himself.

The two men's expressions hardened. Lord Brucker took a step toward Brennerman, but his son put his hand on his shoulder to stop him. He looked Brennerman up and down. "Captain, I'll put your rudeness down to surprise. I'm not sure how you managed to inveigle your way into this affair, but you are above your station. If you turn around and walk away, I won't change my mind."

Brennerman glanced at Lord Brucker's smirking face, then turned on his heel and strode toward the exit. Their laughter chased him out the door. He crossed the veranda, nearly tripped descending the steps, and strode blindly away from the manor, only stopping when he reached the middle of the circular lawn created by the driveway. When a carriage making its way around the left side of the circle drew his eye, he noticed two familiar men walking slowly toward the garden. It was dark, but even in the moonlight, he recognized Alar's long blond hair.

He watched them, surprised he had no impulse to follow. What did that mean? Letting his head fall back, he gazed up at the stars. Belden was two years ahead of him at the Imperial Military Academy. Normally, a plebe, a first year, would never come to the attention of men like Belden and his entourage. But Brennerman's excellence caught their attention. At first, he was flattered to be allowed into the fringes of their circle. But it was the worst thing that could have happened to him.

Conscious of his low caste, Brennerman tried to hide the fact he was Baird. It was a mistake. Caste and social position were important enough to the Volloch they had many ways to discover a person's true status. When they discovered he was hiding his caste, they turned on him. It was worse than if he simply admitted it to begin with. Social humiliation was their primary weapon, but it wasn't the only one. The instructors ignored what was happening. Some of them joined in, no doubt hoping to curry favor with Lord Brucker's son. They made his life a misery.

Fortunately, after Belden and his immediate cohort graduated at the end of Brennerman's first year, the intensity of the harassment diminished, allowing Brennerman's quality to shine through. By the time he graduated, two years later, he had pulled himself from the mire they threw him into.

After Victor Storm promoted him to captain, Brennerman entertained fantasies of meeting his chief tormentor as his superior. It never crossed his mind anyone in the Imperial Cavalry would reward that indolent prima donna with a promotion. But not only had they promoted him, the emperor made him a general over the heads of much more qualified men. And he wore the eagle on his collar.

It had to be a sop to his father, Lord Brucker. Bergamot was a powerful man, but his influence paled compared to Brucker. That they would elevate a man so obviously incompetent to curry favor with a man like Brucker was... He lowered his gaze and shook his head in disbelief. Coming on the heels of everything else he experienced recently, it felt like the final straw.

Brennerman's career was over. They might let him stay in command of his company in Argren, but he would remain in that backwater until he resigned his commission. The promise he made to his wife that he would bring her honor would go unfulfilled. Turning back to the manor, he gazed through the open doors at the frolicking upper caste Volloch. He promised she would one day be welcome among their kind. He would make it so by proving his worth. It was the reason he still tried, despite the petty humiliations, the insults, the disappointments. Striving to fulfill the promise was the only way he could keep his wife's memory alive.

"Captain Brennerman."

Brennerman turned his head toward the speaker. Alar watched him with an uncertain smile on his face. "Alar," he said and returned his gaze to the manor as the Bruckers appeared on the veranda. "Lord Brucker." He glanced at Alar, who stepped up beside him. Seeing the rebel's uncertain frown, he said, "The loud one."

"Someone you know?"

Brennerman nodded. "He killed my son." He paused, then clarified. "Technically, the driver of his carriage did, but they were driving too fast because Brucker was late for a social engagement."

Alar was quiet for a moment. "I'm sorry."

Brennerman let out a soft chuckle. A true sentiment from the rebel? It didn't matter. His grin faded. "It destroyed my wife. We managed to stay together for a few months, but I had to leave when the war started. When I returned, she was gone." He watched the Bruckers, now the center of a group of fawning Volloch. "I never found out what happened to her."

"What happened to Brucker?"

"Nothing."

"Why?"

"He's one of the most powerful men in the Empire." Brennerman gestured with both hands to Bergamot's estate. "He could buy Bergamot." He chuckled bitterly and looked at Alar again. "What would you expect to happen to such a man in the Empire?"

"No more than what happened to the men who slaughtered my family."

Brennerman held his gaze for a long moment, searching his face for animosity, anger, resignation. But all he saw was a quiet resolve. A day from the previous autumn came into his mind. Images of smoke, blood and broken bodies from his raid on Lirantok. Those *Alle'oss* didn't die at his hand, but he was responsible. What seeds of hatred had he sown that day? Whose lives did he put asunder? And who could blame them for wanting justice?

Putting the manor and the carefree lords and ladies to his back, he turned and watched a carriage receding on the drive.

"So, what is it that brought you to the wedding?" Alar asked.

Brennerman heard the wariness behind the question and understood where it came from. The moment had come to make a choice. He had plenty of time to think about what Commander Krueger told him about the *Alle'oss* artists. The arrest warrant would list rebellion and treasonous acts as their crimes, but it was a charade. They only wanted an excuse to eliminate *Alle'oss* artists.

Brennerman was not naïve. Though he never encountered it before, he was sure this sort of subterfuge was a common Inquisition tactic. And it was one Brennerman might once have supported if it meant truly eliminating threats to the Empire. But there was one thing the commander said that nagged at him. "Whether the art they create for this wedding represents a threat to the Empire is immaterial." Brennerman saw the painting. There was no crime. Krueger intended to arrest them for potential future crimes only because they were artists.

They were rebels. Brennerman may be the only one who believed that, but he was surprised to discover he didn't care anymore. Let them cast themselves against the Imperial edifice. It was futile, but he reckoned men like Alar had as much right to their anger as he did.

And besides, his career was over. Ruining these three people's lives wouldn't change that.

He looked at Alar and said, "Nothing. Nothing worth mentioning." He extended his hand to Alar. Alar hesitated, then took it.

***

Alar watched Brennerman walking toward the stables, as surprised as if the captain had grown another head. He noticed the captain standing alone when he looked back to watch Adelbart's baggage being loaded. Confronting him was a snap decision. It was risky, but he needed to know Brennerman's intentions so he could plan their next move.

Leaving Gerold under the willow tree where Alar eavesdropped on the three Desulti during the opening ball, he approached the captain. The interaction confirmed something he always believed. Everyone had a story, and it was always useful to learn that story to understand what made them tick.

Brennerman's story was tragic. It didn't redeem him, in Alar's mind. He had committed too many crimes against the *Alle'oss*. But unlike many of his fellow rebels, Alar didn't expect purity from *Oss'stera's* allies. To win their freedom, they would need the help of many people. People who had their own motives to resist the Empire. As unlikely as it seemed, the captain who was such a bogeyman to the *Alle'oss* in Argren, had an epiphany. Watching him fade into the shadows, Alar hoped it was a lasting change. Maybe Brennerman would discover he had common cause with the people he tormented.

The sound of the man Brennerman called Brucker guffawing drew his attention. He watched for a moment, then turned away and headed to the willow tree. He needed to get Gerold up the servants' stairs to his room. And soon. It was growing late, and he still had work to do. He found Gerold sprawled across a bench like an old, frayed afghan.

"They're gone," Gerold said, his voice flat.

"That's a good thing, isn't it?"

Gerold's gaze wandered up to Alar's face. "Yes. Though I worry about what is to come."

Alar took him by the arm and pulled him up. "Don't worry about the future. Plan for it."

As they ducked beneath the drooping branches, Gerold said, "Yes, yes, of course." They were making their way around the family's wing of the manor house, headed to the entrance to the servants' stairs, when Gerold asked, "So, what is the plan? For tomorrow anyway?"

"Tomorrow, we — Scilla, Ukrit and I — act as surprised as everyone else. You stay in your room until after the midday meal. We'll bring you something to eat. When someone asks you what you know, tell them you wish to speak to Lord Bergamot in private. Tell him Violette and Adelbart confessed their love for one another and are going to be married."

"Married? So soon?"

There was still activity in the kitchen, but the courtyard was deserted. Alar unlocked the door to the servant's stairs that led to the guest wing, pulled it open and stepped back to allow Gerold to enter. "Never lie if you don't have to."

Gerold hesitated before entering. "But Bergamot may send men on horseback to bring her back."

"He might. But they won't catch them until they're nearing Richeleau. Can you imagine if Bergamot were to forcibly stop a carriage conveying an Imperial governor?" Alar gazed steadily at Gerold. "It's a risk, but lying to a man like Bergamot would be a mistake."

Gerold nodded, looking somewhat relieved, then he entered the door. Halfway up the stairs, he asked, "How am I getting to Richeleau?

Alar, following behind him, grinned. "We'll arrange a ride."

When they arrived at the top, Alar extracted the key Violette gave him and unlocked the door he locked earlier. He led Gerold down the hall to his room. The governor's assistant followed without another word. Just before the door closed to Gerold's room, Alar glimpsed him flopping like a wet rag onto a divan.

One more task to accomplish. He exited the guest wing onto the balcony and looked down into the Entrance Hall. It didn't appear anyone had noticed Violette's absence yet. Scilla and Ukrit stood near the exit. He waved to get their attention, then raised a fist, the sign *Oss'stera* used to indicate success. The change in their posture was instantaneous. Ukrit headed directly to the Reception Hall, undoubtedly in search of one last ale. Scilla blew Alar a kiss with a smile, then followed her brother.

Alar crossed the balcony, glanced around to make sure he wasn't observed, then slipped into the family wing. There were doors open down the hall that led to the rooms he searched the first night he was here. He heard low voices, but he didn't see anyone, so he hurried down the hall that contained the family's bedrooms. As he passed Violette's room, he grinned, wondering if her friend was still in there. The door to the servants' stairs was closed.

He listened at the door to Bergamot's bedroom, then slipped the key into the lock and twisted it. The room was empty. The chest was visible in moonlight on the floor at the foot of the bed. He unlocked it, lifted the lid, then had to lock his legs in place to stay upright. Even in moonlight, the gold glittered. There must be hundreds of gold Imperial Eagles. His awe was tempered by the smallest flash of anger. This man was willing to pay this much just to marry off his daughter. How much wealth did one family need? Just the coin in this chest was enough to feed and house all of *Oss'stera* for years.

But he didn't have time for such thoughts now. He propped the lid open, counted out ten coins and slipped them into his pants pockets. That was the amount Violette and Holden agreed to let him take. He was reaching for the lid when he hesitated, his eyes on the gold. Removing ten coins barely made a dent in the pile. If Bergamot was going to miss them, he would miss twenty just as easily as ten. Counting out ten more coins, he divided them among his jacket pockets.

He eased the lid down, locked the chest, then hurried to the door. Hearing no sound, he cracked it open, peered out, and found a guard glowering down at him. He stepped into *annen'heim*. Once in the realm of the dead, he clenched his teeth. So what if he escaped? Scilla and Ukrit couldn't disappear into *annen'heim,* and they would certainly take the blame if they couldn't capture Alar. Resigned, he recrossed the boundary.

When he saw the guard's eyes widen, he almost laughed. What would that have looked like? Even though Alar barely moved, it must have looked like Alar flickered. He pulled the door open and adopted his most winning smile. "*Lehasa.*"

The guard's frown resurfaced from beneath his surprise. "Lord Bergamot wants to see you," he growled.

"Lord Bergamot?"

The man stepped aside and gestured to the door on the opposite wall. It was the room Trell said was Bergamot's private study.

"Oh, Lord Bergamot."

The guard knocked on the door, then pushed it open after a muffled response from inside. He stepped back and waved Alar inside.

Alar entered, expecting the guard to follow, but when the door closed behind him, he glanced over his shoulder and found himself alone.

"Alar."

Alar looked toward the voice. Lord Bergamot stood behind a small bar in front of shelves containing a variety of bottles and decanters. The room was illuminated by several lamps mounted on the walls and moonlight coming through double doors open to a balcony. The lord was pouring an amber liquid into a snifter from a crystal decanter.

"Lord Bergamot," Alar said and crossed the room.

Bergamot held the bottle up and lifted his brows. When Alar nodded, he retrieved another snifter and poured a small amount into it. Setting the decanter aside and inserting the stopper, he handed the snifter to Alar, lifted the other in toast, and sipped.

Alar took a sip and nearly choked. His throat was on fire. He tasted brandy before, but that was an *Alle'oss* style that apparently had far less alcohol.

Bergamot laughed and came out from behind the bar. He put his arm around Alar's shoulders and led him firmly out onto the balcony.

When they stood at the railing, Bergamot relinquished his hold on Alar and looked down. He gestured with his glass for Alar to look as well. The kitchen was across an alley paved with brick. They could just make out the edge of the courtyard between the kitchen and the manor house.

"Pay attention," Bergamot said. "It should be any moment."

The courtyard was as empty as it was when Alar led Gerold through it earlier. A few servants emerged from the kitchen, but they passed below the balcony without drawing the lord's attention. Alar was beginning to wonder what he was supposed to see when two familiar people appeared from the kitchen and headed between the wing of the manor house and the kitchen. They looked as if they were heading to the servants' quarters.

"There," Bergamot said and sipped his brandy.

Alar glanced at him. "Trell?"

"No, the other one."

"Vint." He was one of the servants Alar met while tagging along with Trell.

"*Brother* Vint," Bergamot said with a small lift of his brows.

Alar stared at him, then watched the pair disappear around the corner of the kitchen. He looked at Bergamot again. "Brother? Inquisition?"

Bergamot nodded. "Inquisition spies are everywhere, even on the staffs of powerful lords."

This was a revelation. Alar never considered the Inquisition would feel the need to spy on wealthy Volloch. After all, weren't they on the same side? "Why?"

"Leverage." Bergamot shrugged. "He's looking for something the Inquisition can hold over my head. To gain influence over me."

Alar considered this while he sipped the brandy. Ready for the burn this time, he managed to swallow without embarrassing himself. "How do you know about him?"

"I have a spy in the local Inquisition house. I knew about Vint before he arrived. I could have refused to hire him, but they would have just tried again. Better the spy you know than the one you don't."

Alar stared at him. "How do you Volloch live like this?"

Bergamot laughed, a sound so free and easy Alar found himself grinning. The lord turned away from the railing and gestured for Alar to follow.

Alar entered the study, wondering what the lord was up to.

Bergamot sat in one of the squashy chairs in front of the hearth. Alar took another.

"Why are you telling me this?" Alar asked.

"Because I approve of what you arranged between Violette and Adelbart. It demonstrates a surprising resourcefulness. In fact, I've watched you operate with some admiration since you arrived."

Alar froze, his snifter halfway to his mouth. Seeing no hostility in Bergamot's expression, he took a sip and asked, "How?"

Bergamot shrugged. "In the Empire, you must always assume the walls have ears." He settled himself in his chair. "Violette and Adelbart... It is a clever solution to an almost intractable problem. I have to admit, I'm a bit chagrined I had not thought of it." He took a sip and gestured with the glass. "Of course, Violette's mother will not approve. She and Adelbart's mother..." He paused and gazed over Alar's head. "Well, let's just say sneaking my daughter out in the middle of the night was likely the only way you could have brought those two together." He gave an odd shake of his head and focused on Alar. "Not looking forward to tomorrow. It's going to be an ugly scene. Angry wife. Wedding guests. The gossip mill will be primed for months. Years." He shuddered and sipped his brandy, then grinned and lifted the glass in a toast. "Might as well enjoy a quiet moment while it lasts, eh?"

"Then why do you approve?"

"Gossip doesn't worry me. There will always be gossip. My wife will eventually accept the situation." Bergamot smiled. "I believe Violette will be happy and isn't that the most important thing?"

"Is it?"

"We aren't all as cold-blooded as we appear." Bergamot cocked his head. "Although I will admit to an ulterior motive. We both know who will be in charge in that marriage. My daughter will be the governor of Argren in all but name."

Alar was about to sip his brandy, but he lowered the glass and studied Bergamot. "And that's important to you?"

"Power, Alar, is always important. Never forget that. Even if one doesn't know to what use it can be put. There are many in the Empire who would say it's only Argren, but I believe that is shortsighted. Argren has a lot to offer. There are riches to be made." He gave Alar a sly grin and said, "Especially for a clever young man."

Before Alar could think of a response, Bergamot set his snifter aside, stood and invited Alar to stand. He rested a hand on Alar's shoulder and urged him toward the door. "Now, Violette's mother will need someone to blame for her daughter's disappearance and it won't be me." They came to a stop in front of the door. "I'm afraid I will have to let Olson go."

"But Olson had nothing to do with it."

"Of course not. But someone's head will have to roll. Better him than you, right?" He grinned at Alar's frown. "I wouldn't worry about Olson. A man with such extraordinary gifts will always find a place." He winked and took Alar's snifter.

While Bergamot reached for the doorknob, Alar asked, "Why did you tell me about Vint?"

Pausing with his hand on the knob, Bergamot said, "Oh, right. I nearly forgot." He released the doorknob. "Your companions are really quite extraordinary artists. It may be immodest of me to claim a certain knowledge of such things. I'm a patron to many less talented artists."

Alar felt a surge of hope. A wealthy patron would be a steady source of income.

"Unfortunately, I can't find my way to supporting an *Alle'oss* artist of the new school." He grinned. "Not openly, in any case. Let us keep the small donation from Violette's dowry our little secret."

Alar studied his face. He could try to deny the theft, but he had a feeling he didn't need to. Letting a small grin curve his lips, he said, "I'm sure Scilla and Ukrit will appreciate your support."

"I'm sure. One more thing. Vint reported the fact there were new school artists at the wedding to the Inquisition. Inquisitor Anders and I had an interesting discussion about what was to be done with Scilla's painting. Holden spoke eloquently in her favor, by the way. Fortunately, Anders is a more reasonable man than many in the Inquisition and he found nothing that would require Inquisition action." He gave Alar a pointed look. "But they will not forget. Make sure Scilla and Ukrit don't produce anything that would change their minds."

"Thank you, Lord Bergamot. We'll take your advice to heart."

Bergamot opened the door to reveal the guard waiting in the hall. "Please, collect Alar's companions and escort them to their rooms."

"Should I stand guard at their door?"

"That won't be necessary."

The guard couldn't hide his surprise.

Bergamot said to Alar, "I would prefer you and the others stay out of sight for now."

"Of course." Alar stuck out his hand. When Bergamot raised his hand, Alar took his forearm in the *Alle'oss* fashion.

23

Plans

Alar opened his eyes to Scilla's smiling face. He grinned lazily, wrapped his arms around her, and pulled her on top of him.

"Hey, hey," he heard Ukrit say. "You two aren't married yet."

Scilla rolled across him and propped herself on her elbow against the wall. "We pulled it off."

"All according to plan," Ukrit said. He was sitting on his bed across the room. "Maybe. I assume because we're still here, you took care of Brennerman and the inquisitor somehow."

By the time the guard herded them back to their rooms, it was after the fourth bell and Alar only told them they were safe. He was too exhausted to explain everything. "It was very strange. Brennerman seems to have had a change of heart."

"About?" Scilla asked.

"I'm not entirely sure. But he left without talking to the inquisitor." He told him about his conversation with the cavalry captain.

After he fell silent, they considered, then Ukrit said, "That doesn't absolve him of what he did in Lirantok." It was during a raid led by Captain Brennerman that Scilla's and Ukrit's parents were killed and their home burned.

"No, nor other crimes against the *Alle'oss*," Alar said. "But if Brennerman can have a change of heart, then maybe others can as well."

"Maybe," Ukrit said, doubtfully. "What about the dowry? You said you got the coin."

"I did," Alar said. "But I got caught." He explained what happened and everything Bergamot told him. When he was done, they remained silent as they digested the news.

"So, what is his game?" Ukrit asked. "I'm having a hard time believing a Volloch lord is a good guy."

"I'm not really sure, but I got the impression he knew exactly what we were doing with the governor. I mean the black market deal. He obviously knew we stole from the dowry," Alar said. "He doesn't have to be a good guy for his goals to align with ours." As soon as he said it, he remembered having the same thoughts about Ragan. Ragan, Brennerman, Bergamot. They all had their own goals. Their motives might not align perfectly with *Oss'stera's*, but did that matter? "There are possibilities here."

"Possibilities?"

When Alar, staring at the ceiling, didn't answer, Scilla knocked on the wall behind her. "What worries me is the bit about the walls having ears. How much did he hear?"

"Apparently, not enough to get us arrested," Ukrit said. "Once again, blind luck is on our side."

"Spirit's luck," Alar said, then focused on Ukrit. "I have a feeling Bergamot knows a lot more than he's letting on." He rolled out of bed. "I'm hungry. Let's go see if there is any fallout yet."

A sharp knock on the door brought them all to a standstill.

"Spoke too soon," Scilla said, and scrambled to sit on the edge of the bed.

Alar lifted his hands in a calming gesture and went to the door. Cracking it open, he peered out and found Helmut standing in the hall.

"Helmut." Alar opened the door wider and forced some humor into this voice.

Helmut's eyes flicked down to Alar, then he gathered himself, stared straight ahead and said, "Lord Bergamot has ordered me to escort you from the grounds." He finally met Alar's eyes. "Immediately."

"What about our art?" Scilla asked after the words sank in.

"There is a carriage waiting. Your works have been loaded already." When no one moved, he said, "Now!"

That got them moving. Fortunately, packing their few belongings only took moments. As they were leaving, Alar asked, "Breakfast?"

"No," Helmut said.

It was early enough that the estate was eerily silent as they crossed the lawn from the artists' dormitory to the drive, where a carriage waited. Ukrit's sculpture and Scilla's painting were lashed to the luggage rack on the top. When the driver asked where they wanted to go, Alar told him the Tipsy Rooster Tavern on River Road.

Helmut opened the door and held out a hand to help Scilla step up into the carriage. Then he stepped back and held the door for Alar and Ukrit to climb in on their own. It wasn't until they were on the road beyond the gate that anyone spoke.

"You think they're taking us to prison?" Ukrit asked.

"I doubt they would have allowed us to keep the art, if that was the case," Scilla said.

"The Inquisition might be confiscating it," Ukrit said.

"Bergamot said they decided it was okay," Alar said.

They watched the city pass by through the windows. As they entered more familiar neighborhoods, they smiled at one another. If they were heading to the Inquisition, they were taking a long way around. When the Tipsy Rooster came into view, the driver pulled the team to a stop and shouted, "Everyone out!"

As they clambered out, Alar said, "Scilla, go get us a room." He handed her a pouch with an odd assortment of coins, then he and Ukrit unloaded the art while the driver looked on impatiently.

The carriage was rounding a corner onto a side street when Scilla emerged from the tavern. Ukrit grinned at them and said, "We got away with it."

"Never had a doubt," Alar said with a wide smile.

"Now what?" Scilla asked.

"You get us a room?"

"The only room left was a common room on the top floor. Four straw mattresses on the floor. The owner remembers us. Thought he was going to have a heart attack when I handed him the coin."

"Okay," Alar said. "Let's get this all up there. Then we'll go see if we still have horses and a wagon."

***

They picked up fried rolls with goat cheese from a street vendor on the way. The shack was just as dilapidated as they left it. In the back yard, Fin was brushing one of the horses down. When he heard them, he looked over his shoulder, then turned to face them.

"They're still here," Ukrit said.

Fin scowled. "'Bout time you got back. Only got another day of feed and they nearly bit the grass to the roots." He gave Sigurd another swipe with the currycomb. "Plus, some little man with a big red beard came looking for you. A really angry man."

"Taavi?" Ukrit asked. Seeing Alar's question in his expression, he said, "Our barge captain."

"Didn't say his name, but he said he wants to see you and you would know where to find him."

Alar looked at Scilla, who nodded, then approached the boy and rested a hand on the horse's rump. "It was Fin, right?"

Fin squinted up at him and nodded.

"We really appreciate the job you've done. It's obvious Sigurd and Olafson were in good hands." He grinned at Fin, but the boy only gave him a quizzical frown. "We're going to need people we can trust.

People who know how to get a job done. How would you feel about working for us full time?"

Fin paused and gestured to the horse with the currycomb. "Taking care of the horses?"

"In part. But there would be other tasks."

"You pay me?"

"Of course."

"How much?" A speculative gleam softening the boy's frown.

Alar exchanged a grin with Scilla. "We'll negotiate. Are you interested?"

Fin hesitated, then gestured to the shack. "Can I keep sleeping in the shack?"

Alar glanced at the ramshackle building. "You don't have a home to go to?"

Fin shook his head.

"I think we can do better than this old shack. What do you say?"

The elements of a grin played at the edges of the boy's expression before being banished. "Okay."

"You can start by helping us hitch the horses to the wagon."

***

They drove north on the road that ran along the western bank of the river. Ukrit drove with Fin beside him on the driver's bench. Alar and Scilla sat, shoulders pressed together, in the bed of the wagon. The trees pressed up against the side of the road opposite the river thinned, then disappeared as a great body of water came into view.

"There it is," Scilla said. "That's the fishing village."

As they drew closer, the pitiful state of the village became apparent. A few people were unloading fish from a small sloop and others were tending a smoke hut. But most of the buildings appeared to have been abandoned for some time.

"That's Taavi's barge," Ukrit said, pointing toward the dock. The captain stood on top of the cabin in the stern, watching them approach, arms hanging by his side.

Alar led Scilla and Ukrit down the dock, leaving Fin in the wagon. The captain glared at them as they approached.

"He's a jerk, but don't let him put you off," Scilla whispered.

When they stepped onto the deck of the barge, a woman rose from a circle of crew members playing a dice game on the deck and greeted them.

"This is Sinta," Scilla said. "She's the first mate."

Alar extended a hand and took her forearm. "Sinta. I'm Alar."

Sinta handed a folded stack of papers to Scilla. "Your paperwork." Then she nodded to Taavi and returned to the game.

Alar approached the stern of the barge under the glare of the captain. "I'm Alar."

Taavi tossed a pouch at him so suddenly, Alar barely had time to get his hands up to catch it. He hefted it, then loosened the drawstring and peered inside. He would have to count it to be sure, but it appeared to be more coin than he expected. More than they sent to the Ishien River Valley by a considerable margin. He handed it to Scilla.

"You already take your cut?" he asked, then gaped at the flood of angry *Alle'oss* that emerged from the captain. He only knew a couple of the words, but they were enough to guess at the nature of the rest. He glanced back at the crew, who were obviously waiting to see his reaction. When he saw their smiles, he turned back to Taavi and smiled. "I assume that means yes."

"Sold it faster'n we could get it off the barge. You got more?"

"Soon," Alar said, hoping it was true. This produced another stream of curses, this time in Vollen. He waited until it petered out, then asked, "This where you usually dock?" Taavi only glared harder, so Alar walked to the railing and looked at the small village. He glanced up at Taavi. "We need a warehouse."

Taavi's brows disappeared beneath the fringe that protruded from his hat, then he turned and surveyed the village.

Sinta, Scilla and Ukrit stepped up beside Alar at the rail. "No one owns this land," Sinta said. "Nor the abandoned buildings. There's a lot of useful lumber here already." She met his gaze, then gestured to the men standing beside the sloop, watching the exchange. "You put a little money into the infrastructure here, you might have a willing workforce."

Alar took in the pitiful state of the village. "What do they do with the fish?"

"We've been shipping smoked fish south for them," Taavi said from his perch on the cabin. "That's why we're here. About the only load the Imps let us have. Not enough profit in it for them."

"Not enough for us either," Sinta said. "That's why we were so anxious to take you on." She gave Taavi a sly grin and whispered, "Would have done it for fifteen percent."

Alar studied Sinta for a moment, then nodded at the sloop. "This the only boat they have?" She nodded. "More boats, more profit. Right?"

She nodded and returned his grin.

***

After introducing themselves to the residents of the fishing village and taking a tour, they didn't make it back to the Tipsy Rooster until early evening. When they set a bowl of stew in front of Fin, his eyes nearly popped out of his head. After he ate, they took him up to the room and showed him where he would be sleeping. He threw his arms around Alar, moistening Alar's shirt with his tears. After hugging Scilla and Ukrit, he flopped down onto the mattress and was asleep before they left the room.

Back in the common room, the server set a second round of tankards in front of them. "You three look a sight better than when you first came in here," she said. "You have a turn of luck?"

"Indeed, we did," Alar said. They all offered her a toast before she turned away. Feeling pleasantly mellow, he sipped his ale and let out a deep sigh.

"Now what?" Scilla asked.

Alar sat back, looked across the tavern, and saw a familiar figure. It was Olson, sitting alone, looking far less pulled together than when they met him in this tavern. Returning his attention to his companions, he said, "Now, you and I go to Richeleau. You make contact with Violette. Make sure she's still as enthusiastic about our deal as she was before she escaped. I'll take the art and talk to Siofra."

Scilla's lips pursed.

"And… you have a wedding to plan," Alar said. "I'll be back in a month or so to help. I've always loved the early autumn."

"What about me?" Ukrit asked.

"You have a warehouse to build."

"A… Me? By myself? I don't know anything about construction."

"Let me see if I can get you some help." Alar slipped out of the booth. He made his way through the crowded tavern until he stood next to Olson's table.

Olson looked up. "Oh, Alar," he said, surprise lifting some of the weight from his expression.

"I'm sorry, Olson, for what they did to you. It wasn't your fault."

"Ah, you heard." A hint of speculation entered his expression. He looked past Alar to where Scilla and Ukrit sat. "I'm a little surprised to see you here. I was under the impression the artists were being detained until after the investigation."

"Lord Bergamot granted us permission to leave. In fact, he hustled us off the estate before anyone noticed."

Olson gazed at him, possibilities obviously running through his mind. "Have a seat, Alar." When Alar sat across from him, he said, "Someday you might tell me what actually happened to Violette, but I sense you have something else on your mind."

"Yes, I do." Alar rested his elbows on the table, inviting Olson to lean forward so they could speak more confidentially. "I belong to an organization called *Oss'stera.*"

Olson's brow furrowed. "It's *Alle'oss,* but I don't know more than a few phrases."

"It's an old construction that means our struggle."

"Our… Struggle."

"We have ambitions to follow the Desulti's example." Alar let it hang there, hoping Olson would put the pieces together.

Olson stared blankly at him, then he gazed across the tavern to where Ukrit and Scilla were watching the conversation. When he returned his attention to Alar, he cocked his head. "The Desulti made themselves wealthy and powerful to protect themselves from the Empire."

Alar nodded but didn't speak.

"You realize the Desulti are feared and hated throughout the Empire. The only reason the Volloch tolerate them is because they've become so entangled with the Empire's economy, it would create chaos to get rid of them."

"I suspect they are *tolerated* because they make a lot of coin for the Volloch lords." Alar held his gaze. "Never underestimate the greed of the lords."

Olson shrugged. "Both can be true." He glanced to the side, then murmured. "The Desulti are also not above murder to get their way."

Alar shrugged and let a small grin curve his lips. "But always as a last resort."

Olson studied Alar's face, then he sat back and gave Alar a sly smile. "You certainly are ambitious, young man."

"Well, someone I admire once told me to set my sights high, and I took her advice to heart."

"How do you plan to accomplish this… fantasy?"

"It's only a start, but we have a deal with Governor Adelbart that allows us to export goods from Argren, free of taxes and regulations."

Olson's face went slack.

Alar sat back. "Lord Bergamot told me you are a man with extraordinary gifts."

"You had a conversation about me with Lord Bergamot?"

Instead of answering, Alar said, "I think he meant it as a hint."

"What is it you want of me?"

Alar smiled. "What we need is a man with extraordinary organizational skills. A man who knows how to get projects done. Someone with connections."

Olson sighed and let his gaze wander. "I don't suppose I have any other options at the moment."

Alar stood. "Why don't you come join us?"

***

Brennerman crouched in the same spot where he first observed the rebel village with his head scout, Schenk. The early morning sun back lit the trees that clung to the top of the granite edifice that protected the village, but its golden disk wasn't visible yet.

He could almost feel the eagerness exuding from Captain Hoch, who knelt beside him. Their men, rangers on the left and troopers on the right, hid in the underbrush behind them. They hadn't encountered the *Alle'oss* sentries Schenk warned him about on their approach and there was no sentry on top of the granite outcrop. It appeared as if they achieved total surprise.

"Remember, Hoch," Brennerman murmured, "I am in command of this operation. You follow my orders."

A scowl darkened the shiny anticipation in the ranger's expression. "Yes, yes. You have already told me."

"Only *if* we find proof there are rebels here, do we take action against the *Alle'oss.*"

"We'll find it."

Brennerman studied his profile for a moment, then turned to his adjutant on his other side. "Move out."

The order was passed along, and the men crept forward, the rangers first, followed by Brennerman's troopers. He had to admit, the rangers were impressive, moving through the twilit forest like ghosts, silent and leaving no trace of their passing.

At the base of the hill that descended toward the entrance to the village, they emerged from the underbrush and crossed the rocky clearing toward the twin ravines. Still, no one raised an alarm. They paused while the lead rangers slipped into the dark opening of the ravine on the right, where Brennerman glimpsed the crates from the supply caravan.

A moment later, a lieutenant emerged and shook his head. Hoch, crouching at the back of his men, rose, strode forward and disappeared into the ravine.

Brennerman waited, though he already knew what they would find. When shouts emerged from inside, he rose and held his hand up to tell his men to stay where they were, then he walked forward. As he neared the ravine, Hoch appeared, anger blotching his face. His men followed, dragging a large *Alle'oss* man between them. Blood trickled from the corner of the man's mouth.

Hoch stopped within a pace of Brennerman, pointed back toward the ravine and growled, "You said you saw evidence from the missing supply caravan in this ravine."

"Actually, I didn't say that. You may have heard a rumor to that effect, but it didn't come from me."

Hoch stared. He whirled around, searching for his adjutant. Finding him, he said, "Search the other ravine. Search the village."

His men poured into the ravine, leaving the *Alle'oss* prisoner standing by himself, watching in horror. Hoch followed, but before he disappeared, Brennerman shouted, "If you find anything, report to me before you take any action."

Hoch only waved a hand in a gesture of disgust before he disappeared from view.

"Have the men keep an eye on the rangers," Brennerman told his adjutant. "Make sure they don't harm the *Alle'oss* without my orders."

"What do we do if they try to?"

Brennerman turned to make sure the man understood him. "Intervene. Forcefully, if necessary."

"Yes, sir." His adjutant saluted, then passed along the orders. His men swept past their captain and disappeared, leaving Brennerman alone with the *Alle'oss* man.

Once he was sure they were alone, Brennerman asked, "You removed anything that might give the rangers an excuse?"

"Aye, we did," the man said. "Not that men like that need an excuse."

That was true. Brennerman knew this could go badly, despite the warnings he gave to the *Alle'oss*. But when Hoch heard rumors the village harbored rebels, this raid became inevitable. The ranger captain wouldn't rest until he personally lay the rumor to rest. To prevent Hoch from acting on his own, Brennerman agreed to lead the raid. "The children?"

"Staying in nearby villages." The man glanced at the ravine as angry voices emerged. "Not sure why you, of all people, warned us, but we appreciate it."

Brennerman gave him a stiff nod, then strode forward and entered the ravine.

24

Unions

It took Alar and Lief three weeks to drive the wagon from Richeleau to Téama, the Desulti's home village. Ukrit's sculpture, which Siofra purchased, was securely lashed in the bed and Scilla's painting, rolled up in a leather tube, was secured in a chest to keep the weather off.

"Looks a little like Kartok and a little like Richeleau," Lief said, gazing around at the outer buildings of the village.

Alar had to agree. Richeleau still retained much of its *Alle'oss* character, whereas the Empire had imprinted their staid aesthetic on Kartok. Their arrival created a stir among the pedestrians. He assumed most of the Volloch women were Desulti, but there were also *Alle'oss*, including some men.

Lief pointed to a burned-out building and broken windows in other buildings. "Something bad happened here."

"Yeah. And not long ago, by the looks of it." The worries he harbored for Tove spiked. Did this have anything to do with what he overheard when he eavesdropped on the three Desulti beneath the willow tree, the news that sent Siofra back to Téama in the middle of the night?

The village was larger than most in Argren. More a town than a village. They had to stop an *Alle'oss* man to ask for directions. He told them where the livery was and where they could find Siofra.

As they made their way through the streets to a large plaza at the center of the village, Lief asked, "You reckon Tove lives in one of these buildings?"

"I keep thinking we'll come around a corner and see her."

They arrived in the plaza and pulled up in front of an enormous stone building the man called the Great Hall. Alar climbed into the back of the wagon and retrieved the tube with the painting, then hopped down to the cobbles.

"See to the wagon and horses, then meet me back here."

"What about the statue?"

"We'll take care of that later."

As Lief drove the wagon back across the plaza, Alar climbed the stairs of the broad porch that extended the width of the Great Hall. Two massive doors stood open, revealing a large room inside.

A Volloch woman standing in the doorway eyed him warily as he approached. "Can I help you?"

"I'm looking for Siofra," Alar said with his most winning smile.

"Is she expecting you?"

"She is. If you could direct me or let her know that Alar is here to see her."

Recognition lit her eyes when he said his name. "Alar?"

"Yes, that's right."

"You're Tove's friend."

"You know Tove?"

"Of course."

He gestured to fire damage in the building across the plaza. "I've been worried about her. Is she well?"

"Rest assured. She is more than well. Now, follow me." She turned and entered the Great Hall.

A wave of relief watered Alar's eyes and almost robbed him of the ability to walk. When he didn't immediately follow, the woman paused and waited for him to catch up. They crossed a room as large as the ballroom in the governor's mansion in Richeleau, but much more spartan. The walls were bare, unadorned stone. Rows of columns flanked the central space and left darkened alleys along the walls. Windows high on the walls lit the ceiling but had little effect on the rest of the room. A rectangle of sunlight from the immense doors illuminated the center space.

They passed through a door on the right side of the room and entered a hallway. Eventually, they came to an open door and entered a large office. The woman paused. "My name is Eithne. I'm Siofra's assistant. Wait here." She slipped through a door at the back of the room. Moments later, she emerged. "Siofra will see you." She stepped back and held the door open.

The room was the most elaborately decorated room Alar had ever seen. There were many exotic objects which would normally draw his attention, but he kept his attention on Siofra. She stood in the middle of the room, smiling warmly, her hands clasped at her waist.

"Alar. This is a surprise, and your visit is on an auspicious day."

Alar's brows rose. "Auspicious?"

"Today your friend Tove is to be initiated into the Murtair."

Alar stopped in his tracks. He stared at Siofra for a moment, then a smile leapt onto his face. "Truly?"

"Yes. She has made quite an impression on the Order. I understand from Brie, we have you to thank for sending her out way."

"Brie is being generous. I only made a suggestion." He cocked his head. "I take it you made it back in time to avert catastrophe."

She hesitated. "Yes, and no. I assume you noticed the damage as you passed through the village."

"I did."

"Courtesy of Imperial soldiers from the fort in Ka'tan." Ka'tan was the *Alle'oss* city a league north of Téama. "However, we survived, and the information you provided proved immensely valuable in the aftermath. You have my gratitude."

Alar was tempted to ask for details, but he had a more important topic to discuss.

"So," Siofra said. "What can I do for you?"

He lifted the leather tube containing Scilla's painting.

"The painting," Siofra said and extended a hand.

Alar pulled it back and cocked his head. To Siofra's uncertain smile, he said, "You haven't made an offer."

"Ah." Siofra's warm smile returned. "Wine?"

"Of course."

She went to a credenza and retrieved a bottle of white wine. "An *Alle'oss* white this time," she said with a mischievous smile. After pouring them glasses, she led him to the windows that looked out at the towering mountains north of the village. They stood quietly, sipping their wine until Siofra said, "Your friend, Brie, ran into one of your *Oss'stera* companions in Lirantok."

Alar glanced at her. There could only be one reason Brie was in Lirantok. She must have been there to convince the *Alle'oss* in the valley to work with the Desulti instead of *Oss'stera*. "Lief."

Siofra nodded. "That was it. A boy, by Brie's estimate."

"But mature beyond his years."

Siofra nodded, her eyes on the mountains. "He shamed Brie."

"That doesn't sound like Lief."

"He called out her… our hypocrisy." Siofra gazed up at him. "Years ago, we sought refuge in your mountains. Wouldn't have survived without the *Alle'oss* who came to our aid. And we set about making ourselves safe by becoming wealthy and dangerous."

"Yet you would prevent us from doing the same." Alar held her gaze.

"That was the gist of his argument. It has been the topic of lengthy discussions in our ruling council."

"And what have you concluded?"

Siofra returned her gaze to the mountains. "There is some sentiment that we have been remiss in our treatment of our hosts."

Alar may have been a simple farm boy until he had eight summers and a ragged social outcast for most of the rest of his life, but he recognized a delicately phrased political answer when he heard it. The question wasn't settled. It complicated what he was about to propose. He had been considering what *Oss'stera* had to offer the Desulti since his discussion with Ragan. During his long trip through the mountains with Lief, he finally concluded there was only one thing they could offer.

"There will be war," he said. "Perhaps not for another ten years, but eventually the *Alle'oss* will grow weary of the Empire's brutality and resist. The Imps will react the only way they know how."

"That is what I believe, as well," Siofra said. "The revolts in Styria held the Empire's attention for a time, but after a period of peace, this emperor appears restless. Presiding over a peaceful Empire doesn't seem to appeal to him. Yet, the Empire finds itself hemmed in. Styria has been subdued. The Tsadan navy rules the seas. The Kaileuk have stymied the Imperial armies in the south. There is nothing left for the Empire to exploit save Argren. There is already speculation among the Volloch lords about what riches might be extracted from your mountains."

Alar looked at the towering peaks, still covered by snow. "A great woman told me I should follow the Desulti's example. That I should make *Oss'stera* powerful enough to lift Argren from the ashes when that conflagration comes." He paused, shrugged and said, "That's what I intend to do." He turned toward her, inviting her to face him. "We can't compete with you commercially. You have no interest in raising an army. But you will need one. There is enough animosity within the Empire toward the Desulti that they will take advantage of war to settle old scores. It seems to me the Desulti and *Oss'stera* have more reason to cooperate than to compete."

Her lips twisted, and her eyes narrowed. "I have had similar thoughts. There are many within the Order who would disagree. But Tove has wrought change, opened eyes. There are now some who feel we have more in common with the *Alle'oss* than the Empire."

Alar smiled. That didn't surprise him in the least. He worried for Tove when she left Richeleau with Brie to come to Téama. From what he read in Siofra's journal and what Ragan told him, he was right to worry. But the truth was, the Desulti had no idea what was coming their way when they allowed her into their Order. Tove had suffered and survived more in her short life than anyone he knew. It would have broken most people. But in the time he knew her, he watched her emerge from the shadow of her trauma, hard as iron and nursing a white hot resolve.

"This is what I propose," he said. "Let's find ways to cooperate. I don't know what that means, right now, but let us, you and I, agree to work toward common goals. A relationship based on openness and trust. You help us become wealthy and we'll become strong."

Siofra studied him. "You trust me?"

Alar nodded.

"Just like that?"

"Yes. I've been told you are someone I can trust."

Siofra smiled. "I've been told the same about you." She extended her hand. "Agreed. You and I will work to find a way forward together. Eventually, we'll bring the rest of the Desulti along with us."

Alar took her hand, then retrieved the tube with Scilla's painting and held it out.

"But I haven't made an offer," Scilla said with a sly smile.

"A gift. A token of friendship. A reminder of what we forged today."

***

Siofra walked with him back through the Great Hall until they emerged onto the porch in front of the building. Despite it still being summer, Alar regretted not wearing his cloak. The higher altitudes were cooler than in Lachton or Richeleau. They were discussing plans for the evening when Alar looked across the plaza and spotted a familiar figure. Leaving Siofra, he ran down the steps and across the plaza.

Tove ran to meet him. She threw her arms around him and pressed her face into his chest, then fought free and pushed him with both hands.

"What was that for?" Alar asked, his smile widening at the familiar ritual.

She thumped him on his chest. "That's for not telling me you were in Téama."

"Had to find out where you lived, didn't I?" Alar pulled Tove into a hug, squeezing her, then letting her go. He noticed a Volloch woman looking on uncertainly. He knew from Siofra this must be Danu. "Heard you were making friends. Is this Danu?" He extended his hand to Danu. She took his forearm in the *Alle'oss* fashion.

"You're late."

Alar turned to find Siofra waiting nearby.

"Right!" Tove said. She took Alar's arm and said, "I have something to do right now, but we're going to the tavern in Ka'tan after. You're coming."

"Of course." He said to Siofra, "You want to come?"

"I wouldn't miss it. It's time I start making connections in Ka'tan. Plus, I've heard rumors about a stew that are difficult to believe."

"You're late." Brie had appeared on the top step of the Great Hall. She wasn't smiling when she said, "Not a good start."

"Wait here," Tove said to Danu, then she jogged up the steps and followed Brie into the Great Hall.

Lief appeared as Siofra returned to her office.

"What is Tove late for?" Alar asked Danu.

"She's being initiated into the Murtair," Danu said.

Noting her worried frown, Alar asked, "You're worried about her." Danu nodded.

"I don't know," Lief said. "If anyone has to worry about Tove being Murtair, it would be the rest of the Empire."

He said it without smiling, but it coaxed a smile onto Danu's face.

"Come on," Alar said. "Let's walk. You can tell us how Tove has been."

***

Alar moved as fast as was safe down the rocky slope that led to the entrance to *Honutok*. Looking up, he had a disorienting sense of *déjà vu* when he found Lief waiting for him. The last thing he needed on his wedding day was Ragan showing up with one of her dire pronouncements.

"You're late," Lief said as he drew near.

"You waiting for me?" Alar asked cautiously. When Lief nodded, he asked, "Ragan isn't here, is she?"

"She is. But she says she's only here for the wedding."

Alar studied his face. "Then why are you waiting for me here?"

"You're late. Scilla is… She's unlike herself."

Alar grinned. "Well, what are we waiting for?" He led Lief into one of the ravines that led into the village, waving to the sentries on the top of the granite outcrop.

The population of *Oss'stera's* home village had grown significantly since the small band of rebels founded it the previous winter. Some of the recent newcomers still lived in temporary roundhouses, but most of the citizens lived in more permanent log and stone structures. Like most *Alle'oss* villages, *Honutok* was organized around a community space and community building. The new building was draped with traditional blue and green bunting and blue and green streamers fluttered in the freshening breeze from every home.

What looked like the entire population was assembled in the center of the village. Many of them were dancing. Alar stopped. "Why does it look like they've already started the celebration?"

"Because you're late," Lief said and set off without waiting to see if Alar followed. He led them around the crowd. It looked as if the village was preparing for a festival, which was what a wedding usually was. In addition to the music and dancing, the breeze was rich with the enticing aromas of festival foods. Alar offered to delay the wedding until the harvest festival, but no one would hear of it. They acted as if they were doing Scilla and him a favor, but he knew they just didn't want to pass up the opportunity for an extra festival.

He was so focused on what was happening in the center of the village, he didn't pay attention to where they were going until he collided with Lief.

"Sorr —" He looked past Lief, stepped to the side and asked, "What's this?"

"You and Scilla need a place to live, don't you?"

Alar stared at him, then looked at the house. It was two stories, constructed of timber and stone. There were four double-hung glass windows. A rare luxury in rural *Alle'oss* villages. Glass wasn't that uncommon, but windows which could be raised and lowered were as rare as hen's teeth outside the larger cities in Argren. The house was perched on a rise from which they could look out over the rest of the village.

"What… How…"

"Come on," Lief said and led him up the stone walkway to the front door. He opened the door and entered what looked like a typical *Alle'oss* family room. Two rocking chairs were arranged in front of a stone hearth on one side of the room. The floor in front of the hearth was covered by the same shaggy bear pelt that once swaddled Ragan and her newborn daughter. A small trestle table was centered in the rest of the space. Their bows and arrows were propped in one corner and an artist's tools sat on a table in the opposite corner, Scilla's latest unfinished work on an easel beside it. There were two doors on the wall opposite the hearth, one of which led to stairs to the upper floor. The other likely led to a pantry.

"Ukrit!" Alar said.

The big man turned away from the hearth when Alar and Lief entered.

"You're late," Ukrit said with a grin. "Scilla is —"

"I know." Alar gestured to the room with both hands and lifted a brow.

"Almost everyone in the village contributed," Ukrit said. "In one way or the other."

"Where did the lumber come from?" Logs were relatively easy to acquire, but cut boards were much more difficult or expensive.

"Olsen," Ukrit said. "Some he liberated from… somewhere. I didn't ask. Some came from that old shack we lived in when we first got to Lachton. I thought it appropriate."

"The windows?"

"Didn't ask."

"We can talk about all this later," Lief said. "Scilla is going —"

"Right!" Alar said. "Bath first."

"You don't have time for a bath."

"I'm not getting married without one."

Twenty minutes later, Alar was in the bedroom on the second floor, getting dressed, when he heard a knock at the front door. Muffled voices drifted up from the family room as he was pulling on his boots. Standing, he faced Lief and asked, "How do I look?"

"You get that in Lachton?" Lief asked, examining Alar's suit.

"Yes, how did you know?"

"It looks…"

"Too much?" Alar tugged on the jacket, which was still tight across his shoulders. "Scilla bought it for me."

"Well, then," Lief said with a shrug. "It's perfect."

When they arrived in the family room, Adelbart and Violette smiled at him.

"Governor, Lady," Alar said. "I didn't know you were coming."

Adelbart came forward and took Alar's hand. "We couldn't possibly have missed the occasion." He gestured to Violette. "And of course, you and Scilla will attend Violette's and my celebration next month. Gerold and Violette have planned —"

"Now, Adi," Violette said. "This is Alar's day." She rested her hand on his arm and said, "We were directed to tell you, you're —"

"Late. I know," Alar said.

"Yes." Violette smiled. "Adi, let's go find a place to watch."

When the door opened, the volume of the music rose. Alar, who was following Adelbart and Violette, stopped at the threshold. Whirling around, he stared at Ukrit. "*Sheoda*, I forgot about the wedding dance!"

"It's too late, now," Ukrit said.

"You don't know the dance?" Lief asked.

"Why would I know the wedding dance?"

"You must have seen it before," Ukrit said.

"Where would I have seen that?" Alar asked, throwing his arms out to his sides.

"Well… You're just going to have to fake it," Ukrit said. "No one will care if their fearless leader trips over his own feet at his own wedding." He paused and frowned. "Well, nobody but Scilla."

"I know it."

Alar, who was staring down at the gathering in the center of the village, turned around and found Lief nodding at him.

"How do you —" Ukrit started to ask.

"Never mind." Alar grabbed Lief's arm and pulled him into the yard. "Show me."

"I'll do Scilla's part," Lief said and held out his hands, palms up.

Alar took his hands.

Ten minutes later, Inga, the woman who ran the school, arrived at a run, her brow shiny with sweat. "Alar, you're late! Scilla is in a right state!"

Alar looked at Lief, who gave a small shrug and said, "Maybe let Scilla lead."

Alar dropped his hands and took off down the hill.

Cheers rose when he emerged out of the crowd into the community space. He caught sight of Holden, Adelbart and Violette joining in with the others, then hurried to the side of the square where an arbor constructed of yew boughs stood. Ecke, the witch Alar saved from the Inquisition the previous autumn, smiled at Alar as he approached. She had only twelve summers, but for centuries the *Alle'oss* considered it good fortune to have a *saa'myn* preside over a marriage. The last of the old *saa'myn*, Beadu, was too old to travel to *Honutok*, so it fell to the first of a new generation. Ecke would be the first *saa'myn* to perform the rites in nearly one hundred years. No one knew the words of the ancient ceremony, but that didn't matter. They were starting their own traditions.

Alar greeted Ecke, then turned and took his place, with Ukrit and Lief standing at his side. The residents of *Honutok* stood in an arc, smiling at them. A few jeers rose at his expense for making them wait. He spotted Ragan standing in the front row beside Zaina, Keth, and the boy named Aron.

Taking a deep breath, he blew it out, trying unsuccessfully to catch his breath and slow his speeding heart. "So much for the bath," he mumbled to Ukrit. "I'm sweating like Adelbart."

"I've seen you scared, worried, angry," Ukrit murmured. "But I don't believe I've ever seen you nervous."

"I'm not nervous. I'm just…"

"Nervous."

"Yeah. I'm —"

And then the crowd across from them parted, revealing Scilla. She was surrounded by Inga and some of the other women of the village. She wore a traditional *Alle'oss* wedding dress and sandals. Small yellow and blue blossoms were woven into her curls. When her blue eyes met his, she smiled and everything else faded into the background.

Murmurs rose in the crowd when she appeared, but as she crossed the clearing, the crowd grew quiet. She joined him under the arbor and Lief and Ukrit withdrew. They faced one another, lifted a hand and entwined their fingers. Looking into Scilla's shining eyes, Alar was barely aware of Ecke binding their wrists together with a blue ribbon.

"Today we celebrate the union of Alar and Scilla," Ecke said, "in the sight of the *Ian'and* who have gathered, attracted to our joy." She lifted her arms up. No one else except Ragan could see the small glowing orbs, but Alar imagined them whirling around them.

He didn't hear the rest of what Ecke said. The words didn't matter. He and Scilla had been one since long before they agreed to marry. The ceremony was for *Oss'stera* and for their friends, to allow them to celebrate their love. Alar thought of his parents. His memories were more misty emotions than reality. He couldn't even remember what they looked like. But he was sure the home they made for him and his sister was filled with love and joy. Despite the tragedy of his early life, fortune had smiled on him in many ways. But all else paled next to the day Scilla crossed his path.

Noticing Ecke had fallen silent and chuckles rippling through the audience, Alar focused on Scilla's wry smile.

"It's time for the dance," she whispered.

"I didn't say my part," he whispered.

She leaned toward him and whispered, "Yes. You did."

Alar stared at her, a grin growing slowly on his face.

With their hands still joined by the ribbon, they walked to the center of the community space and faced one another, where the entire village would watch their first dance as a married couple.

Scilla held up her other hand. Taking in Alar's uneasy frown, she asked, "Did you learn the dance?"

"I did, but…"

"But?"

"Lief suggested I let you lead?"

A smile blossomed on her face as the first notes of the wedding song rose. She flipped one of her hands over and said, "Let's both lead."

About the Author

Ross Hightower and DL Heim have been partners in crime for more than 38 years. While Ross built a career as a professor and Deb worked on four advanced degrees, they managed to raise two wonderful people and launch them into the world. When Ross started writing his first novel, *Spirit Sight*, they never dreamed they would work together, but after a rocky beginning, they discovered they loved writing together. It took a few beers, many intense conversations, and a few arguments to produce *Oss'stera*, the third novel in the *Spirit Song: Rebels Rising* series. There will be many more books to come.

Other Titles by Ross Hightower and Deb Heim

Note from Ross Hightower and Deb Heim

Word-of-mouth is crucial for any author to succeed. If you enjoyed *Desulti*, please leave a review online—anywhere you are able. Even if it's just a sentence or two. It would make all the difference and would be very much appreciated.

And if you would like to read a bonus chapter from *Desulti*, let me know at author@rosshightower.com.

Thanks!
Ross Hightower and Deb Heim

We hope you enjoyed reading this title from:

www.blackrosewriting.com

Subscribe to our mailing list – *The Rosevine* – and receive **FREE** books, daily
deals, and stay current with news about upcoming
releases and our hottest authors.
Scan the QR code below to sign up.

Already a subscriber? Please accept a sincere thank you for being a fan of
Black Rose Writing authors.

View other Black Rose Writing titles at
www.blackrosewriting.com/books and use promo code
PRINT to receive a **20% discount** when purchasing.

www.ingramcontent.com/pod-product-compliance
Lightning Source LLC
Chambersburg PA
CBHW030017200726
48283CB00012B/665